Praise for *And Union No More*— a must-read for history lovers:

"Stan Haynes uses a turning point in the evolution of America as the template for this thrilling adventure. His storyline infuses actual flashpoints in history in such a fluid manner that it is practically impossible to tell them apart. The characters are unique in every sense of the word . . . The subplots flow naturally and fit into the overall story arc like cogs on an effective wheel . . . I daresay And Union No More is a story without comparison in its genre."

—Readers' Favorite (5-star review)

"[A] novel rich in US history, providing the reader with something enticing that is also highly educational . . . Haynes . . . is able to mesh fiction together with historical record, creating a piece that is well worth the reader's time . . . While using history as a guide, there are some twists embedded within the larger story that help keep the reader on their toes . . . Kudos, Mr. Haynes, for keeping me highly entertained and educated throughout this novel."

—Reedsy Discovery

"Haynes does a splendid job of portraying the tense circumstances that enveloped the Kansas Territory during its journey to becoming a state. The characters he introduces, along with the historical figures, are immersed in a death struggle for the soul of the nation . . . Historical fiction fans will likely find much to enjoy in this novel that explores events that will eventually lead to one of the most devastating chapters in the nation's history."

—US Review of Books

Reviews of Stan Haynes' prior novel, *And Tyler No More*:

"Haynes paints a historically authentic and dramatically gripping tableau of the tumultuous politics of the time . . . This is a rigorously researched novel . . . [A]n impressive literary feat . . . ."
—**Kirkus Reviews**

"Haynes's accomplished debut novel sets an arresting historical mystery during the administration of President John Tyler when the federal government was in the process of annexing Texas . . . The question . . . 'What if thousands of enslaved people, if not those living now, at least their children or grandchildren, could be brought closer to freedom by a single death?' Haynes establishes the stakes and context with clarity and power, threading a wealth of fascinating history into his telling . . . History enthusiasts will ponder 'what if' in this memorable novel . . . ."
—**BookLife**

"Washington hasn't changed all that much since the 1840s—it was just as nasty and . . . perilous back then. This is a well-written, well-paced tale with a nice feel for the times. It's history that goes down easy, my favorite kind."
—**Burt Solomon,** author of *The Murder of Willie Lincoln* and *The Attempted Murder of Teddy Roosevelt*

Other books by Stan Haynes:
President-Making in the Gilded Age
The First American Political Conventions

AND UNION NO MORE

A NOVEL

STAN HAYNES

This is a work of historical fiction. Where historical figures appear in the story, they are portrayed fictitiously, with details and events that are products of the author's imagination, and should not be construed as real.

AND UNION NO MORE
A NOVEL

SMH Publishing

Cover design by White Rabbit Arts

ISBN: 978-1-7377669-2-6 (print)
ISBN: 978-1-7377669-4-0 (e-book)

Printed in the United States of America

To Nate and Katie

CHAPTER 1

May, 1856— A cool, late-spring dawn had just broken over the Kansas prairie. Monty called Robert's name, quietly, a couple of times. With everything that had gone on in the past few days, he knew that startling a man sleeping with a loaded pistol at his side was not a good idea.

He saw Robert's eyes dart open and the instinctive grab for the weapon, stopping when he recognized Monty standing next to the pile of straw that he had been resting on. He and the younger Robert had become close friends after both had arrived in Kansas several months ago.

"Get up, we need to go!," said Monty. "Something terrible has happened. I've already got the horses saddled." He shoved a cup of hot coffee into Robert's hands. "Drink fast, and grab your gear."

"What now? What is it? Where are we going?," asked a puzzled Robert.

"I'll tell you once we get going."

Monty watched as Robert gulped down the weak coffee and pulled on his boots. Having slept in their clothes, both were already dressed. He looked in his saddle bag and the only extra clothes he had brought along, a few shirts, some drawers, and a couple of pairs of socks, were still there. The events of the last few days raced through his mind. It was Monday, he was pretty sure. It had been less than a week since it all began. Last Wednesday, the long-anticipated attack on Lawrence, the town that served as the headquarters of the free-state movement in the Kansas Territory, had finally occurred. He had seen it all, crouched beside Robert, as they hid in a shed. Proslavery thugs from neighboring Missouri, with the backing of federal authorities, had stormed into the town. They called themselves a "sheriff's posse," but to Monty and others in Lawrence, they were nothing more than an invading mob. They burned the town's main hotel, destroyed the offices of its newspapers, and looted most of the shops. Monty and Robert had been frustrated and angry, disagreeing with the command from their superiors in the free-state militia to stand down and not oppose the attack. Since then, however, they had come around to believing that it had been the correct decision, as they had been hopelessly outnumbered. Any resistance would have been futile, and would have resulted in many deaths.

In the aftermath of the attack, Monty and Robert had fled Lawrence. The men in their unit had scattered. There was no one to lead, at least for now, and Robert had insisted on getting Monty away from danger. It would have been a coup for the degenerates who attacked the town to get their hands on such a prominent figure in the free-state cause as Monty, a former congressman and a captain in the militia. Several of the movement's leaders had already been captured and imprisoned. Monty and Robert had first headed east of town, but the roads were blocked by the ruffians, forcing them to turn and head south, toward Ottawa. They covered almost twenty-five miles, resting only a few hours in the darkest hours of the night. Early the next morning, they came across a friendly settler, a free-stater living in an isolated cabin with his family, who welcomed them and let them stay in his barn. They had hoped to get on their way the next day, to circle around to the west and eventually make their way back to Lawrence, but the settler told them that slavers continued to patrol all the nearby roads and paths, and that it was not safe to leave. Each day, the settler ventured out as a scout, but he came back with the same news. They had been in hiding for four days, growing more impatient with each. But last evening, Monty had learned of something even worse.

Monty was glad to now finally be on the move, but he was worried. The danger had not passed. They could still be ambushed at any minute. Despite this, whatever the risk, he had to go and see for himself what had happened, if the news received last night was correct. He wanted it to not be, but he had a sinking feeling that it was.

As they rode, he could sense Robert's annoyance at the lack of information. After their horses had been trotting to the southeast for a few minutes, the inevitable question came.

"Anytime you want to tell me where we're headed, and why, I'm all ears."

"We're going to Pottawatomie Creek," Monty responded, "About twenty miles away. After you retired to the barn last night, a man stopped by the cabin. Said that there had been an attack around there. Several men hacked to death with swords. I need to investigate and report back to our militia leaders. I doubt any of them are as close to the place as we are."

"Hacked to death, you say? Goddamn border ruffians," responded a dismayed Robert. "First the attack on Lawrence, and now this. Have the slavers lost all decency?"

"It's worse than that," replied Monty.

"How could it be?"

3

"If what I was told last night is true, the victims were slavery men and the killings were done by our men, by free-staters."

"That can't be. I don't believe it," replied a shocked and skeptical Robert.

"The fella last night seemed pretty sure of it."

As they rode on in silence, Monty sighed and shook his head in disgust. Another day, and more violence in Kansas. How had it come to this? Americans not only killing their fellow Americans, but now butchering them. Could this have been done by the side that *he* was supporting, that *he* was fighting for? Had he been a fool, he wondered, to leave a safe and prosperous life in Ohio to come here and join the fight against slavery? On most days, when such questions entered his head, he eventually answered no, concluding that being part of this cause was worth it. On this brisk morning in late May, as he headed toward the site of a massacre, he was not so sure.

CHAPTER 2

*J***une, 1854**— "May Senator Douglas burn in hell for the evil that he has unleashed." Montgomery Tolliver said angrily, shaking his head in disgust. He took another sip of his coffee and stared at the newspaper spread out before him on the table in the small kitchen.

"Now, Monty, calm down" scolded Theresa, his wife. "You will wake the children. We don't wish such a fate as that on Senator Douglas, or anyone."

"Seems like a fitting punishment," responded Monty. "We had slavery locked in a box and Douglas and his friends in Congress just gave the South the key to get out, to expand their dreadful institution. And our weak-kneed president has signed it into law."

Monty and his wife were discussing the Kansas-Nebraska Act, enacted two weeks earlier, on May 30, 1854, with the signature of President Franklin Pierce. Under it, the vast lands west of Iowa and Missouri, which had been part of Jefferson's Louisiana Purchase, would now be open to slavery. Folks in Ohio and all across the North were enraged. Over the past week or so, Monty had not had a conversation with anyone in Dayton without it having come up. This had all been settled, everyone was saying, by the Missouri Compromise in 1820. Other than in Missouri, slavery had been forbidden anywhere north of that state's southern border, *forever*. The compromise had been a compact between the states, forged by Senator Henry Clay of Kentucky, Monty's former boss and mentor. The Great Compromiser, Clay had been called, and it had been one of his greatest achievements, easing sectional tensions between the North and the South for a generation. A line had been drawn on the map. Slavery would be tolerated where it already existed, and south of Missouri, but not one inch farther to the north. And now, with this new law, that line had been erased. This land, now formally christened the Kansas-Nebraska Territory, inhabited mostly by Native Americans who had been resettled there by the federal government, would now be open for settlement, and slavery within its borders would be determined by a vote of its citizens. Popular sovereignty, they called it.

"It was clever of them to frame it as a voting rights issue. It *sounds* good," commented Theresa.

"Douglas and his cronies are nothing if not shrewd. With this, they can expand slavery and wash their hands of it. They'll just say it's what the people wanted."

"Did you know Senator Douglas when you were in Congress?"

"Only enough to know that I couldn't stand him. A man short in stature but big in ego. Like most senators, believes he's destined to be president someday."

Two years earlier, disgusted with his party's refusal to take a stronger stance against slavery during the last presidential campaign, and with its pompous nominee, General Winfield Scott, Monty had resigned his seat as a Whig member of Congress from the Tenth District of Ohio. Since 1852, he had returned to his home in Dayton, avoided politics, gotten married, and had started a family. The Whigs had been defeated in that election, in a landslide, by the Democrats and their candidate, Franklin Pierce of New Hampshire. The Whig Party was now in shambles and the Democrats, dominated by slaveholding southerners and their northern allies, now ran the federal government. There was little that could be done to stop them.

As a former congressman, Monty knew how Washington worked. Things were not always what they seemed to be, and the true motivation behind new policies was often hidden. He suspected, and some of his friends in Congress with whom he remained in contact had concurred, that the origin of the Kansas-Nebraska Act was likely more about greed and power than about slavery. A railroad all the way to the Pacific Ocean was coming. It was only a matter of time. Those who owned land along its path would get rich. Congress had two likely routes to choose from, a northern one and a southern one. Neither section of the country had the votes to get their preferred route enacted into law. Senator Stephen Douglas, of Illinois, wanted the route for the railroad to begin in his home state, in Chicago, and to take a northern route. But senators from the South refused and had been intransigent. Why, they argued, would they support a northern route for the Pacific railroad that would go through land where slavery, under the Missouri Compromise, was banished? There was nothing in that for the South, they said. Instead of Chicago, their position was that the railroad should start in St. Louis, or New Orleans, and take a southerly route to California.

Monty had heard that Douglas and many of his friends and supporters owned land and had business interests along his proposed northern route. He explained to Theresa that he suspected that a deal was cut, and that this was how the new law had come about. They would open the land to settlement, so that the railroad could be built and, to attract the votes of a sufficient number of southern senators needed for passage, eliminate the prohibition in the Missouri Compromise against slavery there. Instead, let the issue of slavery be decided by a vote of the people living in those territories. Monty believed that it was a bone that Douglas was more than willing to toss to his southern colleagues to get what he wanted. They could sell it to their constituents. Losing out on a southern route for the Pacific railroad was a small price to pay for getting rid of the Missouri Compromise, long hated in the South, and opening a path to expanding slavery where, previously, it could not exist.

"That's how they do things. You scratch my back, I scratch yours," he said to Theresa, adding, "And, of course, Douglas will pick up support among his newfound southern friends for the Democratic presidential nomination in 1856. Mark my words, money and a lust for power are behind all of this."

"You are certainly in a cynical mood today," said Theresa.

"I've been there. I know how they think. Letting slavery expand to line their own pockets, and for political gain, is not beyond them."

* * *

Laws often have unintended consequences. If the politicians in Washington had assumed that settlement of the Kansas-Nebraska Territory would follow natural migration patterns and that, once sufficiently populated, peaceful elections would decide whether slavery would exist there or not, they were naive and did not understand the passions over slavery that existed in both the North and the South. Instead, by their new law, they had created a free-for-all in Kansas, with northern abolitionists determined to transplant as many opponents of slavery to the territory as possible, to make it a free state, and with southerners, especially those from the neighboring slaveholding state of Missouri, equally determined to do everything within their power to make sure that Kansas would enter the Union as an enslaved state. Guerilla warfare resulted. The mid-to-late 1850s became known to history as the era of "Bleeding Kansas," a precursor to the Civil War, which followed soon in its wake.

CHAPTER 3

ugust, 1854— It had been a while since Robert's shadow had darkened the doorway of a church. When was it, he wondered, in '49 at Christmas Day services with his mother? Or was it '50? May God rest her soul, he thought, as an image of her sweet face flashed in his mind. That had been at the Methodist church a few blocks away, where the family had attended services when he was a child. He did not recall ever having entered the large white wooden building with the high steeple that he saw before him, although he had passed it hundreds, if not thousands, of times during his life. The Trinity Episcopal of Newport, he had heard, was the largest church in Rhode Island. It was not religion that had brought him here but, rather, the handbill for tonight's meeting that he had seen posted a few days ago on the board in front of the post office. "MAKE KANSAS A FREE STATE," the headline had proclaimed in large letters.

For the past few months, the Kansas-Nebraska Act had been the main topic of conversation around town. The consensus in Newport was that the South had hoodwinked the North and, shamefully, it had been northern legislators who had steered the new law through Congress and provided the votes to make it a reality. Slavery, since 1820, everyone was saying, had been contained and forbidden anywhere north of Missouri's southern border. Now, the Kansas-Nebraska Territory would be open for settlement, and people there could vote on whether to allow slavery. It did not sit well among folks in the North, and Robert strongly agreed. You can't change the rules on something so important, he thought, and not expect people to be upset.

Robert slid his boots back and forth several times on the worn braided rug just inside the entrance to the church, successfully removing most of the mud that had clung to them. There had been a steady rainfall most of the afternoon, not unusual for Newport in the late summer. He removed his soggy slouch hat, revealing his red hair, combed back and extending to the base of his neck. Like the other men in his family had been, he was a redhead, with green eyes and light, freckled skin. Thirty-one years old, he was of average height and build, and had a triangular face that most considered handsome. He took a seat on one of the wooden pews near the back of the church. The arched ceiling kept the room cool, although the humidity in the air was noticeable. He looked around. The high pulpit located at the end of the center aisle, painted white and with three different levels, was the room's most noticeable feature. The sanctuary was much larger, and fancier, than the church his family had attended. He had always thought that Episcopalians were highfalutin and the ornate nature of their church confirmed that opinion. About fifty or so people were spread around the room. Most were young men, like him, sitting alone or in pairs, who appeared to be in their late teens or twenties. There was no idle chatter. He sensed that most felt about the evening's topic as he did, that they had a feeling of eager anticipation, but also of seriousness. Decisions made tonight would change lives. He spotted a couple of families, with small children, who, surprisingly, Robert noticed, were mostly being quiet. In his youth, he recalled his father hustling him and his older brother out of church services, more than a few times, due to their unruliness. His eyes then focused on the backs of the heads of several men on the front pew, older men, some bald and most of the others well on the way.

At the appointed time, a short, rotund man with spectacles stood and walked to the plain wooden lectern that had been placed in front of the pulpit. He identified himself as a deacon of the church, but Robert did not catch his name. He welcomed all and proceeded into a brief denunciation of the Kansas-Nebraska Act. When one door is closed, he said, the Lord opens another. He then introduced the featured speaker of the evening, Eli Thayer, a businessman from Worcester, Massachusetts, who he said had a plan to confront the crisis brought on by the new law.

A young, balding man with a bushy black beard and a thin, slightly hooked nose, walked to the lectern. He appeared, Robert guessed, to be in his mid-thirties. The man began to address the crowd.

"I have spent the past few months traveling throughout New England, its towns and hamlets," Thayer began, "to speak to others, like you, who are concerned about recent events in Washington City and what they mean for the future of our country. Will the evil of slavery be allowed to spread beyond its current borders? The answer lies in your hearts, in your resolve, and in the actions that you, and thousands like you, are willing to take."

Thayer's tone, thought Robert, was more conversational than emotional. Almost professorial. Having identified the problem, he moved to his proposed solution.

"Some months ago," he continued, "I founded the New England Emigrant Aid Company, and have raised money from investors to support its goal, which is to populate the plains of Kansas with freedom-loving souls such as yourselves, and to defeat at the ballot box any attempt to stain that virgin land with the evils of human bondage. Our politicians wring their hands and despair over this new law, and have readily accepted defeat. All is lost, they say, and Kansas is destined to be a slave state. Others, the extreme abolitionists, want revolution. They denounce our Constitution and advocate the dissolution of our Union over slavery. I follow a different path, a middle one, between these two extremes of resignation and revolution. I say, we can meet the challenge, operating under our Constitution and within our laws. We need freedom-loving folks in Kansas. Live your dream of a new and bountiful life, in a place where you are needed, and support the cause of freedom. Join us in this crusade!"

Robert had read in the newspaper about Thayer's brain-child, this endeavor that he was promoting. The concept was simple, but also daunting. Offer discounts on travel, including the accommodations along the way, and the promise of cheap land, to those opposed to slavery who were willing to relocate to Kansas. The company would set up towns, build schools and public buildings, and help fund the construction of saw mills, flour mills, blacksmith shops, and the like. All the conveniences of New England, transplanted to Kansas.

The crowd in the damp church listened attentively to the remarks and gave Thayer an endorsement of applause after he concluded. There was no whooping or cheering. That, Robert knew, was not the New England way. These people, his people, did not wear their emotions on their sleeves. They generally reacted with a quiet determination, instilled in them by a sense of duty.

After the talk, as Robert stood, he recognized a couple of friends, really just acquaintances, who had been sitting behind him. Both said they were interested in joining this new enterprise. It seemed to be the right thing to do, they said. Maybe this is what he needed, Robert thought. A move to Kansas. What did he have left here in Newport? Just entering his fourth decade of life, he was alone, the only surviving member of his family. The last several years had been brutal. First, the death of his beloved older brother, his only sibling. That had been just over ten years ago. After that tragedy, Robert had then, like his father and brother before him, joined the Navy. He did not find military life to his liking and did not reenlist after his three-year stint. He had then returned home to Newport and, about five years ago, had married Harriett, the love of his life. After only one blissful year, she had died, in childbirth, along with their daughter. And then, just two years ago, he had lost both of his parents to an epidemic of cholera that had swept through Rhode Island.

After leaving the Navy, Robert had gotten a job at a local newspaper, the *Newport Mercury*, and had remained working there through all of his personal tragedies. It was what had saved him, he believed, keeping him busy and from sinking into depression. He could set type faster than anyone he knew and, most of the time, could diagnose the problem with and repair a faulty printing press with ease. He had also begun writing some articles for the paper, but not as often as he desired. He wanted to be a real newspaperman, a reporter, full time. But he knew it was not likely that this would ever happen at the *Mercury*, where the owner and his two sons did almost all of the writing.

Robert thought back to family conversations when growing up. His parents and his brother had despised slavery, and it had been a frequent a topic at the dinner table. The Declaration of Independence means what it says, he remembered his father saying. *All* men are created equal. Why is it that we in the North, his father had argued countless times, continue to turn a blind eye to this evil within our nation's borders? Before his brother left home to join the Navy, he had been just as resolute against slavery. Robert had adopted their beliefs, but never seemed to have had the passion that they did. Maybe that is what he needed, he thought. Some passion in his life. Something to believe in, to go to Kansas, to start a new life, and to take a stand against slavery. It would have made, he was sure, his father and brother proud.

At the rear of the sanctuary, he looked over the papers spread out on a table. The man seated behind the table extended his hand.

"Good evening, and thank you for coming. I'm Amos Lawrence, treasurer of the New England Emigrant Aid Company. Any questions?"

"Will you be having newspapers in your Kansas settlements?," asked Robert.

"Oh yes," Lawrence responded, "we will have full towns up and running, within a matter of months. Newspapers, churches, shops, you name it. We will get you there, at reduced cost, and help get you set up once you've arrived. Here, take the full brochure. It explains everything."

"Thank you."

"Here's my card. I'll be at the hotel next door for a couple of days. Stop by if you have any questions."

"I will."

"What is your name, young man?," inquired Lawrence, as he grabbed a pencil to jot down the information.

"It's Geddis, sir, Robert Geddis."

CHAPTER 4

*O**ctober, 1854**—* Raven stood beside a crooked cotton-wood tree and stared into the darkness before her. The lone sound she heard was the lapping of the water of the Ohio River on the muddy riverbank, a few feet away. She felt the moisture from the soft mud ooze into her well-worn boots. The stars shone above on this crisp and moonless autumn night. She continued to look intensely at the river. Finally, there it was—she saw it! A brief flicker of light, about thirty degrees to her right. She lifted her lantern up from the small hole that she had dug in the moist dirt to conceal its light, held it at chest height, waved it for a couple of seconds, and quickly returned it to its damp hiding place. Seconds later, she saw another momentary burst of light from the river. Her signal had been received.

She figured it would be about five minutes before the small rowboat reached land. While waiting, she reflected on how she had gotten to this place in her life, waiting beside a river on an autumn night a couple of miles outside of Cincinnati. The extra burst of energy from the cup of coffee that she had hours ago before leaving her home had worn off, but it was not like she needed an artificial stimulant. This work stirred her. It was, by far, the most exciting and rewarding part of her life. Others told her that she was too old for it, but she felt that her age was an advantage. White folks were not suspicious of a Black woman approaching sixty years. She would not be someone, they thought, who would take the risk of being a conductor on the Underground Railroad. She believed that she was almost sixty, but she really didn't know. As a formerly enslaved person, she had no official record of her birth. She was taller and more muscular than most women, had rich ebony skin and an oval face, with amber eyes, a broad nose, and full lips. Her shoulder-length wavy hair was parted in the middle and tied in the back.

Raven's earliest memories were of growing up on a large tobacco farm in southern Virginia. It was in Pittsylvania County, she had been told. A couple of years ago, one of the men she worked with on the Underground Railroad had pointed the area out to her on a map. Near the border with North Carolina, she remembered him saying. There, she helped tend to her two younger siblings, a brother and a sister, and had been taught to sew by the slaveholder's wife. Then, at around age thirteen (she believed), she went to work in the tobacco fields, alongside her mother. She hardly knew her father. He was an enslaved man on a neighboring farm and had visited a few times, but there was tension between him and her mother, who had told Raven to stay away from him. In time, she had relations of her own, but had never given birth, nor been with child. Her mother told her that it was a blessing. Why bring another enslaved child into the world, she had said. Raven was not so sure, and often thought that she would have liked to have been a mother. But the Lord, she told herself, had decided differently.

Life continued in the same dreary pattern until she was around thirty or so, when the wheel of a wagon loaded with tobacco ran over her right foot, fracturing the bones in three places. It was an accident. The horse pulling the wagon had been startled. Unable to continue working in the tobacco fields, the slaveholder sold her a few months later. He said she was no longer of any use to him. She learned that her new owner was a cousin of her former one. Abruptly being torn from her mother and siblings had been bitter and painful, a trauma that she never got over. Her new home was farther north in Virginia, on a large farm in Loudoun County, almost two hundred miles away. The work there was less physical. She tended to the animals—goats, cows, and pigs—and did some work in the fields, where corn and other vegetables were grown. She sewed and mended clothes for the slaveholder's family and became an accomplished seamstress. She had an eye for precision and took pride in the beautiful things that she could create with a needle, thread, and fabric. Over time, her foot got better. The pain mostly went away, but she was left with a limp.

After several more years, her life took another turn, unexpectedly so. The slaveholder put her up for sale at an auction, along with two others. Rumor was, she'd heard, that he was having financial problems and needed cash. It wasn't like the farm couldn't run without her. She was expendable. A young man purchased her and, expecting the worst (something that she had conditioned herself to be prepared for throughout her life), he then told her that he was setting her free. He took her to Washington City, where the paperwork was done. He had told her to head north, to Canada, beyond the reach of bounty hunters who kidnapped freed Blacks and sold them back into slavery in the South. Along the way, she had been helped by the Underground Railroad. Older, alone, and having no way to contact her family (if any of them were still alive), she decided she wanted this to be her work for the rest of her life. Helping others like herself get to freedom. What was there, she wondered, for her in Canada?

That had been more than ten years ago. She had first lived in Pennsylvania, crossing down into Maryland and escorting small groups of enslaved people, some of whom had started their journey in the Deep South, across Mason and Dixon's Line and into free territory. Then, about three years ago, she had been asked by the folks she reported to at the Underground Railroad to move to Ohio, where more help was needed. They resettled her in Cincinnati, on the Ohio River, the dividing line between the slave state of Kentucky and the free state of Ohio. At first, she ventured into Kentucky and guided her charges into free territory but, more recently, she remained on her side of the river and met those crossing it into Ohio and guided them farther north. Being the person who led them through their first miles in free territory was exhilarating for her, but it was also dangerous. Under the Fugitive Slave Act, passed in 1850, anyone caught helping or sheltering an escaped slave could be fined and imprisoned, especially Blacks, and everyone was required to assist in the law's enforcement. Bounty hunters seemed to be everywhere. Even if they were not, folks imagined them to be lurking about. Some of the work was at night, but daytime movement could not be avoided. She guided the souls under her care to a safe house, where they would meet up with the next conductor, who then took over.

For this particular mission, Raven was to take her charges farther north, about fifty or so miles. The journey would take at least a couple of days, mostly in a horse-drawn wagon. Some conductors preferred walking through forests and fields at night, but, due to her foot injury and limp, her pace was too slow and made any extended travel on foot impossible.

Raven was her code name, as were the names by which she knew of all of the people that she worked with. The less she knew about the others, and that they knew about her, the better. That was how the system operated. After all, each of them was a criminal under the Fugitive Slave Act. Her superiors in the Underground Railroad had her travel to different towns and cities, and told her to vary her routes to each, so as not to establish any pattern, decreasing the chances of being detected. She had made this same trip a few times before. The last time, there was a new safe house that was used and she was instructed to again deliver her charges there. It was some sort of industrial site; exactly what, she did not know. She had only seen it in the dark. There, she would meet a white man, the same one as on the last trip. He was, she judged, in his early sixties, and she knew him by the code name of Coyote.

She looked before her into the darkness over the Ohio River, called the River Jordan by many of enslaved souls she met on its banks, a watery crossing that, for them, led to the Promised Land. Outlines of figures in a rowboat slowly began to appear and she heard the sound of oars trudging through the water. It was time to get to work.

CHAPTER 5

eptember, 1854— He was ready for a change, Billy Rutledge had decided. Twenty-one years old and his life was going nowhere. Ever since his widowed father had died three years ago and left the family farm, about fifty acres, to his older brother, Billy knew that, at some point, he would have to strike out on his own. He had been allowed to finish his second year of college at the newly opened University of Mississippi but, after his father's debts were paid off, there was no money left for him to continue. Like many southern families, the Rutledges had lived beyond their means. In the South, appearances were important. So much for Billy's dream of becoming an engineer.

His only sibling, older brother Charles, had graduated from Jefferson College, down near Natchez. Charles had the better education and, now, he had the land. The first-born son always got the best. That was the southern way, Billy had observed, ever since he began thinking about such things. Five years younger than Charles, the two had never been all that close. He wasn't sure why. They didn't even look like brothers, everyone said, even when they were boys. If pressed, most would agree that Billy had grown into the more handsome of the two. Standing a little less than six feet, he was trim and fit, had a clean-shaven oval face, thick black hair, which he combed back and which touched his shoulders, a thin nose, and hazel brown eyes.

Their father's will had specified that Billy would always be allowed to live, rent free, on the farm, but that was the extent of his inheritance. For the past two years, he had been living in the house, now owned by Charles, that he had grown up in, along with Charles and his wife, and their two young daughters. Billy was not married and had no prospects along those lines. He worked as a laborer on the farm, and oversaw the handful of workers that they hired during the planting and harvesting months. The family had never owned any enslaved people, but not out of any philosophical or moral reason. They just couldn't afford them.

"I gotta do something," Billy had caught himself muttering several times over the past couple of months. He learned about this evening's meeting a few days earlier when he'd spotted a flier that had been posted in nearby Jackson, the state capital. It was about the Kansas-Nebraska Act. "COME TO THE RESCUE!" the headline had proclaimed. That had been on his last visit to town to buy supplies for the farm and, while there, he had observed that talk of the new law was on everyone's lips. Mississippians couldn't stand idly by, folks said, and let the Yankees make Kansas a free state. That could not be permitted to happen, as far as they were concerned.

As he walked up the steps and past the four white marble columns of City Hall, he was pleased to see many others headed the same way. Looks like it will be a good turnout, he thought. Once inside, this was confirmed. The public meeting room was mostly full. He took a seat where he could find one, near the middle. Gotta be more than a hundred people here, Billy observed. Almost all were men, split between young and old. The familiar smell of tobacco filled the room. If it was not being smoked, it was being chewed.

The featured speaker was introduced, followed by applause, cheers, whistling, and the stomping of feet. No one could ever accuse southerners, Billy knew, of not expressing their emotions, especially when the topic concerned the region's "peculiar institution." Senator David Atchison, from Missouri, was one of the South's leading statesmen in Washington City. It was rare that someone of such stature came to speak in Jackson. Billy watched as a stern-looking man of medium height and build, with a prominent nose and chin, and jet-black hair, walked to the podium.

"People of the slaveholding State of Mississippi," Atchison began, "a crisis is at hand. Prompt action must be taken, or we can bid farewell to our southern rights and independence. Over the past months," he continued, "the good people of the western counties of my state of Missouri have been heavily engaged, both in time and effort, in fighting the battles of the South. They have attempted to uphold southern interests in this struggle, unassisted by our friends. The Yankee abolitionists, staking their all upon the Kansas issue, are moving heaven and earth to settle that beautiful territory and render it not only a so-called Free State, but a den of Negro thieves and New England scum."

Billy heard a shout of "Never!" from a man in the row in front of him.

The senator went on, "The time has come when Missouri can no longer stand up, single handed, as the lone champion of the South, against the onslaught of the entire North. It requires no great foresight to perceive that, if the Yankees succeed in their crusade in Kansas, there will be a war upon the institutions of the South, which will continue until they shall cease to exist anywhere."

"How, then, shall these impending evils be avoided?," asked Atchison. "The answer is obvious. Settle the Kansas territory with emigrants from the South. Is it in the nature of southern men to submit without resistance? Of course not. We take action! Those who cannot go to Kansas can contribute money to support those who can. Will you, our brethren here in Mississippi, help us?"

"Yes, yes!" came the cries of men from around the room. Billy found himself caught up in the emotions of the moment and was sitting on the edge of his seat. "We will!," shouted the man sitting next to him.

"The great struggle will climax at the first election held in the territory, scheduled in only a couple of months. The time for action has arrived." The senator paused briefly, raised his right hand, index finger extended, and shook it violently at the crowd. "We must have southern men in Kansas, and soon, by the thousands. Falling short is not acceptable. Let all who can, come, and do so at once. There are hundreds of thousands of acres of rich land in Kansas, worth from $5 to $20 per acre, open to settlement for only a fraction of its value. Let the farmer come and bring his slaves with him. Let those without slaves come to protect our way of life. The loss of Kansas to the South will be the death knell of our institutions."

Atchison's voice got stronger as he closed in for his conclusion. "Missouri has done nobly, thus far, in overcoming those sent to Kansas by the abolitionists, but we cannot hold out much longer unless the whole South comes to the rescue. We need men! We need money! I urge you, send us both, without delay!"

The crowd stood as one and cheered the senator. Billy had never seen anything like it. He felt a surge of patriotism. Southern patriotism. Without action, and soon, his section of the country would be wronged. He grabbed a copy of each of the papers in the back of the room and stuffed them into one of his pockets.

As he rode his horse the three or so miles back to the farm, he pondered if this was the solution to his problem. In Mississippi, he would always be Charles' little brother, a man with no inheritance. This was an opportunity to better himself, and to do some good for the South. Was this a cause that he was willing to uproot himself and change his life for? He didn't see why not. Abolitionists taking over Kansas just didn't seem right. The senator, he thought, had made a lot of sense. Yes, he decided, he was going to do it.

CHAPTER 6

July, 1852— Monty had been looking forward to going home. During his years in Washington City, he had made the trip to Ohio several times, sometimes in the winter, when it took up to two weeks. This time, in the nice July weather, he expected that it would take less than half that. He would be following his usual route, taking the Baltimore and Ohio Railroad to Baltimore, and then traveling by stagecoach on the National Road in an almost straight line westward through Maryland, dipping briefly into Virginia and Pennsylvania, and across central Ohio, past Columbus to Springfield. From Springfield, it was only a few miles south to Dayton.

For the first couple of days, he kept rethinking his decision to resign from Congress. Had he been too rash, too temperamental? He kept coming to the same answer—no, he had not. How could he, in good conscious, have remained a member of Congress from the Whig Party when he did not support the party's position on slavery in the upcoming 1852 election, and when he loathed the party's presidential nominee, General Winfield Scott? Better to sit out the election, maybe even leave politics for good, he reaffirmed in his mind, than be a hypocrite.

In the afternoon of the third day out of Baltimore, the stage-coach came to a stop. Monty saw the driver get down from his seat and check the rear wheels. He and the four other passengers in the cramped coach looked at each other anxiously, hoping that their trip would not be delayed by any mechanical problems. Everything had been progressing smoothly so far.

"Just a loose bolt on the axle," said the driver, as he peered into an open window on the coach. "Nothing serious. I tightened it some and it will hold until we get to Gooding's Tavern in Wheeling and put in for the night. I'll fix it then. Only about five more miles."

"That's a relief," muttered the man sitting directly across from Monty, to no one in particular.

An hour or so later, as they entered Wheeling, on the Virginia side of the Ohio River, a woman in the coach pointed to a statue atop a large pedestal on the south side of the road. "That certainly looks interesting. I wonder what it is."

Monty, having stopped there before and read the inscriptions on the pedestal, responded. "It is a monument to Senator Henry Clay. Been there about twenty-five years. Clay was influential in getting the National Road extended and in bringing it through Wheeling, and the family that lives in the mansion there behind it had it erected to honor him and express their appreciation. The statue on the top represents a goddess, Liberty."

Every time he passed it, Monty had a feeling of pride that he had gotten to work for, and to know, the man for whom this monument had been built. It had only been only a couple of weeks since Clay's death. During the seemingly endless hours on the stagecoach, he had been reflecting on his visits with the ailing senator a month or so ago at the National Hotel in Washington City. They had talked about some uncomfortable things. Clay, although very ill, had shrewdly figured out Monty's failed plot to kill President Tyler back in 1844. The senator had not approved. He had bluntly told Monty that assassination, no matter how dire the political condition of the country may be, can never be the answer in a republic. But they had also gotten the opportunity to talk about the good times they had when Monty worked on the senator's staff. As the monument receded into the distance behind the stagecoach, Monty pondered what a testament it was to the longevity of Clay's career. He had been a child when it had been built. Even then, Clay had been a revered national figure, one to whom monuments were erected. No need for him to tell his traveling companions, he decided, of his personal connection to Clay. Bragging was not his style.

"Thank you. Much appreciated," responded the lady who had made the inquiry.

"A good man, Senator Clay," said the man sitting next to Monty. "God rest his soul. Damn shame he never became our president."

Monty and another man nodded in agreement.

The stagecoach pulled up to Gooding's Tavern. It was late afternoon, and the weary passengers got out and stretched their legs, while the driver retrieved their bags. Two other coaches had already arrived and had been pulled to the building's side, their horses unhitched. Monty looked at the three-story stone structure. He had stayed here before. A bit run down, but more than adequate for a brief overnight stay. The Widow Gooding's food was always some of the best that he experienced on his trips to and from Ohio. He hoped that she would be serving her fried chicken and apple cobbler tonight. The layout of Gooding's was standard for taverns on the National Road. On the first floor, there was a large dining room with a long table, seating about twenty, where dinner would be served family style. Across the foyer, there was a parlor, for after-dinner drinks and conversation, and the kitchen. The ladies would sleep, dormitory-style, on the second floor, and the men on the third. Monty, and most others, slept in their clothes, as the stagecoach drivers usually departed early, before seven in the morning.

An hour or so after arriving, Monty sat down for dinner. He was the second from the end of the table. Several others were already seated and had filled their plates. He saw a platter of fried chicken just to his right and reached out with his fork and stabbed a thigh. Good thing, he thought. The other meat was boiled mutton, a dish not to his liking. He added some potatoes, pickled beets, and a biscuit, still warm from the oven. The two men sitting nearest to him were already talking politics, about the upcoming 1852 election.

"I have to say," said one, "I don't care for either one of 'em. Pierce just doesn't have the experience we need in a president and Scott, well, I just don't have any confidence in him. He's past his prime. Do we really need another old general in the President's House? The last two we elected, Harrison and Taylor, died there."

"My view is that we have to go with the lesser of two evils," responded the other man. "The southern slavers got Pierce nominated and they have his ear. They already got more than they deserve under the compromise that was passed a couple of years ago. That Fugitive Slave Act still makes my blood boil. Pierce will give them more, whatever they want, in my opinion. So, it'll be Winfield Scott for me."

A couple of other men at the table chimed in with their opinions, one for Pierce and one for Scott.

"How about you, young man?," the man seated across from Monty asked, looking directly at him.

Monty always listened more than he talked during these dinner conversations in taverns with fellow travelers. This evening, he decided, would be no exception. Sure, he thought, he

could tell them that he had been, until last week, a congressman from Ohio, that he had gone to the Whig Convention
in Baltimore to try to keep Scott from being nominated, and
that he was leaving the Whig Party in disgust over Scott and
the party's timid position on slavery. He could be the center of
attention for the rest of the meal, and during the after-dinner
conversation in the parlor over cigars. But talking to impress
others never suited him. Instead, he looked at the man who had
asked him the question and responded, "Not sure. Could you
pass the apple cobbler, please?"

CHAPTER 7

July, 1852— It had been three days since the overnight stay at Gooding's Tavern in Wheeling and the long journey was finally nearing its end. This was Monty's second homecoming to Dayton in seven years. He was now thirty-six years old. The last time he had returned, in 1845, after working in Washington City for Senator Clay and for the staff of the Senate, he had only stayed about three years. Then, he had not left by choice, he always told others. He had been recruited by the Whig Party to run for Congress in 1848, not something that he had sought. But, if it had not been to serve in Congress, he had to admit to himself, he probably would have left for some other reason. As much as he enjoyed being with his parents and siblings, he wanted more out of life than spending the rest of his days in Dayton and working at the family's foundry. Exactly what, he did not know. At least not now. Politics, and particularly the issue of what to do about slavery in the United States, kept gnawing at him. It was something that remained in his thoughts, every day. After all, he had once plotted to kill a president to keep slavery from expanding. As he began to see familiar scenes just outside of Dayton, he had a feeling, even a hope, that something would come along and lure him away again.

There was barely enough room in the small carriage that Monty had hired in Springfield to hold himself, the two trunks he had shipped there, and the canvas travel bag that he had been using on the trip, the sum total of his life's possessions. It was early afternoon when the rig pulled up in front of the three-story brown clapboard house on Fourth Street with a large front porch. It was the only home that he remembered, his family having moved there before he was five. Before he could settle up with the driver, he heard footsteps on the porch and turned to see his mother, who had been sitting by a window in the parlor most of the day, eagerly awaiting the arrival of her first-born son. Elizabeth Tolliver was now fifty-six and the years had been good to her. She remained trim and had only a few flecks of gray in her brown hair, her spectacles the most noticeable concession to her age. Betsy, as she was known, was from Cincinnati and had married Monty's father, Roger, there when she was seventeen. Almost thirty-five years ago, with two small children, they had moved to Dayton for Roger to start his foundry. Two more children had followed. Since then, there had been some lean years for the foundry, but more good ones than bad. Her three other children had married and had given her five grandchildren, with one more on the way. Monty knew that Betsy was close to all of her children, but he felt a special bond with her. Since childhood, she had told him she believed that he was destined to do great things in life.

Mother and son embraced midway between the street and the porch. "Mother!," said Monty, "It's good to be home."

"I have missed you so much! How was the trip from Washington City?"

"Not bad at all. Good weather and it only took six days. Where's father?"

"Where do you think? At the foundry. He asked that you ride out there once you get settled, if you're up to it. Come inside, I've baked your favorite."

In the kitchen, over apple pie and coffee, Betsy filled her son in on the latest family news. His older sister, Martha, who lived in Cincinnati, was doing well. She had two children, a son and a daughter, who were entering their teen years. His other two siblings, Betsy continued, were still living close by in Dayton. His younger brother, Stuart, also had two children, both girls, and he still worked as a foreman at the foundry. Unlike Monty, Stuart had chosen to not go to college. Betsy's youngest child, Samantha, had married a local doctor and had one son, who was now three, and was expecting another child.

"Any news from around town?," Monty asked.

"I saw Theresa Copeland at the market the other day. She seems to be holding up as best as one could expect."

"Theresa Copeland?"

"Used to be Theresa Bennett. You remember her. You met her a few years ago."

"Yes, yes . . . Theresa. I had forgotten her married name. What do you mean she's holding up as best as one could expect?"

"She's a widow now, you know. Pretty sure I told you that before."

"No, you didn't," Monty insisted. "I definitely would have remembered, if you had."

"It was about a year and a half ago. Maybe two years. Her husband was killed in a carriage accident."

"That's terrible. What a tragedy. I seem to recall that they had a child?"

"Yes, a boy. Precious little thing. He's about six now, I reckon. I see him at the market now and then with his mother. Both of them now live with Theresa's parents."

"I must stop by and pay my condolences," replied Monty, "if that is what it would be called at this late date."

"Yes, that would be kind," Betsy replied. "I do recall how fond you were of her." She smiled. She could have updated Monty about any number of people that he knew in Dayton, but had chosen Theresa for a reason. It seemed to have worked. Monty was going to pay her a visit. Mothers had intuitions about such things.

Monty ate the last bite of his pie, took a sip of his coffee, and wiped his lips with a napkin, "Delicious, as always. Thank you," he said, adding, "Is Princess in the stable out back? I think I will head out to the foundry to see father and Stu."

"Yes, she's out there. A bit long in the tooth, but still a good ride, either under saddle or pulling the buggy."

The ten-year old, white-faced strawberry roan mare neighed as she saw Monty walk toward the stable. "Good girl," he said, holding out his flat hand with a sugar cube that he had taken from the kitchen. Bribery through food, he had learned at a young age, was the best way to get animals to cooperate. Within a few minutes, he had the tack and saddle in place and he mounted Princess for the three-mile trip to the foundry.

During the ride, he kept thinking about the conversation with his mother. Although tragic circumstances had brought it about, Theresa was now available again. To the extent that he ever had one, she had been the love of his life. He remembered the timing of it well, in late 1843, when he had come home for Christmas. He had called on her several times. She was intelligent and well-read, with auburn hair, blue eyes, and an infectious smile. A potential wife, he had thought.

Then, when he had returned to Washington City in early 1844, he had gotten involved in the plot to assassinate President Tyler. Not a good time to pursue romance, he had decided, and delayed contacting her. The death of his best friend, Ben, soon followed and, with his grief over that, there was more delay on his part. By the time he decided to contact her again, he learned that she was engaged. Theresa, he remembered, was about six years younger than he. That would make her thirty now, give or take a year. He had let her slip through his fingers back then. If it was within his power, he decided, he would not make the same mistake twice.

CHAPTER 8

July, 1852— Monty could see a dark plume of smoke rising from Tolliver's Metal Works long before he could see any of the buildings. It was a hot and dirty business, but one that had become increasingly important to the country's economy over the years. His father had started the foundry on the banks of the Miami River when Monty was just a child and when the uses of iron and other metals were primarily for carriage and wagon axles and wheels, kettles, and other assorted items. Now, boilers for steamships, locomotives, and other steam machinery, cast iron stoves and storefronts, and other large items, constituted most of the orders from customers. More than thirty men worked at the foundry, making it one of the largest employers in Dayton. Roger Tolliver was a good businessman and he had done well in providing for his family. They were not rich, but did not want for anything. As he got closer, Monty saw one of the large water wheels by the river, which helped to provide power to the machinery, turning. The structures then came into view—the foundry shop, machine shop, blacksmith shop, sawmill, carpentry shop, and a handful of storage build-ings—all crowded onto the four-acre property. He tied Princess to the hitching post in front of the storage building just past the entrance, where the offices were located.

Through the opened barn-like door, Monty saw the familiar figure of his father, whose face was turned away, moving a crate that appeared to be too heavy for him and struggling a bit with it. Just like him, Monty thought, still doing things that were better left for younger men with stronger backs.

"Excuse me, sir," Monty inquired, "do you have any jobs available?" He tried to disguise his voice, although not sure if he had done it successfully.

"It depends," responded Roger, rather tersely, as he began to turn around. He then laid eyes on his son, whom he had not seen for a year and a half. A broad smile came across his face. "For you, most definitely!"

Monty observed that his father had aged some, with a bit more gray in his full head of black hair, and perhaps some more wrinkles on his clean-shaven face. He may also have added a few pounds, Monty suspected, but still looked more fit than most men in their late fifties.

"It won't be hard work, will it?," asked Monty, jokingly, as father and son embraced.

"It is good to see you, son. Your mother and I were hoping you would arrive today. We weren't sure. She parked herself by the front window before I left this morning. I assume you already stopped by the house?"

"I did. Mother looks good."

"She always does. How was the trip?'

"Uneventful, and quick, thank goodness. Sure beats traveling in the winter."

"Come into the office, so we can catch up," said Roger, motioning toward the open doorway to the right side of the structure. There were three offices off of the short hallway, each with pine lumber walls and a window. Plain and rustic, as Monty had remembered the place. They went into Roger's office, the one farthest down the hall, and the largest. The first one was empty. That was the one Monty had occupied when he had worked at the foundry a few years ago, before he left for Congress. The second office was used by the bookkeeper. "Jeff is off today," said Roger, as they passed the middle door. Monty planted himself in the uncomfortable wooden chair in front of his father's desk.

"I saw in your last letter that you got to spend some time with Senator Clay before he passed last month."

"I did," Monty responded. "Had a few good visits with him at the National Hotel. He was sick and weak, but was as mentally sharp as ever. We talked about a lot of things."

"Sorry to hear that the politics got so bad that you had to resign your seat and leave Washington City," said Roger. "Fillmore has been an adequate president. Wish he had gotten the nomination. I don't see either one of those two jokers we'll be choosing from in November doing any better."

"I just couldn't stay on. I'm not sure I will even remain a Whig and I'm damn sure not voting for a Democrat. I'll either write in a name, or not vote at all."

"Well, Washington City's loss is our gain. We are glad to have you back home. Are you open to what I wrote about in my last letter?," asked Roger.

"The job? Yes, of course, if you will have me," Monty confirmed.

"Definitely. Pick up where you left off in '49. Be the face of the foundry in the community, and work to get more business. You were great at it before. With your experience in Congress, I'm sure you'll be even better at it now. You have those skills, much better than I do. You know that I have always preferred the practical side more, working with the men and making sure that our work is done to specifications and made with quality."

"What about Stu? Won't he be offended if I step back in? He has been here with you for a long time?"

"I talked with your brother. He's on board one-hundred percent. Excited about it, in fact. He's more like me, and would rather be sweating in the shops with the men than putting on fancy clothes and talking business."

"Then we have a deal," said Monty.

"Excellent," said Roger. "Your old office down the hall is still empty. You can start tomorrow."

CHAPTER 9

*O**ctober, 1852—*** "Thank you, sir, for coming." Monty said as he stood up from the table to greet his dinner companion. He had arrived early. This was one meeting to which he did not want to be late. The gentlemen had suggested the restaurant, one of the nicer ones in Dayton, when Monty had advised that he had something important to discuss and would like to do so over dinner. It was early October, three months since he had returned home. There was a crispness in the fall air and the leaves on the trees were starting to turn.

"Of course, glad to do so," replied Nathaniel Bennett, the owner of a local dry goods store.

It was not his guest's business, but his daughter, that was the intended subject of the dinner conversation. Monty had first met Theresa Bennett, now Theresa Copeland, on a visit home from Washington in December 1843. A friend from school had suggested that he call on her and Monty knew from the several times that they were together over those couple of weeks that she was special.

Now thirty years old, Theresa's current status was due to two tragedies. At nineteen, she had been engaged to a local man who died of cholera a few months before their intended wedding. In her grief, she had withdrawn from society for a couple of years. At her parents' suggestion, she then began teaching at a primary school. Her work and her interactions with the children had improved her spirits and she had begun to see gentleman callers again around the time that she met Monty. She felt the same way about him as he did about her, and was disappointed when she did not hear from him for months after he had returned to Washington City. By the time he contacted her, she was engaged to another man. They had married in 1845. The marriage was a happy one and they, a year later, had a child, a boy they named Joshua.

Three years later, fate again struck a blow to Theresa's young life. Her husband was killed in a carriage accident while on a business trip to Cincinnati. She and her son were taken in by her parents. After two years, the grief had lessened, although it was not gone. Theresa pushed herself to move forward with her life. She was still young, did not want to remain known as "The Widow Copeland" for the rest of her life, and wanted Joshua to have a new father. Her heart had jumped when she heard that Monty had resigned from Congress and was moving back to Dayton.

When Monty visited her to express his regret over the loss of her husband, they both felt a rekindling of the feelings that they had had for each other almost a decade earlier. Both now in their thirties, they knew that the clock of life was ticking. Monty asked to call on her and Theresa had readily agreed. They picked up where they had left off and their relationship grew into one of love. They visited each other's families, went out with friends, took long walks, read poetry together, and did the things that young couples do. Little Josh developed an affection for Monty and Monty adored him.

Monty was more nervous than he had thought he would be. "Mr. Bennett," he said, after they had ordered their meals and were waiting for the food to arrive, "You are no doubt aware that I have grown very fond of Theresa. She is a very special woman. I am not one to beat around the bush. I would like to have your daughter as my wife and I would like your blessing."

Bennett smiled. "I suspected that this might be the purpose of your dinner invitation. I discussed it with my wife. We are both very pleased and excited. You have our wholehearted blessing and support and we would welcome you as part of our family." He reached across the table and extended his right hand to Monty.

Over dinner, they discussed wedding plans. "I was thinking sooner, rather than later," said Monty to his father-in-law to be. "Neither Theresa nor I are getting any younger and I see no reason to wait. How does New Year's Day sound to you?"

"That sounds splendid!," replied Bennett. "A good way to start the new year. I will need to get Mrs. Bennett's approval, of course."

"And I will need to get Theresa's."

CHAPTER 10

November, 1853— Monty sat, nervously, in the parlor of the small house that he had purchased upon his marriage to Theresa. Their wedding on New Year's Day had been a relatively small affair. It was, after all, Theresa's second marriage. A service at the Methodist church that Monty's parents attended, with family and a few friends looking on, was followed by a reception at the home of the Bennetts.

In the year since then, Monty's life had been happy, and relatively quiet. He enjoyed resuming his job at the foundry and being able to work with his father and brother there. He was not a technical expert in metallurgy, as they were, but his experience and knowledge from his work in Washington City had brought other skills to the business. His likable personality and his ability to remember names and faces served him well. As a former congressman, he was well known in Dayton, somewhat of a local celebrity. His ideas for pursuing new lines of business, including making parts for weapons for the military, and locomotive parts for railroads, had already produced new contracts. The foundry had hired a few more employees.

He continued to be frustrated with the political situation in the country. Since their heavy losses in the 1852 election, the Whigs remained in decline, maybe a fatal one, he thought. The Democrats ran things now. In the South, slavery continued, as it always had. The abolitionists in New England made anti-slavery speeches and published their newspapers, but were viewed as cranks and extremists throughout much of the North. A year after arriving back in Ohio, Monty continued to only observe, not participate. One day, he kept telling himself, he would get back in the fight.

But it was what was going on upstairs in his home that concerned him the most now. Theresa had become pregnant a couple of months into the marriage. They were both happy about it and were excited. Josh, who was looking forward to having a sibling, had been picked up by Theresa's parents the previous day to stay with them for a while. Monty heard the footsteps of the midwife, Mrs. Sullivan, every now and then. He felt confident that she knew what she was doing. She was experienced and had been recommended by his parents. Her mother had delivered Monty's two younger siblings. He could not sit still for more than a couple of minutes at a time. He got up from his chair and paced around the room, and then into the dining room. Occasionally, a groan from Theresa made its way down the stairway. The last time the midwife had called down to him, she said it would be at least another hour. He pulled his watch out of his pocket. He got up and paced some more. It had now been another hour and a half. Why is this taking so long, he kept asking himself. He resolved to be patient and decided to wait fifteen more minutes before calling up to her. Then, a few minutes later, he heard it. The unmistakable sound of the cries of a baby. Relieved, he let out a sigh. Then, he became worried again. What about Theresa?

It seemed like another hour, but it was likely only a couple of minutes before Mrs. Sullivan, in her Irish accent, called down to him. "Mr. Tolliver, you have a baby boy. Congratulations! Mrs. Tolliver is resting and is doing well. Give me another fifteen minutes and you can come up."

Now, he was truly relieved. He looked at his watch again. He waited. Finally, it was time. He then ran up the stairs and into the bedroom. There, he saw his beautiful wife, propped up by pillows in bed, holding a bundle wrapped in a yellow blanket across her chest. She appeared to be exhausted, but looked up and gave Monty a big smile when she noticed him at the doorway. Mrs. Sullivan motioned for him to come over to the bed. He walked over and gave Theresa a kiss on the forehead.

"Meet our son. Would you like to hold him?" she asked.

Monty bent down, picked up the baby, and gently began to sway him in his arms. He looked at the red face, squinty eyes, and the tuft of dark hair on the top of his head. After only a minute or so, as he had feared, the child began to cry. He held him to his chest and tried to calm him, without success.

"I think he's calling for his mother," said Mrs. Sullivan.

He gently placed the baby back in Theresa's arms and the crying stopped.

"Have you decided on a name?," asked the midwife.

Monty looked at Theresa. "Are you still agreeable to what we discussed?," he asked.

"Of course, I am honored to have our son named after your late friend."

"Benjamin. His name will be Benjamin," Monty said, proudly, to Mrs. Sullivan. "Benjamin Bennett Tolliver."

CHAPTER 11

*O*ctober, 1854— "Will I ever get there?" Robert muttered to himself, as he stood on the deck, near the bow, of the *Morning Star*, a rundown steamboat that he had boarded in St. Louis. He imagined how the ship might have looked in its prime. Now, it just looked old. The deck boards were gray, split and, in a few spots, warped. What had once been white walls were smudged with dirt and grime and, where there was any exposed metal, it was mostly rusted.

It was the latest leg, but not the last, of his long trip to the Kansas Territory, and to his new life. Although the travel had been slow, he had no regrets. He had been aboard for four days now, and there were at least three to go. Maybe more, depending on the fickle conditions of the Missouri River. He would disembark at Kansas City, and then take an overland route the last forty or so miles into Kansas, to Lawrence. This town, named after Amos Lawrence, the treasurer of the New England Emigrant Aid Company, whom he had met at the church back in Newport, was to be the main settlement for free-staters moving into the territory. He had written to George Washington Brown, who was going to be the editor of the *Herald of Freedom* newspaper in Lawrence, seeking employment and advising of his experience in the newspaper business. He had worked in all aspects of it in his years at the *Newport Mercury*, he advised his prospective employer, but it was writing that he had become passionate about. He wanted it to be his life's work. Be a real reporter, for a newspaper that made a difference in people's lives. The *Herald's* editor had responded that he would hold a job open for Robert, until the beginning of December. If all went as planned, he would beat that deadline by a few weeks.

He stared at the muddy water. It had been a long trip. He had already grown tired of life on a riverboat. A few days ago, his wish had been to never have to set foot onto a railroad car again. He had been jerked, bounced, and jostled so much that every muscle in his body had ached. Now, he thought, he probably preferred being on the rails to being afloat. At least the scenery passed more quickly on a train.

The journey had started with great fanfare. He and his fellow clients of the New England Emigrant Aid Company (twenty-four, by his count) had been given a grand sendoff at the train station in Boston. Abolitionists had gathered to show their support, as if the Israelites were heading out to smite the Philistines. A brass band played, folks lined the platform and shouted, sang, and cheered. They were excited to be seeing one of the first colonies of Yankees off to save Kansas from slavery. Two days later, when Robert's group arrived in Albany, there had been an equally enthusiastic reception, to encourage them in their journey. The farther west they traveled, however, the fewer the well-wishers to greet them at each station. By the time they reached Buffalo, they were just like any other passengers, unnoticed. Robert liked that better, he didn't need to be in the limelight. He just wanted to start a new life, and help a cause that he believed in.

Onward, westward, the trains had chugged, to Cleveland, to Chicago, and then south to St. Louis. One day, they had been delayed for hours, sweating in hot railroad cars, when a broken-down locomotive had to be repaired. That had been somewhere in Indiana. Although the Boston agent for the Emigrant Aid Company had promised that there would be first-class accommodations at the hotels they stayed in along the way, in reality, they had been, most of the time, less than desirable. He was glad that there were no women or children in their group, given some of the conditions.

As the days on the rails passed, one song that had been sung enthusiastically by the crowd at the Boston station stuck in his mind. He hummed it to himself, over and over, on the trains. Set to the tune of *Auld Lang Syne*, it had become the anthem of Kansas emigrants. Of the words, he mostly remembered the refrain:

> *We cross the prairies, as of old*
> *Our fathers crossed the sea;*
> *To make the West, as they the East,*
> *The homestead of the Free!*

At St. Louis, the mode of transportation shifted from rail to water. From bad to worse, in his opinion. It rained heavily the first two days. The food served on the *Morning Star* was barely edible, and the sleeping conditions were worse. Robert could not afford a cabin, so he slept, along with dozens of others, on mattresses spread out on the floor of the ship's dining room. The third night, when the weather had been nicer, he had pulled his mattress out onto the deck. At least the air there had been fresher, and the snoring of his fellow travelers had been less bothersome.

The ship was crowded, and getting more so. At each westward stop in Missouri, a few more passengers got on. Most were men, rugged looking, some with no baggage at all. The travel information given out by the company in Boston had warned New England emigrants to Kansas to be suspicious of the locals once they reached western Missouri. There had been stories of intimidation, threats, even beatings, by proslavery thugs—dubbed "border ruffians" by the eastern press—to persuade emigrants to have second thoughts about life in Kansas, and to turn around and head back home.

Robert first saw the three of them get on the *Morning Star* at Lexington, around noon, and made a mental note. Stay away and keep your distance. If they weren't some of the border ruffians that he had been warned about, then they should be. They certainly looked the part—burly, bearded men, clad as much in leather as in cloth. One stood over six feet, with the two others several inches less, but just as menacing looking. Like a grizzly bear, Robert thought, with two nearly grown cubs. A bowie knife and a revolver hung from each of their belts. He could not help but feel that the big one kept staring at him.

A couple of hours later, while Robert was standing at the ship's railing taking in the wooded coastline, he heard a noise from behind. He turned and looked. Papa bear stood no more than a foot from his face.

"Where you from, boy?," the man asked, in a gruff tone.

Robert resisted the urge to object to being called a boy. He was, he judged, just as old as, or older, than this character. "Back East, from Rhode Island," he responded. As soon as the words left his mouth, he wished he could have taken them back. Too much information. Why hadn't he said "Here and there" or "Who's asking?" Still, with his accent, there was no way he could lie and say he was from anywhere other than New England, even if he had wanted to.

"Are you sound on the goose?," came the next question from the man/beast.

"Come again?," asked a puzzled Robert.

"Are you sound on the goose?," the man repeated, this time more forcefully.

"I don't understand."

"That's all I need to know," replied the man, as he turned, spat a wad of brown tobacco juice onto the deck, and walked away.

CHAPTER 12

September, 1854— "Father, is everything alright?," Monty asked, as he stood in the doorway of Roger's office at the foundry.

"I'm fine," responded Roger. "What do you mean?"

"I stopped by the house last night after dinner. Needed to pick up one of the boys' coats that we left there last Sunday. Mother said you had come back here to the foundry to work for a couple of hours. I wasn't aware that we had any rush projects. Anything I can help you with?"

In the two years since Monty had returned to Dayton, he had often tried, in vain, to convince Roger to cut back on his work and delegate more tasks to others.

"No, no. Nothing like that," said Roger. He then bit his lower lip and sat silently for a few seconds. "I probably should have told you about this before now," he added.

A puzzled look came across Monty's face. "About what?" he asked, as he squinted his eyes and cocked his head to one side.

Roger got up, walked past Monty, and closed the door to his office. "As you know," he said, lowering the volume of his voice, "sometime the workers will drop by to ask me questions.

Can't be too cautious when talking about this." He returned to his chair behind the desk.

"Talking about what?," Monty asked.

"Over the past few months, I've been going to meetings of abolitionists here in Dayton. I decided to become more involved with them and, a few weeks ago, agreed to let runaway slaves hide out here, at the foundry, for a night or two. A safe house, they call it."

Monty was overcome with a feeling of pride, manifesting itself as a grin. He knew that his father opposed slavery, but this news was a surprise. A welcome one. Roger was not a man to take unnecessary risks. Although the door to the office was closed, following Roger's lead, he spoke softly, but in an excited manner. "My father, a conductor on the Underground Railroad. Good for you!"

"Not a conductor," Roger corrected. "Just providing a place for them to stay. A station master, they call it. The conductors do the hard work, taking on the challenge of leading the poor souls from stop to stop, moving them farther north."

"Well, they couldn't do it if they didn't have safe places to stay. Where do you put them up?"

"In a building behind here, the one closest to the river. You may remember that we used it as a sawmill until we built the new one. It's fairly secluded and is used for storage now. None of the workers go around there anymore. Big enough to pull a wagon inside and hide it. I built a small pen in the woods near there to keep a couple of horses overnight. Also have a rowboat around the back, in case the authorities come looking and a quick escape on the water is needed."

"Does Mother know about this?"

"Yes, she does. You know that I've never been good at keeping anything from her. It worries her, because of the risk, but she is supportive. She cooks some extra things when we have our guests and I bring them in."

"How does all of this work?"

"You know that boarding house on Ohio Avenue, the one run by Mrs. Pierson?"

"The gray one with the big porch?"

"Yes, that's the one. I pass by there on my way to work each day. If she has a red quilt hanging on her laundry line, that's my signal to expect visitors that night. I either stay here late, or come back after dinner, like I did last night. After it gets dark, I get a signal from the conductor, get everyone situated, and then I head back home. They're usually gone before dawn. There was one group that had to stay over two nights, because we got word there were bounty hunters in the area looking for them."

"How often do they come through?"

"Well, I've only been doing it for a bit more than a month. Seems to be about once every ten days or so. Had three groups so far, including the one that came through last night."

"I'm proud of you, father. I was a congressman and you've actually done more for the fight against slavery in a few weeks here in Dayton than I was able to do in over three years in the House of Representatives."

"Every little bit helps, that's for sure. Wish I could do more."

CHAPTER 13

O *ctober, 1854*— Raven took a few steps into the cold water of the Ohio River, reached out, and grabbed the end of a rope. It had been tossed by a young white man, who was leaning over the bow of the small rowboat. Although it was dark, she recognized him from the last couple of runs across the river. She knew him as Merlin, his codename. Beyond that, she knew nothing else about him, nor he about her. Theirs was an enterprise in which stopping to chat was not encouraged, nor wise. As she walked backward a few steps and pulled the boat toward the bank, she asked him, barely above a whisper, "How many we got tonight?"

"Three," he responded, just as quietly.

She was pleased with the information. Three was always a good number to transport, she thought. All could fit in the bed of her wagon, they could easily stick together when walking through woods, and a smaller group meant it was less likely that someone would make a mistake and get them caught. She had guided a group of five once, a few months ago, and that had been a challenge.

In the darkness, she could barely see the three figures, two men and a woman, as they eased themselves over the side of the rowboat, into the shallow water, and made their way to the muddy riverbank. She motioned to one of the men to come over and stand next to her, and both of them then gave the front of the rowboat a strong shove. She watched as Merlin's face faded into the darkness.

"This way," she said, as she led them up to the top of the riverbank, and then down a path, to her horse and wagon. Fallen leaves crackled under their feet. Old Red, her aged chestnut gelding, stood just where she had left him, patiently waiting. Raven lifted up the canvas tarpaulin that covered the bed of the wagon and motioned for her three charges to get in, lie down, and cover themselves. After an affectionate rubbing of Old Red's soft white nose, and a treat of half a carrot that she pulled from her pocket, they were on their way.

The ride to Raven's home, about two miles away, over familiar dirt roads, took, in the darkness, over an hour. It was now well past midnight and she neither passed nor saw anyone. Always a good thing, she thought to herself. Because of its age and rundown condition, her house, on the outskirts of Cincinnati, was really more of a shack. It was fairly secluded, at the end of a path, with two small rooms on the main floor, and a loft above. One room, containing the fireplace, was where she slept, cooked, and lived. Raven supported herself as a seamstress and the other room was where she worked, filled with pieces and bolts of cloth, a comfortable chair for sewing, and a large waist-high table. But it was what was under the table that made the place perfectly suited for Raven's other job. Beneath the rug, a trap door led to a root cellar, about eight feet deep and six feet square. It could hold three people comfortably, up to five if needed, for hours at a time. An underground pipe, leading to a vent in the rear of the shack, provided some fresh air.

"Y'all must be exhausted," said Raven, as she pulled up the corner of the tarpaulin, and pointed to the back door of the shack. "Let's go, and be quick about it. Never know who may be watching."

Once inside, she lit a few candles, pulled up chairs for everyone, and got a good look at her new guests. They were young. Of course, she thought, everyone looked young to her these days. Their skin tone was a bit lighter than her own. One of the men and the woman were holding hands and were a couple, she surmised, likely in their early twenties. The other male was younger, probably in his mid-teens. They were dressed in well-worn and dirty garments, made of homespun coarse cotton. The men had loose-fitting shirts and trousers and the woman a frock, pulled over what appeared to be a silk blouse that had seen its better days. Their shoes looked worse, with at least one good-sized hole on the outside of each.

"I'm Raven," she said. "Y'all are now in the free state of Ohio." She loved how that statement always brought smiles to faces. "You must be thirsty and hungry," she continued, as she pulled a large chunk of bread from a loaf she had baked a couple of days before, poured some water into a gourd, and started to pass them around. "Ain't much, but it'll have to do for now."

"Bless you, Miss Raven," said the older of the two men. "The Good Book says, 'They that serve only the Lord their God shall be blessed with bread and water.'" He continued, "I'm Josiah, and this here's my wife, Eliza, and my brother, Jacob."

"How long y'all been traveling?" asked Raven.

"About three weeks, give or take. We was on a cotton plantation in Alabama. How far we got to go?"

"I'm a-taking you farther north. Y'all be with me a couple of days and then somebody else gonna take over. You can go clear on to Canada, if you want. That's another three weeks, maybe more."

Eliza spoke up, for the first time. "What do you suggest, Miss Raven?"

"If you stay in America—Ohio, Michigan, anywhere—there's always a risk of bounty hunters coming after you and taking you back down South. You can get fake freedom papers, but ain't no guarantee they'll be accepted. Or you can go to Canada. That's for you to decide. You'se free now."

"Thank you for helping us, ma'am," said the younger man, Jacob.

Raven walked over to the work area and motioned to the two brothers, "Help me move this table. You gonna need to sleep in my root cellar. Never know if we was followed from the river. Don't want any white folk pounding on my door and finding you."

After the door was opened, she handed each of them a blanket. "Wrap this around you," she said. "Can get cool down there. Careful on the ladder."

"Thank you, Miss Raven," said Eliza.

"Get some rest. We'll head out in the morning."

Later, as she lay in her small bed, although exhausted, Raven found it hard to get to sleep. The next two days would be full of risks and challenges.

CHAPTER 14

*O**ctober, 1854***— "Monty, did you *hear* me?," Theresa asked, the tone of her voice clearly expressing her annoyance.

"I'm sorry, dear, no, I did not. What did you say?"

"I already asked you twice. Would you like more coffee?," she repeated for the third time.

"Yes, please, and thank you."

Theresa grabbed the coffee pot from the cast iron stove and walked over to the kitchen table and refilled Monty's cup. "You're certainly captivated by that newspaper. What's so interesting?," she inquired.

"Finally, a politician is talking some sense about the Kansas-Nebraska Act, confronting Senator Douglas, face-to-face, and putting him in his place."

"And who might that be?"

"A fellow named Lincoln, from Illinois. Abraham Lincoln. He used to be a Whig congressman a few years ago. Served a single term, the one before I started there. I met him briefly on the day that I was sworn in."

"Where was this speech?"

"Some town in Illinois. Pe-or-i-a, according to this article. Not sure if I'm pronouncing that right. At a joint appearance with Douglas. Says here that Douglas spoke first and argued why, in his view, letting people in the territories vote on having slavery is a good thing. Democracy in action, he said. He also spewed out, as he always does, his hatred of Negroes. Lincoln responded and refuted all of Douglas' arguments. He said a lot of the things that I have been thinking. Of course, he expresses them much better than I ever could."

"Tell me what he said."

"The gist of it is that slavery is morally wrong, an evil, and that everyone, including southerners, knows it. That is why, he argued, since the founding of the republic, restrictions have been put on it, with the support of southerners, so that it cannot spread. The Founding Fathers accepted it in the South, only out of necessity, to get the country formed. But they then banned it in the Northwest Territory and banned the importation of more slaves, making it piracy and punishable by death. Then, in 1820, the Missouri Compromise banned it in more territory, again with agreement from the South. Why do all of that, Lincoln asked, if there was not a recognition of, and a consensus, that slavery is morally wrong and should not be allowed to grow?"

"That makes a lot of sense," commented Theresa.

"The Kansas-Nebraska Act," Monty continued, "said Lincoln, reverses all of that. It allows slavery to spread, under the false guise of democracy. He says the Missouri Compromise should never have been repealed and that it must be reinstated."

* * *

After one term in Congress from 1847 to 1849, Abraham Lincoln left politics, returned to his home in Springfield, and practiced law. He was out of the public eye for a few years. It was his opposition to the Kansas-Nebraska Act that caused him to speak out again and be heard. In October 1854, Lincoln squared off against the law's primary author, Senator Stephen Douglas, in Peoria, in their home state of Illinois. Hundreds gathered on the lawn of the courthouse, in a foreshadowing of the famous debates that the two men would have four years hence in their campaign for a seat in the United States Senate. Douglas spoke first, for about three hours, arguing that the new law was democratic, and stating that he did not care one way or the other if slavery was voted up or down in Kansas or Nebraska, only that the process of deciding the issue should be by a vote of the people, under the doctrine of popular sovereignty.

Lincoln's extended remarks in response, also lasting about three hours, are viewed by historians as his reentry into politics, the first public airing of his refined views on slavery, and an expression of the political beliefs that would propel him to the presidency in the election of 1860. Lincoln was not an abolitionist, but favored containment of slavery to where it already existed. He argued that this had always been, since days of the Founding Fathers, the policy of the country, a policy that existed because of a fundamental American belief that slavery was morally wrong. Despite this, he argued, the Kansas-Nebraska Act undid all of this and provided a method for slavery to expand. In one of the speech's most famous passages, Lincoln derided Douglas' statement that he had no personal opinion whether slavery should or should not be approved in the new territories:

> "This *declared* indifference, but as I must think, covert *real zeal* for the spread of slavery, I cannot but hate. I hate it because of the monstrous injustice of slavery itself. I hate it because it deprives

our republican example of its just influence in the world—enables the enemies of free institutions, with plausibility, to taunt us as hypocrites—causes the real friends of freedom to doubt our sincerity, and especially because it forces so many really good men amongst ourselves into an open war with the very fundamental principles of civil liberty—criticizing the Declaration of Independence, and insisting that there is no right principle of action but self-interest."

* * *

"Sounds like you have a new hero, this Mr. Lincoln," said Theresa.

"I wouldn't go that far, but it's always good to know that there's someone out there publicly expressing what you believe in. Maybe there's some hope yet for us Whig congressmen who've been put out to pasture."

"Perhaps another one is chafing to get back into the arena?"

"Me? No, of course not."

Theresa gave him one of those looks, the kind that spouses do when one knows the other is not being entirely truthful.

"I hear the boys stirring," she said. "I need to go up to them."

"And I need to get on my way to the foundry."

As he went out the door, Monty pondered how, in only a couple of years of marriage, Theresa always had the ability to read him so well. He had said no, but in his heart, he knew she was right.

CHAPTER 15

ctober, 1854— Raven pulled the reins to her right side. Old Red compiled and the wagon rounded a curve on the narrow dirt road. It was then that she first saw him, a man mounted on a motionless black horse about a quarter of a mile ahead. Her heart sank. The day had been going so well, at least up to now.

She turned her head to the side and covered her mouth, pretending to cough. "Could be trouble ahead," she said to Josiah and the two others, in a voice loud enough to be heard over the noise of the moving wagon. "Stay still and quiet." She hoped that Josiah, lying on his back in darkness, was able to get his hands on the knife that she had given him.

It was early afternoon. They had been on the road about six hours, having left Raven's home shortly after sunrise. The evening before, she had pulled the wagon around to the rear of the shack, close to the back door. Despite only having a few hours of rest, she had awakened early, with energy. Days like this, moving runaways in her care farther away from the South, always excited her. She lit a fire in her small fireplace, made some oatmeal and coffee, and helped her three guests up from the root cellar. As they ate, she explained what to expect. She would be taking them to Dayton, about fifty miles away, to a safe house. There, they would be met by another Underground Railroad conductor, who would lead them farther north. It would be a two-day trip and, en route, they would be hidden in her wagon. Most of the traveling, about two-thirds of it, would take place this day, to Springboro. That town, she explained, was a friendly community with several safe houses. They would overnight and spend most of the next day there, until mid-afternoon, and then head out for the remaining miles to Dayton, to arrive there in darkness, and to another safe house.

Outside, as dawn started to break, Josiah, Eliza, and Jacob had laid down, faces up, in the bed of the wagon, with their heads nearest to the driver's bench. Josiah was between the two others. Raven then placed an insert made of thin boards, cut the width and length of the wagon and nailed together, into grooves cut about half way up the bed, concealing her secret cargo underneath. They had more than enough room to move around a bit. On top of this false bottom of the wagon, she had then loaded several bolts of cloth, pieces of folded loose fabric, along with some of her sewing tools, and then covered them all with a tarpaulin, which she tied down tightly.

From past trips, she knew the route to Dayton well. In the late morning, she had passed Monroe. Springboro would be the next town, still a few miles away. It was good traveling weather. A perfect June day, Raven thought. The ground was dry, the temperature warm, but not hot, and only a few puffy clouds in the otherwise deep blue sky.

As she approached the man, he edged his horse into the road, blocking the wagon. She slowed and brought it to a stop.

"Afternoon, sir. Ain't it a beautiful day? Praise Jesus!," she said, in a cheerful tone, trying to mask her fear. From experience, she always liked to start the conversation in these encounters. Sometimes, a friendly demeanor made them back off. Being rude and hostile, she had found, usually fed their natural dislike of Black folk. She noticed that the man wore no badge, making her more suspicious that he was a bounty hunter. He had a neatly trimmed dark beard, a black slouch hat, and a revolver dangling from his belt.

"Where ya headed?," he asked, gruffly, as he dismounted his horse and walked toward the wagon.

"Up to Springboro."

"You sure got a big load there," he said, eyeing the tarpaulin covering the wagon. "What ya hauling?"

"Bunches of fabric and sewing supplies," Raven replied. "I'm a seamstress. On my way to see Mrs. Dempsey in Springboro. She's the mayor's wife. I'm gonna be making new draperies for her house. Did some work for her before. Got a meeting set up this here afternoon. Said she wanted to see every color and style I got, so I done brought it all."

As soon as she spoke the words, she worried that her lie had conveyed too much information. Maybe she shouldn't have made up a name. What if this miscreant decided that he would accompany her into town and to the non-existent Dempsey house? She decided she would deal with that if and when the time came.

"Is that so?," the man responded, skeptically. "Seems like a lot of fabric."

He's not gonna go away easily, Raven thought. She hoped that Josiah had gotten a firm grip on that knife.

The man walked over to the rear of the wagon and began to loosen the rope on one of the corners of the tarpaulin. As he did so, Raven noticed dirt and grime on both of his hands.

"Mind if I take a look?," he said.

Raven knew it was a statement of intent, not a request for permission. She breathed in and out slowly, trying to control her anxiety, and brought a forced smile to her face.

"Look all you want, mister. I don't got nothing to hide. Just be careful not to get your dirty hands on any of the fabric. Mrs. Dempsey won't take too kindly to that."

As the man began to peer under the tarpaulin, Raven heard a sound coming from behind. Hoofbeats. Unless it was another bounty hunter, she thought, it had to be a good thing. Perhaps there would be a way out of what was looking to be an ugly and violent situation. She turned around and saw a one-horse buggy with two men in it. The driver pulled his rig to the right side of the wagon and slowed to a stop.

"Good day to thee," the driver said to Raven and to the man, doffing his hat. "May we be of any assistance?"

Raven looked at the two men in the buggy and had an instantaneous feeling of relief. Her tense muscles loosened and her heavy breaths eased. "Quakers, thank God!," she whispered to herself. They were clean shaven and plainly dressed, with broad-brimmed black parson hats, collarless white shirts, and gray trousers, held up by suspenders. Both had fair complexions, thin noses and lips, and prominent chins. Brothers, she suspected. In her training for the Underground Railroad, she had been taught to look out for Quakers when on journeys and to seek help from them, if needed, as they would likely be friendly and sympathetic to the cause. She knew that many Quakers lived in and around Springboro.

"Good afternoon to you!," responded Raven.

The bearded man looked up briefly from underneath the tarpaulin, but said nothing.

"This gentleman here asked to inspect my load," Raven continued. "I'm a seamstress from Dayton. Heading up to Springboro to see Mrs. Dempsey, the mayor's wife. Gonna be making new draperies for her house and just bringing her a load of fabrics to look over."

The man lifted the tarpaulin higher, revealing an assortment of rolls of fabric, in shades of greens, reds, and blues.

"Mrs. Dempsey, you say, wife of the mayor?" said the Quaker who held the reins, more in the tone of a question than a repetition of her words. He hesitated for a couple of seconds and then added, "We are from Springboro."

Raven swallowed hard and felt a pain in her stomach, certain he was about to say that he knew almost everyone in Springboro and that there was no Mayor Dempsey, nor a Mrs. Dempsey, revealing her lie, and prompting the bounty hunter to inspect her wagon more closely.

"Caleb," the other Quaker quickly chimed in, "I thought I told thee that I saw Mrs. Dempsey at the market recently. I believe it was on Third Day, and she mentioned that she had retained the services of a seamstress from Dayton to do some work for her. None too soon, I have to say, from my recollection of the look of the draperies in that house."

"Abner, I do believe thou did."

"Ma'am," Abner continued, "we are headed into Springboro ourselves and will be glad to accompany thee. It would please us to have a visit with our old friends, the Dempseys."

"That would be much appreciated, thank you," said a grateful Raven.

"At your service," said Abner, as he tipped his hat and bowed slightly in her direction.

The bounty hunter, overhearing it all, lowered the tarpaulin, retied it and, with a look of disgust on his face, said good day to all, mounted his horse, and headed south, in search of easier prey elsewhere.

All stared intently at him until he was a good distance away and until they were certain that he was not going to turn his horse around, raise his gun, and come charging back.

As the Quakers pulled their buggy even with the front of the wagon, Raven noticed Caleb shake his head and look at his brother.

"Thou shall not lie, Abner," he said, and then broke into a slight grin.

"The Lord will understand and forgive," Abner responded, "I am quite certain."

"As will Mayor and Mrs. Dempsey, wherever they may be," added Caleb.

They both chuckled, as did Raven.

Raven leaned back and to the side, closer to the bed of the wagon.

"All's good," she said, "We're on our way again," as she gathered the reins and started northward again toward Springboro.

CHAPTER 16

*O*ctober, 1854— Robert stood at the stern of the *Morning Star*, staring at the seemingly endless ribbon of water through which the ship had passed. A screech from above attracted his attention, his eyes focusing on a hawk, flying low, just to the left of the ship, hot in pursuit of some prey. Probably a sparrow, he thought. Just as both disappeared into the woods by the riverbank, he felt his upper body lurch forward, and then suddenly backward. He still had a slight pain in the base of his neck from the last time.

"Dang! Not another sandbar! Second one today," he heard a young man, standing a few feet away from him, exclaim. The words had been spoken in Robert's direction, and with a decidedly southern accent. He had noticed the speaker, whom he judged to be a few years younger than he, walking around the ship for the past couple of days, but they had never met. Can't just ignore him, Robert decided, thinking it would be awkward and, unlike many of the others, he didn't look menacing.

"I've lost count," Robert responded. "Hope they get us moving again quicker than last time." He extended his hand. "I'm Robert. Robert Geddis."

"Billy Rutledge. Pleased to meet ya," came the response, as the two shook hands. "Low water level on the river and an overloaded ship will do it every time. I reckon we're gonna get stuck on every last one of 'em."

"Hope not. Where you headed?"

"Lecompton. Gonna stake out some farm land around there. Judging from your Yankee accent, I 'spect you're one of those abolitionists and headed for Lawrence?"

"I am going to Lawrence." replied Robert, "Got a job waiting for me there." He was not ready to confess his politics to this stranger. That was one of the things that the literature from the Emigrant Aid Company had cautioned against. When in mixed company, keep your beliefs on slavery to yourself.

"Traveling alone?," inquired Billy.

"Yep. You?"

"I am."

They talked about where they were from—Robert from Rhode Island and Billy from Mississippi—about their family situations, and what had led both of them to this dilapidated steamship headed up the Missouri River to the Kansas Territory.

"Biggest part of it for me is to start a new life," said Billy, "but I haveta say, protecting southern rights ain't no small part. What do y'all think you're doing here?" It was a comment, more than a question, not asked in anger, but in a matter-of-fact way. Billy continued, "You Yankees can have Nebraska. Only fair. But Kansas is our neck of the woods. Heck, Missouri is right next door. I'm no slave master, but if our institutions, our property, ain't respected in Kansas, what's that gonna mean for Missouri? Or back home in Mississippi? The Negroes will run away and flock there."

"Same here," responded Robert, "I mean about the starting over part. Definitely. I sure am ready for a change." So much for not sharing his opinions with strangers, he decided, and continued. "But the other part is important to me, also. To me, it's about fairness. We had this thing solved, ever since 1820. Everybody was fine with the Missouri Compromise. You can't change the rules after near a quarter century and expect folks won't be upset."

"Times change. Nuthin wrong with fixing mistakes, if they need a fixing. We own these territories just as much as y'all Yankees. A man oughta have the right to take his property wherever he wants in his own country."

"Unless that property is a human being."

"That's your opinion."

As they were talking, Robert realized that he had never had an extended conversation with a southerner. His views differed from those of Billy, but the exchange was pleasant. He found him to be likable. In another place, another time, he thought, they may have been friends.

"I got no quarrel with you, Billy. Guess we're just gonna have to agree to disagree."

"May the better side win. By voting. That's what this new law does. Isn't that the fairest way to solve this thing?," replied Billy.

"Shouldn't have to come to that, in my opinion. But if we're gonna decide it by voting, then folks from all over have gotta be able to get to Kansas and settle there freely, without being intimidated. And from what I hear, they ain't. Once they cross into Missouri, they're being threatened and told to turn around and go back home. They have knives and guns pointed at them, and are shown hanging ropes. That isn't right, Billy."

"Can't believe everything you hear. I 'spect it's all blown out of proportion in your Yankee newspapers. They do that, you know. Exaggerate. Nothing to worry about. Prob'ly just a few Missouri boys feeling their oats."

"Like that trio back there?," said Robert, nodding toward the three bears. "Friends of yours?," he added, in a joking manner.

"Nope." Billy then let out a small laugh. "*They* do look a bit wild, I haveta admit. But my guess is that their bark is bigger than their bite."

Both Robert and Billy felt the deck shift under their feet.

"Looks like they got her moving again," said Robert, as he pulled out his pocket watch. "Only twenty minutes. I think that's a record."

"I do believe it is," replied Billy. "Nice chatting with you," as he started to move toward the center of the ship. "Good luck in Kansas."

"And to you, Billy."

With the ship now moving again, Robert felt a cool autumn breeze on his face. He wondered what awaited him in Lawrence.

CHAPTER 17

*O*ctober, 1854— As he rode in the twilight to the foundry, Monty felt a rush of energy, despite the unfortunate circumstance that had led him to this late-night rendezvous. His father had been injured at work in the afternoon. Roger had been inspecting the progress on a boiler that was under construction. As it was being hoisted and moved, a chain broke, causing it to roll and hit him, pinning his left leg underneath. Monty had been in another building, in his office, and rushed to the scene. Roger was conscious, but in much pain. Two of the workers loaded him in the bed of a wagon and took him home, while Monty rushed to the house of the family's physician, Dr. Saunders. The doctor dropped everything and came to examine Roger, diagnosing two fractures in the lower leg. He set the fractures and applied a splint, gave the patient a dose of laudanum, along with instructions to stay off of the leg for two or three days.

The bedridden Roger told Monty that he needed him to do something. It had only been a couple of weeks since he had told his son about his work with the Underground Railroad. That morning, on his way to the foundry, he had seen a red quilt hanging on the line in Mrs. Pierson's yard. That meant there would be arrivals at the foundry that evening. Unable to walk, he needed Monty to go to the old sawmill at the foundry, take some food with him, meet the conductor, and get the charges settled in for the night.

Monty's heart swelled with pride as he headed toward the foundry. The assignment had given him a rewarding sense of satisfaction. He thought back to his days in Washington City and his planning with Ben about the Tyler plot. He was again doing *something* in the battle against slavery, even if he was just filling in for his father.

In the darkness, Monty jiggled the key a few times in the padlock on the door of the little-used building until he finally heard it release. He went in, lit a couple of candles and took a deep breath. It surprised him how the odor of fresh-cut timber remained in the air, although the place had not been used as a sawmill for a few years. It was one of his favorite smells. He put the basket of food he had brought (some ham, apples, and a loaf of bread that his mother had baked) on a table and then went into a storage bin and retrieved some blankets. After pulling up a chair to the open door, he blew out the candles, and sat and waited.

About half an hour later, he saw a flicker of light from the tree line about a hundred yards away. He lit a candle in response, the signal that it was safe to approach. He watched as four figures emerged from the woods. One of them, the one carrying the lit candle, he noticed, appeared to have a limp. He got up to go back inside and relight his other candles.

"You'se . . . not . . . Coyote," he heard a woman's voice say, hesitantly, while he had his back turned and as he was getting the wicks lit again.

"He's my father and I'm filling . . . ."

As Monty turned and took a step forward, the words stopped coming and he froze. Although it had been more than a dozen years, he knew that face. Any doubt he had was overcome by her limp that he had observed seconds earlier.

Raven also froze, as if in shock.

"Delores?," he said.

"Master Tolliver?," Raven responded.

CHAPTER 18

*O**ctober, 1854*— Robert first noticed his head. It was throbbing. And then his jaw and hands. His mouth had a wad of something stuffed in it, and he could feel something tied tightly over it and around the back of his neck. His hands were bound, behind him, and around something. A pole, maybe? He was sitting on the floor of a mostly darkened room, filled with trunks and cargo. He tried to think, back to his last memory. Now he recalled. It was those three burly Missourians, the big one and his two shadows. It had been late afternoon, on the deck. They walked up to him. No one else was around. What had they said to him? Teach him something about a goose? And then one of them punched him. Hard. On the right side of his temple. The blow, or his fall after it, must have knocked him out. And now he was gagged and bound in this dark room. How long had he been here, he wondered. Maybe a couple of hours? Looking toward two partially obstructed portal windows on the other side of the room, it appeared as though the sun had set, or was about to.

A few minutes later, he heard a sound. A door opened behind him, he thought. And then some footsteps. He braced himself.

Was another fist to his head coming? Or something worse? He turned to the left as far as he could and saw a figure coming toward him through the dimness. He could make out that the person had an index finger raised, vertically, across his mouth. As the person got closer, he exhaled, in relief.

"Quiet," Billy whispered. "I got a plan," he said, as he untied the handkerchief around Robert's neck, removed the gag from his mouth, and began untying the knots of the rope that bound Robert's hands to the pole. Robert watched silently as Billy pulled a small candle out of his coat pocket, lit it, and walked around the room. "This'll do," he heard Billy mumble, as Billy took three bricks from a stack of hundreds in the corner of the room (no doubt destined to be someone's chimney in Kansas, Robert speculated) and put them in a small canvas sack. He saw Billy rearrange the handkerchief, the gag, and the rope, and move them closer to the pole where Robert had been tied, making it appear as though he freed himself.

Robert watched as Billy walked over to the door leading to the deck, gently opened it, and peered out. Billy blew out the candle and put it in his pocket. "Come on, not a word," he whispered, as he motioned with his left hand for Robert to follow him, and as he carried the canvas sack of bricks in his right hand. Once out the door, they walked in the twilight, about thirty feet, toward the bow of the ship, until Billy opened another door and they ducked inside. It was pitch black.

"This is a storage closet," he said to Robert. "You'll be safe here. I've been sleeping on the deck in front of it, on my mattress, for the last couple of nights. No one has tried to get in here. I'll set myself up just outside again tonight."

"How did you find me?," Robert whispered.

"I was in line for supper in the dining room, behind those burly fellas that you pointed out to me earlier. Two of them, anyway. The big one and one of the little ones. The third one then came up."

"'How's our Rhode Island rooster?,' the big one asked."

"'Still out cold in the baggage room. Got him tied up real good,' the third one told them."

"Then, the other small one called you a 'cocky abolitionist son of a bitch.'"

Billy relayed to Robert more of what he had heard as he continued to eavesdrop on their conversation.

"'I can't wait until tomorrow morning,' the big one said, 'when we put in at Richfield. Our pals will be ready with the tar and feathers. Just like last week. We'll get him fixed up real good, put a Negro lover sign on him, and parade him around the dock. I love the looks on the faces of those lily-livered Yankees when they see it.'"

"'Puts the fear of God in them, it does,' one of the little ones added. 'They get off their boats, walk straight to the ticket office, and ask for the next passage back to St. Louis.'"

Billy looked at Robert and grinned. "I knew it had to be you. Rhode Island and all," he said. "Came looking for you while they were still standing in line for supper, but they'll be back any minute. I'll slip some food and water to you later, and see if I can round up a chamber pot for necessities."

Robert watched as Billy opened the door, walked out, and left him alone in the darkness. He sat on something, a wooden crate, he supposed.

Several seconds later, Robert heard a loud splash in the river, followed by a shout of "Man overboard!" He recognized the voice as Billy's. And then loud footsteps. People running. Again, he heard Billy speaking, in his southern drawl, "He came past me like a bat out of hell. Red-haired fella. Jumped right over the railing."

That explains the sack of bricks, Robert realized. Clever one, this Billy. He then heard some other voices.

"Anyone down there?" someone shouted.

"I don't see nuthin," said another. "Too dark and the water's too muddy."

And then the first voice again, "We'll never find him. Probably on the bottom already. Tell the captain to keep a-going. What a damn fool."

CHAPTER 19

*O*ctober, 1854— "I told you," said Monty, half-jokingly, "to *never* call me Master, that you didn't ever need to call anyone by that horrible title again."

"That's how I first knew you. *Mis-ter* Tolliver. Is that better?," Delores replied, as she smiled.

"It surely is."

Both took a couple of steps forward and embraced, tears welling up in their eyes.

They explained to Delores' three charges (Josiah, Eliza, and Jacob) how they had first met years ago near Washington City, how Monty had purchased Delores (known as Raven to them) at a slave auction, with the purpose of freeing her, and that he had been true to his word. As the hungry trio began to devour the food that Monty had brought, he and Delores chatted, like old friends who had lost touch with each other and who suddenly had been reunited.

The years, they agreed, had not taken much of a toll on either one of them. Delores told Monty, who was in his early forties, that he looked the same as when she had last seen him more than a decade ago. Delores, Monty observed, although surely now past the age of sixty, had one of those ageless faces, with dark skin that seemed to glisten. Her hair, pulled back tight on her head, had only a few gray flecks in it, as best he could tell in the dim candlelight. Although she was trim, he noticed that she had started to stoop a bit, something that he attributed to her awkward gait from her old foot injury.

"I had some doubts about you when you took me to that whorehouse," Delores teased.

"It was the only place I could think of," Monty replied. "It worked out, didn't it?"

"It did. They were nice and treated me well."

"I thought you were going to go on to Canada. I can't tell you how often I've imagined you living a quiet and peaceful life there. What happened?"

"Got as far as New York. The western part, they said. The folks guiding me along on the Underground Railroad were so good at what they did, risking their lives for me, and for others they did not know from Adam. I wanted to be a part of it, to help others, like you helped me. I thought, what's an old woman like me gonna do in Canada? Don't know a soul there. They took me in and trained me, put me in Pennsylvania for a few years and then moved me out here to Ohio."

"I'm so proud of you."

"So, Coyote is your father?," Delores asked.

"Small world, isn't it?"

"I met him on the last trip. Nice man. I see the resemblance now."

They talked on and on, for an hour, maybe longer. Josiah, Eliza, and Jacob had cuddled up on the straw on the floor, covered themselves with blankets, and were fast asleep. Monty told Delores of his decision to leave Washington City and politics behind, about his return to Ohio, and about Theresa and the children. Delores told him about growing up on the tobacco farm in southern Virginia, how she injured her foot, and of being sold to the farm in Loudoun County. She reached into one of her pockets, pulled out some worn pieces of paper, and showed them to Monty. They were her manumission papers that he had secured for her, with the name of Delores Tolliver on them. A last name, she said, that she has been proud to carry.

They could have talked longer, but Monty looked at his pocket watch and realized it was past time for him to take his leave. Theresa would no doubt be worried, wondering if something had happened to him. Delores, exhausted from her travels of the past two days, agreed that it was time for the reunion to end. She needed to get a few hours of sleep. The conductor who would be taking over for her, she said, should be arriving just before dawn and she would then make her way back to Cincinnati.

Monty asked Delores if she would be back again. Maybe a time or two, she said, but then likely not for a while. They rarely sent her to the same safe house more than a few times in a row. Perhaps again in a year or so, she explained. He stood up, walked over to her, and gave her another gentle embrace.

As he guided his horse slowly through the darkness back to his house, he thought about the result of what he had done all those years ago, and of what Delores had accomplished with her freedom. Like ripples from the tossing of a stone into a pond, his good deed had started something that had benefited many more than just the two of them. He felt good.

CHAPTER 20

ctober, 1854— "What's the matter Monty?," Theresa asked. "You seem troubled ever since your meeting with Delores last week. I would have thought you would have been over the moon after seeing her again."

The children had been put to bed and both she and Monty were sitting in their favorite chairs and reading. He had barely said a word since they sat down. Normally, when reading, he would delight in sharing with her some clever nugget or obscure bit of information from his book.

"I need to ask you something," Monty replied, as he closed his book and placed it on a nearby table.

"Of course, what is it?"

He paused for a few seconds, then rubbed his hands together and bit his lip. "I want to go to Kansas."

"A bit far for a visit, don't you think?"

"I don't mean for a visit. I mean to live there. For all of us to."

"Whatever for?"

"To be a part of the fight. To help stop slavery from taking root there. I've been thinking. Delores had a chance to go away to Canada and enjoy herself. If anyone deserved it, she did, after the life that she had. But she devoted herself to helping others escape slavery, at the risk of being sold back into slavery herself. If she can do that, what can I do?"

"Don't forget that you are the one who gave her the opportunity to do all of that. You gave freedom to her. She would likely now be on a plantation in Mississippi or Alabama, if not for you. Besides, you support the cause, you take risks. Look at what you did last week for the Underground Railroad."

"Buying and freeing her, that was more than a decade ago. I can't rest on that one thing for a lifetime. And the railroad stuff, that's my father's work. I only helped out once, at least so far. I've got this feeling inside that I need to do more."

"You're really serious about this, aren't you?"

Monty thought he detected a slight softening of her tone.

"I am, but only with your blessing. Settlers are pouring into Kansas every day. They will need foundries. We can open one there. We can support a cause that we believe in, and have a prosperous life there, maybe better than the one we have here."

"You know that I will support you. I vowed to do so, for better or for worse. I'm not sure which one this is just yet, but we shall see. When would you expect this great adventure will begin?"

"It will take a month or so for me to wrap up things here and make arrangements to travel there. I'm thinking that I would go alone at first, sometime this fall, to get there before the cold weather sets in. I'd spend the winter scouting out land for the foundry and for a place for us to build a house. My parents, and yours, can help you with Josh and Benjie. I could get things under construction in the spring and then have you and the children join me. It would only be for a few months and then we would all be together again."

Theresa closed her book, got up from her chair, and walked over to Monty and kissed him on the forehead.

"My husband, back in the fight," she said softly.

That night, Monty lay in bed, unable to sleep, excited about something for the first time since he could remember. Awakened to a call to duty. Years ago, he had given Delores her freedom. And now, by seeing her again, she had given something back to him. Inspiration. A challenge. A new purpose in life.

He looked across the bed at Theresa, sleeping peacefully, her features barely visible in the faint moonlight coming in from the window. He was thankful for her support. Life in Kansas, he was sure, would be good.

CHAPTER 21

November, 1854— Robert's boots were covered in mud, despite his best attempts to dodge the puddles from the overnight rain. He walked up what he was sure was Massachusetts Street in Lawrence, a place that was bustling with activity. There were no road signs yet. He had read in a brochure from the New England Emigrant Aid Company that the new town's main street was to be named in honor of the state where the company had been founded. Although the first group of settlers had arrived in Lawrence only four months earlier, there were already a few completed homes and businesses, some of them log cabins and others wood-frame buildings. These were outnumbered by tents, which seemed to be everywhere. Upon his arrival a couple of days ago, he was able to find lodging at the Pioneer Boarding House, a triangular structure, crudely made of logs covered by a roof thatched with clumps of hay from the nearby prairie. It would do for a while. It would have to, he told himself, as there were few other options.

It was late morning and the autumn sun had emerged from the clouds a couple of hours earlier. Robert observed at least half a dozen more buildings under construction, with several men wielding hammers or carrying lumber. He passed a large square hole that had been dug out, which someone told him was for the foundation of a huge hotel that the company was going to construct.

After walking another half-block or so, he thought he found the place he was looking for, one of the completed wood-frame buildings. Any doubt was removed when he read the handwritten sheet of paper nailed to the door—"COMING SOON: The Herald of Freedom, a Free-State Newspaper for Kansas."

Robert's knock on the door went unanswered, so he opened it slightly and peered inside. The room was mostly barren, except for a large wooden crate near its center, which rose more than chest high. He observed the lower legs of a man, on his knees, behind the container.

"Mr. Brown, is that you?," he inquired.

It was not a shout, but almost, and it drew the man's attention. He stood up, walked toward Robert, and dusted himself off. Robert noticed that he was carrying some sort of a metal lever in one hand.

"Yes, I'm George Washington Brown."

"A name to be proud of."

"It surely is."

"My brother was named after Benjamin Franklin," Robert replied, thinking it would be a good conversation starter.

"Another great namesake," responded Brown, as a grin came across his face. "And who might you be? Thomas Jefferson?"

Robert let out a small laugh. "No sir, not so fortunate. My name is Robert Geddis. From Newport. I wrote to you."

As Brown walked closer, Robert could see him clearly from the light that poured in through the room's windows. He had dark hair and a beard, was trim, and appeared to be only slightly older than he. Still in his thirties, Robert guessed.

"Mr. Geddis. You made it! I wasn't sure you would really come all this way."

"I am a man of my word. I hope the job is still open?"

"It most assuredly is. Welcome to Kansas!"

The two men sat on a nearby workbench. Robert knew that Brown was a newspaper publisher who had an agreement with the New England Emigrant Aid Company to start a newspaper in Lawrence. Brown was from Pennsylvania and Robert had written to him there a few months ago asking for a job and outlining his experience working for the *Newport Mercury*. Brown had responded that Robert would be hired, if he could get to Kansas by the beginning of December. Brown advised that he had himself arrived a couple of weeks earlier. The crate that they stood next to, he explained, had been delivered only the day before and contained his printing press from Pennsylvania.

"And, just to confirm, I will be writing articles for the paper, in addition to my other duties?," Robert asked.

"Definitely. If you don't, we are going to have a lot of blank space on our pages. For now, it's just you and me and we're both going to do it all, from writing, to typesetting, to printing, to circulation."

Robert felt a pulse of excitement flow through his body. He was more confident than ever that his decision to uproot himself and move all this way had been the right one. In the first few days after his abduction on the steamship, he had questioned whether he should turn around and go back to Rhode Island. What if Billy had not been there, he often thought. He wondered if Billy had gotten set up near Lecompton, and wished he had gotten the opportunity to thank Billy more before sneaking off of the ship in the predawn hours after his rescue. Their handshake and pats on the back had not seemed enough.

Brown reached down and picked up another metal lever, similar to the one that he had been holding when Robert came in, and handed it to his new employee.

"Let's get this thing out of its crate, oiled up, and ready to go."

Robert took the lever in his right hand, ran the fingers of his left hand along it, and looked his new boss in the eye.

"We're going to do great things here, Mr. Brown. I'm sure of it."

CHAPTER 22

February, 1855— The blindfold around Billy's head was starting to give him a headache. It had been on him for more than an hour. What had he gotten himself into, he wondered?

He had arrived, alone, at the appointed place earlier in the evening, shivering in the near freezing temperature. Someone came up from behind him in the darkness, whispered his name, told him not to turn around, and tied on the blindfold. He was admonished not to speak, unless spoken to. After a wagon ride of about thirty minutes, all in silence, he had been led inside some structure and seated onto a hard, stiff chair. His coat was removed. He sensed the presence of others in the room, but he was not sure. After several more minutes, someone reached under his armpits, pulling him up to a standing position. He then felt both of his hands being grabbed and extended forward. He complied and felt something coarse being tied around his wrists, after which he could hear the sound of breathing, on both sides of him. Billy then felt his left arm move forward and his right arm backward. He was being pulled and, to keep from falling down, he began to shuffle his feet. He was, he realized, part of a moving human chain. After the creaking sound of a door opening, he felt warmth on his blinded face as he entered a different room. He counted his steps. Seventeen paces forward, a left turn, and then five more. Then, he heard the first words spoken since the blindfold had been fastened on him.

"Welcome to this sacred place," said a baritone voice, "May the Supreme Architect of the Earth be praised for His assistance and protection of our holy work."

Billy hadn't made many friends since arriving in Kansas in October, but Ned Watkins was someone whom he had bonded with. Ned (whose given name was Edmund, he had shared with Billy) was about the same age as Billy and they had met in a Lecompton bar. Lecompton, about fifteen miles west of Lawrence, wasn't much of a town yet, but proslavery men coming to Kansas from all over the South had started to settle in and around it, just as free-state settlers were congregating around Lawrence. Ned was smaller than Billy, both in height and weight, had short brown hair, and was rather plain looking. Homely, some would say. But he was a great talker, and Billy had immediately taken a liking to him. Ned was from Illinois, the southern part, he said, and had come to Kansas to make sure that it became a slave state. That seemed strange to Billy, with Illinois being a free state, but Ned said most folks in Illinois south of Springfield thought like he did, and would have slavery there, if they could. He grew up only a stone's throw from Missouri, Ned had said. He spoke with a southern accent, but nothing like Billy's Mississippi drawl. When the two of them were together, some commented that Billy's accent was thicker. Better, Billy liked to think.

Ned had arrived in Kansas last September, about a month before Billy, and had staked out a claim of twenty-five acres east of Lecompton. His title to the land had cleared and he had built a crude cabin on the site before the cold weather had set in. Ned had big plans, he had told Billy. In the spring, he was going to plant hemp. His father, who apparently had some wealth, had promised to send him some money and, within a year or so, he hoped to buy a couple of enslaved workers, as well as some adjacent land. Ned did not suffer from a lack of confidence, something that Billy admired in him.

Billy's plot of land, to the west of Lecompton, was smaller, only about fifteen acres. He had arrived too late last fall to do anything with it. To tide him over until the spring, when he could get some crops in the ground (wheat, he was thinking), and get a cabin built, he had taken a job at a nearby sawmill. The owner of the mill, a Mr. Buford, from Kentucky, was not a particularly friendly fellow, but he did let Billy live in a cabin next to the mill, along with some of the other workers.

Tonight, Ned had told Billy, was going to be something that he would remember for the rest of his life. Billy knew few of the details, only that he was to be initiated into the Lecompton chapter of the Blue Lodge, a secret society of like-minded southern men. He would make new friends, Ned had assured him, support the South, and it would be a stepping stone to rising in Kansas society. Ned had sponsored him. Not everyone got invited. He should consider it an honor, Ned had said. Billy had eagerly accepted.

Seconds after the welcoming, the baritone voice was heard again. "The vice of the soul is ignorance; its virtue is knowledge. Repeat after me. I swear to live each day according to the high standards and traditions of the Blue Lodge."

Billy, still sightless, repeated the words, in a voice as strong he could muster. He heard similar contemporaneous repetitions by others on either side of him.

The voice continued, "I vow to unite myself fraternally with all initiates and members present, to support and defend the

South and her traditions." There was a pause, and Billy and the others repeated what they had heard. And then another sentence, "I will go anywhere, anytime, and do anything that may be commanded of me by my Lodge," followed by more repetitions.

"May this fraternal chain be so strong," the voice concluded, "that nothing can ever break it. So say you all?"

"I do", Billy replied, as did the others he had heard repeat the previous vows.

He felt someone behind him release the blindfold. It took several seconds for his eyes to adjust to the light in the room. He was standing in the middle of a row of five men, each joined together by a rope knotted around their wrists. In front of them, there was a stack of carefully placed stones, shaped like a pyramid, with a lit candle on top. Beyond that, there were several rows of seated men, all clad in the same shade of blue. Aprons, Billy finally realized. He noticed Ned in the first row, staring at him and nodding approvingly. Fireplaces blazed on both sides of the large room. Gotta be a tavern, Billy suspected, but he did not recall ever having been here before. As he was taking in the rest of the room, he was startled by the sound of the deep voice again. He had not noticed that the speaker was standing just to the right side of the row of initiates, and that his apron, unlike the others, was trimmed in gold.

"The rope that binds you together symbolizes the bond of each of you to one another, and to the Lodge," the voice said. "May the Almighty protect us all and our beloved South."

With those words, the man stood before the initiates, cut the ropes around their wrists, handed each of them a candle, and instructed them to go light it from the candle on the pyramid of stones. When all had completed the task, there was clapping and cheering from all in the room.

The rest of the evening was a blur for Billy. The ceremony over, the alcohol began to flow. He had happily imbibed, to excess, judging by his headache the next morning. He vaguely recalled being told of Lodge rituals, of tasks that would be required, and of secret greetings, passwords, and a handshake.

A couple of days later, Billy met with Ned at a tavern for dinner, who went over everything with him again. They practiced the handshake, called a lion's paw (with the fingers separated between the middle and ring fingers), as well as the greetings. Touching a finger to the nose, mouth, or eye, all had different meanings. It was a lot to remember, but Billy felt good about himself. He was an official member of the Blue Lodge. He was making contacts in Kansas society, a good start on his way to fulfilling his dreams.

CHAPTER 23

arch, 1855— Monty was fully awake the moment
he opened his eyes. This day, March 30, 1855, was
a crucial one in his new life, a day for which he
had uprooted himself, had temporarily left his family behind,
and had moved to Kansas. It was the day on which he would
cast his first vote against slavery, the initial step toward making
Kansas a free state.

It had been more than three months since he had arrived in
the territory in December and set himself up in Lawrence. He
was still scouting for two parcels of land, one on the banks of the
Kansas River and a couple of miles from Lawrence suitable for
building his foundry, and another, closer to town, for a house. He
wanted to get the foundry started first. Once a site was selected
and construction underway, the plan was for him to send for
a foreman and a handful of laborers from his family's foundry
in Dayton, who would get the new place operational and then
train local workers in Kansas to take it over. Roger had agreed
to keep the men on the payroll of the Dayton foundry while
they were in Kansas, with their salaries to be a loan to Monty,
to be repaid once the new facility was up and running. It had

all been arranged before he left Ohio. The men had agreed to come, but all of that was still a few months away.

The journey from Ohio to Kansas was not as bad as Monty had anticipated. It had been overland, with a party of about fifty settlers, all eager to start a new life. To his surprise, there were a few women and children in the group. The trip had taken about a month. He had decided to take a northern route after reading stories in newspapers that those who came to Kansas by the quicker southerly route (which took them to St. Louis, and then by riverboat, through the slave state of Missouri, to Kansas City) often faced intimidation and violence from proslavery thugs. From Dayton, Monty took stagecoaches westward through Indiana and Illinois, and then to Iowa City. There, he met his group and they traveled, mostly in covered wagons, southwest through Iowa all the way to Tabor, on the border of the Nebraska Territory. From there, they headed due south to Topeka, where they dispersed to various locations in Kansas. Monty then headed about thirty miles east to Lawrence. Having traveled entirely through free land, the group met with no resistance or hostility and had attracted little attention. Based on his conversations with folks along the way, several in his group were like him and were headed to Kansas primarily to support a cause, to ensure that the territory became a free state. The rest, likely the majority, he suspected, were just looking for a new and better life. They came not only from Ohio, but also from Illinois, Indiana, Iowa, and other free states. They did not support slavery, but stopping its spread had not been their motivation.

Since arriving in Kansas, he had become more confident that he had made the correct decision in not bringing Theresa and his children until he had everything set up. Not only was he glad that they would not have to endure the hardships that awaited the first settlers to any new territory, but he had also become concerned about the increasing threats and violence from proslavery men against free-state settlers. Almost every day, it seemed, he heard some new rumor of someone having been threatened at gunpoint, of livestock being killed, or of homes being burned. He did not want his family in the midst of such an unstable situation.

Monty had arrived too late (ten days, to be exact) to participate in the first election held in the Kansas Territory. That had been in late November, to elect a representative in Congress, and it had been a disaster, at least from the perspective of free-staters. Hundreds of proslavery Missourians (likely well over a thousand, Monty had been told) had crossed the border into Kansas and had voted illegally. Although most did not own slaves, they were southerners, felt strongly about southern institutions, and had heard plenty of speeches inciting them to do whatever was necessary to stop the Yankees from making Kansas a free state. These men, dubbed "border ruffians" by the free-staters, were aptly named, from everything that Monty had heard. Menacing in appearance and behavior, they had arrived on election day armed with knives and guns, and had brought barrels of whiskey.

The rules for voting, as declared by the territory's governor, Andrew Reeder, who had been appointed by the administration of President Franklin Pierce, had been clear. A voter must actually reside in the territory of Kansas, to the exclusion of any other domicile, and have the intention of remaining permanently. So much for the rules, Monty had heard. Some of the ruffians had come over a few days or weeks before the election, found some vacant land, nailed a piece of paper with their name on it to a tree, and moved a couple of logs around to simulate the foundation of a cabin on a land claim that would never be pursued. Most of them didn't even bother to do that.

They just came in groups across the border a day or so before the election to vote in Kansas, voted, and then turned around and went back to Missouri. When Monty had arrived more than a week after the election, it was still all that everyone was talking about on the streets of Lawrence, and the subject of most of the articles in the newspapers. At every major polling place—in Lawrence, in Lecompton, down south in Palmyra, and everywhere in between—the roads into the towns on election morning had been clogged with wagon loads of proslavery Missourians. They crowded the polling places, demanded to vote, and threatened any poll judge who refused to let them do so. Some of the judges, in fear for their lives, quit on the spot; those who remained were helpless to prevent the ballot boxes from being stuffed with votes that had been fraudulently cast. Worse, the ruffians had intimidated and, in some cases, used violence, to keep legitimate residents of Kansas, who favored the free-state cause, from casting their ballots. In some places, Monty had been told, the number of votes cast had exceeded the number of legal residents by three or four times.

It had worked, much to the dismay of the free-staters. The proslavery candidate for Congress, John Whitfield, won the November election with almost 2,300 votes, compared to only around 300 for his closest free-state challenger. Despite the widespread and obvious fraud, Governor Reeder let the results stand. The Kansas-Nebraska Act, the victors had proudly declared, established that the people would vote to decide all issues pertaining to slavery. And vote they had.

Now, three months later, it was time for another election, to select a territorial legislature. This election was far more important than the earlier one, which had only selected a delegate to represent the territory in Congress. The legislative body elected today would write the territory's laws, put it on a course for statehood, and have a large say in whether that would be with, or without, slavery. In the months since November, hundreds more settlers, Monty among them, had arrived from New England and from other free states, most of whom were opposed to slavery. Monty was sure that, if the election were held fairly, a legislature with a free-state majority would be chosen.

Monty rode his horse a mile or so from his rented rowhouse in Lawrence to the polling place, a newly-built cabin on the outskirts of town. It was a cool and clear early spring morning. Along the way, he noticed, a few times, the smell of smoke in the air. Not exactly sure where he was going, he had left early and had arrived shortly after eight o'clock, about an hour before the voting would begin. He noticed that there were already a few people milling about, including a man he recognized, who was standing behind a large open window of the cabin. The man was wearing a top hat, a frock coat, a patterned silk vest, and a cravat. It was attire that was common everyday back East, but, from what Monty had observed, was mostly reserved for churchgoing in Kansas.

"Good morning, James," he said, as he walked up to the window, "you look very official back there."

James Abbott and Monty had stayed in the same boarding house in December, when Monty had first arrived. They had chatted several times there over meals. James was from Connecticut and, like Monty, had come to Kansas with a twofold purpose—to support the free-state cause, and to set up a business. He was a bootmaker, had recently opened a shop in town and, Monty recalled, also planned to do some farming.

"Monty, good to see you. It is morning. We shall see how good it turns out to be," responded James. "The governor appointed me to be one of the election judges here. Come on in, you can help me with the records and the ballots."

Monty noticed that James' face appeared to be flushed and when he picked up a mug of coffee to take a sip, his hand trembled enough to cause some of it to spill.

"You don't look very well, my friend. What's going on?"

"We got word last night," said James, "that those damn ruffians have come over the border again. Someone said the ferries across the Missouri River, around Kansas City, have been packed for the past three days. Wagonloads of the bastards were spotted yesterday, headed here, to Manhattan, to Osawatomie, and to Lecompton. I'm afraid we are going to have a repeat of November, maybe worse."

Suddenly, it dawned on Monty. The reason for the smell of smoke this morning. "They must have camped all around town," he said to James. "I kept smelling smoke on my way over. From their campfires, no doubt."

"Oh, yes, I smelled it too," responded James, as he perused the top page of about twenty-five pages that he held in his hand. It looked like names and addresses, from what Monty could see. "This is a list of who we have as the legal residents," James continued, as he ran his index finger down the page. "Not as up-to-date as we would like, so if someone wants to vote and is not on the list, we're gonna ask them to swear an oath that they are a resident as set forth by Governor Reeder—meaning that they live here and intend to do so permanently." James pointed to two stacks of printed papers on the table before him. "The brown ones are the proslavery ballot with the name of their candidate on them, and the light blue ones are for the free-state voters to cast, with their man's name on them."

"What can I do?," asked Monty.

"When a line starts to form, take some ballots and stand outside. Ask them which one they want, tell them to mark it, and come up to the window. If they're not on my list, I will ask them to take the governor's oath. Then, they can put their ballot in the slot in the box."

"Easy enough."

"Grab some coffee," said James. "Nothing to do but sit and wait."

As James and Monty sat in the cabin and sipped their coffee, a man came in and whispered something in James' ear, making James, Monty observed, look even more worried.

"What's the matter?," asked Monty.

"Bad news. The other poll judge for this precinct, a fella named Blanton, has sent word that he's not coming. Says he had a run-in with some of the Missourians yesterday. They first offered him a bribe to let all of them vote and, when he refused, they threatened to hang him if he showed up today."

"Any back-up judges available?," asked Monty.

"None that can get here in time for the voting," replied James, as he stood and began to pace around the cabin.

About a half-hour later, they heard some noise in the distance, went outside, looked eastward, and saw a cloud of dust headed their way. As the cloud got closer, they could make out wagons, more than a dozen of them, some with banners flying, and each loaded with men. Several of the men were half-standing, and hollering at the top of their lungs, while waving their hats over their heads. Monty could see that one of the wagons had something hitched to its rear. Only when it got closer could he make out that it was a cannon. A small one, but a cannon it was. Good God, he thought to himself, who brings a cannon with them to vote? Not a good omen for the day.

As James requested, Monty took a stack of the ballots and went out to the front of the cabin.

A rugged looking, bearded man, who had been riding next to the driver of the closest wagon, alighted, walked past Monty, and sauntered over to James at the window.

"Mornin', we'se here to vote," he barked.

"Yes sir, good morning. Just give me your name, I'll check it off on this list, and we'll get you a ballot," replied James, his hand visibly shaking as he held the papers.

Other men began to exit their wagons and walk toward the front of the cabin.

"Samuel Young, and you won't see it on no list."

"Very well, then. The governor requires, if you are not on the list . . . that you . . . take an oath of residency in Kansas," replied James, his nervousness and fear obvious in his voice. "Please raise your right hand."

"Here's my oath. I'm a here in Kansas today. That makes me a resident and I'm a voting. And so are all of my friends," Young responded. As he spoke, he pulled a bowie knife from his belt and stabbed it into the board at the base of the window.

CHAPTER 24

*M**arch, 1855—* Monty, James, and the few other free-staters present, stared at the planted knife. Shocked by the action, no one said a word. Any hope for a fair and peaceful election was quickly gone.

"Ain't there supposed to be two poll judges here," the ruffian, Samuel Young, asked James Abbott. "I only see you back there."

"Unfortunately, our other judge, Mr. Blanton, has sent word that he is unable to appear today," said James. "Mr. Tolliver, who is standing behind you, with the ballots, will be assisting me."

Young turned around and gave a sneering look at Monty. Then, turning back toward James, said, "He ain't no official judge, you say?"

"That's correct."

"Well, then I think we need to elect us another judge. We want everything to be official, don't we?" By now, all of the men who had arrived in the wagons, more than fifty, Monty observed, were standing in small groups around the cabin. "What do you think, boys?," Young asked them.

"Only fair!," "Damn right!," and "Hell, yeah!" were some of the replies that Monty heard, which were accompanied by several of the men raising their fists above their heads.

The Missourians then proceeded to select one of their own, a man named Robert Cummins, and, by a voice vote, pretended to elect him as a replacement for the missing poll judge. Cummins, his right hand resting on one of two pistols on his belt, went into the cabin and stood next to James. As he did so, someone reached from behind Monty and snatched away the ballots that he had been holding.

"Samuel Young," Cummins asked Young, who was still standing at the window, "are you a resident of the territory of Kansas?"

"I am, sir," replied Young, as he marked a brown ballot, folded it, and slid it into the slot on top of the ballot box.

"You can't do that, it's fraud!," Monty blurted out.

Immediately, several of the ruffians surrounded him and shoved him toward the back of the crowd, knocking him down into the dirt in the process.

"Come on up boys, one at a time, and cast your ballots," said Young.

Monty noticed that the man who had grabbed the ballots from his hand was marking the brown ballots next to the name of the proslavery candidate for the legislature, and handing them out to the others. He was, Monty decided, probably the only literate one in the group.

James stood, in shock, and stared at the scene in front of him. "I cannot be a party to this," he said to Young and Cummins. He turned and started to walk out of the cabin. "Mark my words, the governor will be hearing from me all about this."

Young and Cummins looked at each other and grinned.

As James approached Monty near the rear of the crowd, Monty was picking himself up from the dirt. He saw a blue ballot on the ground and grabbed it. Determined to vote, he reached into his coat pocket and pulled out a pistol. It was smaller than the weapons that the others were carrying, but it was a pistol nonetheless. He had tucked it in a pocket this morning, almost as an afterthought, not sure what the day would bring. He forced his way through the crowd, to the window of the cabin, and pointed the pistol directly at Young's head.

"Anyone moves, and he's dead. Understand?," Monty shouted, surprising even himself with the forcefulness of his voice. The ruffians looked on, glaring at him, but complying with his demand. He took, with his left hand, a marker that was on the window sill and wrote a large X on his ballot next to the name of the free-state candidate for the Lawrence legislative district. He awkwardly folded the ballot with his left hand, while still holding the pistol with his right hand and pointing it at Young, and placed the ballot in the slot in the box.

Still brandishing the pistol, Monty walked back through the crowd and made his way to James, who was now standing beside their horses.

"Good show!," said James, in a low voice, out of the hearing of the ruffians.

"Thanks," replied Monty, in an even quieter voice. "Quick, let's get out of here, before they figure out that I forgot to bring any bullets."

A small victory, thought Monty, as they mounted their horses and rode away.

CHAPTER 25

April, 1855— As he looked around, Monty thought back to his days in Congress. He could not recall ever having seen a group of men so angry and, God knows, he had been in some heated meetings in Washington City. He had been asked to attend this gathering of free-staters to discuss their strategy in response to the actions of the proslavery men in the recent election for the territorial legislature.

The outrages had continued in the days after the election. Monty was surprised how quickly news of them spread. The fraud had been so blatant that even a proslavery newspaper in Missouri had denounced it, resulting in its office being raided by a mob, its printing press destroyed, and its owner and editor ordered to leave the state, on threat of hanging. In Leavenworth, a proslavery stronghold near the border with Missouri, a lawyer filed a formal complaint about election fraud there, which resulted in him being kidnapped, taken across the river to Missouri, being tarred and feathered, and sold at a mock auction.

No reasonable person, Monty was certain, could look at the numbers from the election and not be shocked. Thousands of Missourians had crossed the border and had cast illegal ballots. A census of Kansas residents just a few weeks before had documented that there were fewer than 3,000 eligible voters. Yet, more than 6,000 votes had been cast and, of those, more than 5,400 had been for proslavery candidates for the legislature. All but a handful of the seats in the legislature went to proslavery men. Moreover, many free-staters, who were legitimate residents of the Kansas Territory, had been unable to cast their ballots, due to intimidation, threats, and violence. An appeal by the free-staters to the territory's governor to toss out the results had ended with a revote ordered in only a few precincts, nowhere near enough to change the outcome.

This meeting had been called by Dr. Charles Robinson, at his home, located about half way up Hogback Ridge, a large hill overlooking Lawrence. The house was still under construction and the men stood outside on what would one day be the lawn. Robinson was an agent for the New England Emigrant Aid Company and had arrived in the territory with the second colony of eastern settlers in August 1854. He quickly became the group's leader and spokesman.

Monty had heard a lot about Robinson since arriving in Kansas, but had not yet had an opportunity to meet the doctor. His initial impressions were favorable. In his late-thirties, balding, with piercing eyes and a dark beard, Robinson had a history of defending those deprived of their rights, and of being idealistic and adventurous. After almost a decade of practicing medicine in his native Massachusetts, he had moved to California in 1849, like others, seeking gold. There, he sided with land squatters who objected to the monopoly on land claims held by earlier settlers, became a leader of the group, and was involved in a deadly riot on the streets of Sacramento. He was injured and arrested on charges of murder and conspiracy, but his popularity with the people led to his election to the California legislature, and the charges were dropped. In 1851, he moved back to Massachusetts and resumed the practice of medicine. It did not last long. Strongly opposed to slavery, he was outraged by the passage of the Kansas-Nebraska Act, became a friend of Eli Thayer, the founder of the New England Emigrant Aid Company, and headed westward once again, this time determined to make Kansas a free state. The good doctor was a man of fortitude and idealism, thought Monty. He listened as Robinson addressed the group of about forty men gathered outside his house.

"We came here to fight slavery. Are we to become slaves ourselves, deprived of our rights, and subject to the whim of mobs of ruffians from Missouri? To let our elections be stolen? Let every man here acquit himself like a man who knows his rights and, so knowing, dares to maintain them. Tyranny is tyranny, and smells even fouler if done under the garb of law!"

The group of men, standing in a semicircle around Robinson, erupted in applause and cheers.

"We must act," Robinson continued. "We defy them! And we will resist them. I call for the formation of militias, here in Lawrence and elsewhere in the territory, among men who support freedom, to defend ourselves, our families, and our rights."

Monty heard shouts all around him. "Fight we will!" "No choice!" "Never again!"

"We are not alone," the doctor said, as he lowered his voice to a conversational tone. "The entire nation is watching. The fraud of the election is in every mind, and on every lip, from Maine to Michigan. Every voice rises, saying to the people of Kansas, 'Do your duty!' So we must, and so we will."

* * *

The March 1855 election for the territorial legislature was a pivotal point in the history of Kansas. The sheer enormity of the fraud committed by proslavery Missourians, who crossed the border and voted illegally, grabbed national headlines and galvanized the free-staters in Kansas to organize and to resist. Wrote Horace Greeley in the *New York Tribune*, "A more stupendous fraud was never perpetrated since the invention of the ballot-box."

Dr. Charles Robinson, a representative of the New England Emigrant Aid Company, became the leader of the free-state resistance in Kansas. Shortly after the election, at Robinson's urging, militias were formed to protect and defend Lawrence and other settlements of free-staters in the territory. Even before the election, there had been episodes of violence against them. With a proslavery legislature ruling over them, the free-staters knew that the threats and violence would only increase. Robinson and others made pleas to easterners to provide arms for self-defense and the response was overwhelming. Thousands of weapons began to flow into Kansas, the most popular being the recently-patented Sharps rifle, a breech-loading single shot rifle known for its accuracy at long range. Early on, because many of the weapons had to be shipped through the enslaved state of Missouri, a good number were confiscated or stolen while in transport. Later, easterners adjusted their tactics and began to ship the rifles under disguise, marked as books or other items. Reverend Henry Ward Beecher of New York, a prominent abolitionist minister and the brother of writer Harriet Beecher Stowe (whose antislavery book *Uncle Tom's Cabin* had been published in 1852), is reputed to have shipped Sharps rifles to Kansas in crates marked as containing bibles, leading many to begin referring to the weapons flowing into the territory as "Beecher's Bibles."

Although elected by fraud, the territorial legislature was recognized by the administration of President Pierce as the legitimate government of the Kansas Territory. When it met in the summer of 1855, harsh proslavery laws were passed. These not only made slavery legal in Kansas, but also made assisting a slave escape to freedom punishable by death, and even made speaking or writing in opposition to slavery in Kansas a felony punishable by up to two years of imprisonment at hard labor.

The free-staters dubbed these "bogus laws" enacted by a "bogus legislature." They boycotted the machinery of the territorial government. They brought no suits in its courts, probated no estates, paid no taxes, and made no calls for assistance from its justices of the peace. They settled their legal matters by arbitration, or by other means, and adopted their own regulations for policing and maintaining order in their towns. Although there were differences among them—some were abolitionists and others opposed slavery only in Kansas—they united politically under the banner of the Free-State Party.

The proslavery faction in Kansas, with control of the territorial government, denounced the free-staters as outlaws and traitors. They also joined together politically, calling themselves the Law-and-Order Party.

Kansas was a tinderbox. All awaited the spark that would ignite a blaze.

CHAPTER 26

May, 1855— Monty looked at the list containing the names of those seated before him, men who had volunteered to join the militia company that he would head in the defense of Lawrence from a potential attack by proslavery forces. Captain Tolliver was a title that sounded strange to him. He had no military experience. Despite his lack of qualifications, the free-state leaders in Kansas, particularly Dr. Robinson, felt strongly that having a former congressman prominent in the militia's leadership would add prestige to their cause. He thought of his friends in Ohio and from his days in Washington City, and how they would be amused by all of this. Monty leading men in battle? Who would have ever believed it? He wondered if he could do the job. Despite his doubts, he was determined to do his best. He purchased some books on military strategy, and others were loaned to him, all of which he had been studying. The most helpful one so far, he decided, was *On War*, written by a Prussian general from the Napoleonic Wars, Carl von Clausewitz. He brought it with him and put it on the table where he was sitting, hoping that it might impress someone. Staring at the list of names again, one stood out. It was not a common last name. Could it, Monty wondered, be *him*?

He pounded on the table several times to bring the meeting to order. The smell of freshly cut lumber permeated the unfinished room which, when completed, would be Lawrence's first schoolhouse. That would take a while. With the continued threat of violence, understandably, very few free-state settlers had yet to bring their children to Kansas. In this precarious environment, there were other priorities. The fifty or so men around the room were sitting on makeshift benches. He noticed a red-haired chap on the right side. *Maybe*, he thought.

"Good morning, gentlemen," he began. "Thank you for volunteering and welcome to this initial meeting of the Second Militia Company of Lawrence. I am Captain Montgomery Tolliver. Our survival here, and the survival of the cause of freedom, may well depend on how well we do our job over the next few months."

Monty explained that the militia would be organized into two platoons, at least at the beginning. If their ranks grew, a third would be added. He would select two lieutenants and advised that anyone interested in those positions should see him after the meeting. He and the lieutenants would then select a sergeant and a corporal for each of the platoons. Drilling would begin immediately, twice a week, on Saturday mornings and Wednesday afternoons. Each man would be provided with a Sharps rifle, which had generously been provided, he noted, by folks back East who supported their cause. A howitzer was on its way, he said, and should arrive in a few weeks. Their assigned territory would be the south side of Lawrence, and extending south and east, more than twenty miles, all the way to Ottawa. In addition to becoming proficient at firing rifles and artillery, their work, he added, would involve digging trenches and putting up earthworks to defend Lawrence from an anticipated attack by the proslavery men.

After the meeting, a line of five men formed in front of Monty's table, those who were interested in seeking the two lieutenant positions. The red-haired young man was among them. Upon viewing him up close, Monty was startled. He was sure that his initial suspicion was correct. The resemblance was amazing, almost as if he was seeing a ghost. After questioning two of the prospects, he looked down at his list and called out "Who's next?," already knowing what the answer would be.

"Robert Geddis, sir," came the reply.

"Where are you from, Mr. Geddis?"

"Rhode Island, sir, from Newport."

Confirmation, thought Monty, if any was needed.

"Any military experience?," he asked.

"Yes sir, I was in the Navy. For three years. Served on artillery crews, as a corporal. Mostly on frigates. Have fired many a cannon."

"What about rifles?"

"Not in the Navy, but I'm a pretty good shot. Did a lot of hunting back home when growing up."

"What brings you to Kansas?"

"The cause, sir. Stopping the spread of slavery. That, and starting a new life here on my own. Was time for a change."

"Thank you, Mr. Geddis," said Monty. "Could you step aside and take a seat? I would like to talk with you further, after I have spoken with everyone."

Monty finished speaking with the rest of those in line. Other than Geddis, only two others had any military experience. Both had been in the army, one a sergeant from Indiana and the other a private, who had served in Michigan. Neither had been involved in any fighting. Kansas, Monty decided, attracted antislavery idealists and farmers more than military types. He told the man from Indiana that he was choosing him as one of the lieutenants and then went over to speak more, one-on-one, with Geddis, whom he had decided would be the other.

Monty informed Geddis of his selection, which was received with excitement. The young man's right leg began to twitch as he sat in his chair and a vein on one side of his forehead became prominent, both characteristics that he remembered from another red-haired man from his past. Still, Monty thought that he may be the more elated of the two. He couldn't wait to write to Theresa about it. Who would have thought it? He then advised his new lieutenant of the personal connection between them.

"I knew your brother."

"Ben?," Robert asked, as he furrowed his brow and a questioning look came over his face.

"Yes, he was my best friend."

Monty's mind flashed back to the first time he met Ben, at a speech given by Senator Clay in the Capitol, and how they had instantly bonded.

"When he was in Washington City?," inquired Robert.

"Yes."

"*Mont-gom-er-y* . . . Montgomery," Robert said slowly, pausing for a couple of seconds, and then making the connection. "You're Monty?"

"I am. Hard to believe, isn't it?"

"Indeed! I remember him speaking of you on his visits back home, and in his letters to my parents. He was very fond of you."

"Likewise. A finer man I never knew. I named my son after him."

"He would have been honored by that, I'm sure."

* * *

That evening, lying in bed, Monty found it difficult to sleep, something he noted had been getting worse recently as the troubles in Kansas increased. There would likely be many challenges over the next weeks and months. Was he up to being the leader of a militia unit? How would he acquit himself of this task? Would his cause, making Kansas a free state, prevail in the coming conflict? He comforted himself with one thought, an unexpected surprise. Whatever might happen, at least he would have Robert, Ben's brother, by his side.

CHAPTER 27

April, 1855— Ned had told Billy to meet at midnight, at a group of trees a few hundred yards up the road leading to the sawmill. Bring your rifle, he had instructed. It had been a couple of months since the Blue Lodge initiation. At the appointed time, a wagon, pulled by one horse, came up the dirt road and stopped by the trees. Ned, who was seated on the wagon's driver bench and holding the reins, reached out a hand and helped Billy up to sit beside him. In addition to Ned, there were three other men in the back of the wagon. It was hard to see their faces in the dark, but Billy thought he recognized two of them from the ceremony.

"Where we headed?," asked Billy.

"To do work for the Lodge," said Ned, proudly. "Gonna burn a cabin that belongs to a free-stater."

"What?," replied a shocked Billy. "Arson?" He could not believe what he had heard. "Burning people out of their homes?"

"Calm down," replied Ned, "Don't worry. It's your first time. You'll just be watching to learn how it's done. We gotta send messages to these damned Yankee abolitionists. We taught 'em in the election that we're in charge. Need to keep up the fight."

"Damn right," Billy heard one of the men seated behind them in the wagon chime in. "They need to leave us alone and git back home."

As the wagon bounced along in the darkness, Billy sat in silence. He felt uncomfortable. How could he be a part of this? He thought about asking Ned to stop, so that he could get off, or maybe just jump out of the moving wagon. He then remembered the Blue Lodge oath that he had taken. Now, its meaning became clearer. He had pledged to go anywhere and to do anything commanded by the Lodge. He thought things through. He was a southerner. Oaths were a matter of honor. How could he now refuse to do something that he had pledged to do? After all, as Ned had said, he would just be watching. What's the harm in that? *He* wouldn't really be doing anything. He had come to Kansas to support the South, hadn't he? Maybe burning down a cabin *would* send a message and help the cause. Ned was his closest friend since he had arrived in Kansas. He trusted him.

The wagon came to a stop behind a patch of bushes. In the distance, about fifty or so yards away, in the dim moonlight, Billy could make out the outline of a cabin. He watched as Ned turned to the three men behind them in the wagon.

"Go to it, boys. And be quick," Ned ordered.

The men hopped out of the wagon, grabbed what looked like poles and began to pour something from a jug over them. Torches, Billy realized, their tips soon consumed by fire. He watched as the three walked up to the cabin, and as two of them continued around to the back. Flames soon began to appear near the eaves of the roof. The two men that had been in the back, now torchless, came running toward the wagon, and Billy watched as the one who had been in front tossed his torch through one of the cabin's windows, turned around, and then also began to run.

Once all had jumped in and the wagon sped off, Billy turned and looked back at the cabin. As the flames rose into the night sky, a man and a woman ran out of the front door, the woman carrying a small child. The anguish on their faces was reflected in the orange light of the fire. The man fired a rifle, aimlessly, in several directions, and then, apparently in disgust, threw it to the ground.

"We sure showed 'em, Ned!" proclaimed one of the men in the back, as they all backslapped one another.

"Good work, fellas!," replied Ned.

Billy sat silently, his stomach turning.

CHAPTER 28

July, 1855— "Captain Tolliver, your men looked sharp in the parade this morning. Between you and me, they were the best of our militia units."

"Thank you, Dr. Robinson. We have been drilling hard for this day. Wanted to look our best on the Fourth of July."

"It paid off. Good work."

The two men were standing amid a throng of revelers, almost two-thousand people, who had gathered in Clinton Park in Lawrence to celebrate Independence Day. What a difference a year had made. When Americans had last commemorated the holiday, the town had not even existed. Now, it was a bustling mecca for free-staters in the territory. The parade featured not only militia units marching in formation, but also a band from Topeka, equestrian units, carriages decorated with flowers, and Native Americans from the nearby Delaware and Shawnee tribes. The program called for music, prayers, a reading of the Declaration of Independence, and speeches. Lots of speeches.

"I hope," Robinson added, "that your unit can shoot as well as they can march."

"Do you think it will come to that, sir?"

"I'm not optimistic. We get more threats from the slavers every day. Any excuse they may seize upon could lead to fighting. Only a matter of time, I suspect. I worry that what happens here is just the beginning. If our experience in Kansas is what happens when northerners and southerners meet face-to-face over slavery, I fear our Union may be no more."

As Monty and the doctor were talking, a third man approached. Tall and thin, he appeared to Monty to be in his early forties, with a mop of unruly dark hair, sunken cheeks, an oval clean-shaven face, and dark eyes. "Good morning, Charles," he said.

"A happy Fourth to you, Jim. Have you met Monty Tolliver? He's the captain of one of our militia units here in Lawrence?"

"I have not. A pleasure, Captain Tolliver."

"Monty, this is James Lane. Jim was a congressman from Indiana. He joined us here in Kansas a couple of months ago. I will be asking him to take over the supervision of our militia, so the two of you will be working together."

Monty was shocked by the doctor's statement of his intent. He did his best to freeze the expression on his face, so as not to reveal his displeasure. He knew of Lane, and what he had heard was not good.

"Pleased to meet you, sir," he managed to get out, he hoped convincingly.

"Tolliver. That name sounds familiar. You were in Congress, weren't you?"

"I was. Surprised that you've heard of me."

"Oh, I make it my business to keep up with politics, and politicians. From Ohio? A Whig, I believe?," replied Lane, with a know-it-all tone in his voice that irritated Monty.

"Correct. Served a term and a half. Left in mid-'52."

"Then we did not overlap. I was there for one term, beginning in '53."

"Jim was a Democrat," Robinson interjected.

"Still am."

"So, you were there in '54 during the debate over the Kansas-Nebraska Act?," asked Monty, already knowing the answer and the position that Lane had taken on the bill.

"I was. Voted for it. Senator Douglas and I were friends. He convinced me that popular sovereignty is the correct way to proceed here in Kansas. Still believe that. Proud to be here and to support the free-state cause."

"We're all on the same side now," said Robinson. "Doesn't matter how we got here."

"Agreed, doctor. I'm happy to have Mr. Tolliver serve *under me* in the militia. I'm sure that we'll get along just fine."

Lane's comment irritated Monty. The man, he thought, is a mixture of arrogance and oiliness. Just as he was about to ask Lane another question, the conversation abruptly ended.

"Excuse me, gentlemen," Lane suddenly added, "I see an old friend from Indiana over there." With a smile and a nod of his head, he moved on to another group of men standing by a decorated carriage that had been in the parade.

"Jim's always working the crowd," Robinson said. "Once a politician, always a politician, I suppose."

"I managed to get it out of my system. Was never one who cared for the glad-handling, or for talking out of both sides of my mouth."

With Lane safely out of earshot, a concerned Monty added, "I'm surprised you've selected him to head up our militia."

"He led Indiana units in the Mexican War, with some distinction, I am told. We don't have a lot of prominent men to choose from on our side with battle experience."

"You do *know* about him, sir?"

"That he used to support slavery? I'm aware of that."

"A friend of mine from Congress, a Whig from Indiana, who still serves, wrote to me about Lane since I've been here. Said to be wary of him. Word in Washington City is that he and Senator Douglas had a deal—that Lane would vote for the Kansas-Nebraska Act, move here and favor slavery, and that Douglas would then support him to be a senator when Kansas becomes a state. A slave state. You're aware he was quoted in the newspapers on his way out here that he would just as soon buy a Negro as a mule? I read one article that said that he had tried to buy a slave, to be a nanny to his children, when crossing through Missouri, but didn't have enough money to close the deal. That doesn't sound like a free-stater to me. *Now,* he's on *our* side? More of an opportunist, or a liar, I'd say."

"Monty, I'm not naive. I trust Jim Lane about as far as I can throw him. But to win this thing, we need a big tent. We can't be turning away folks because of something they may have said or done in the past. We need Democrats, Whigs, abolitionists, free-soilers, all we can attract. Maybe he's sniffed a shift in the political winds since he's been here and wants to be on the winning side. Who knows? The man tells me he now fully supports our free-state cause. And besides, I've heard him talk before an audience. He can sway and motivate a crowd. Something we can use. One hell of a good speaker."

"Most demagogues are," Monty replied.

"Don't be cruel, my friend. It is an enviable talent. Wish I were half as good before an audience. I'm due to give my remarks in about an hour."

"You'll do fine, I'm sure. What's your theme?"

"I have two—liberty and repudiation."

* * *

During 1855, the free-staters in Kansas organized them-selves politically. At a Fourth of July celebration in Lawrence,

Dr. Charles Robinson, who had become the movement's leader, gave a rousing speech that proposed a strategy. Since the territorial legislature had been fraudulently elected, Robinson argued that free-staters should refuse to accept its authority over them, including obedience to any laws that it passed. The actions of an illegitimate body, he argued, must be repudiated. If ever there was an appropriate day to resist tyranny and to declare independence from the laws of the slavers, Robinson proclaimed, the Fourth of July was the day.

A policy of repudiating the elected legislature would require walking a fine line. Free-staters accepted the authority of the federal government over them, and the federal government had recognized the results of the Kansas election and the legitimacy of the territorial government. In Robinson's view, they should walk up to the line of possible treason, but not cross it. Passive resistance to laws was one thing, but active refusal of an order from the territorial government was another. That, he knew, could lead to force being used against them, backed, if needed, by hundreds of soldiers stationed at the two federal forts in the territory, Fort Leavenworth and Fort Riley.

In September 1855, at a convention held in Big Springs, free-staters met under the banner of the Free-State Party and formally adopted Robinson's strategy of repudiation. While all agreed that there should be no slavery in Kansas, they differed on other slavery-related issues. Two factions within the movement developed. Radicals, mostly abolitionists from New England, and led by Robinson, favored banning slavery everywhere and fair treatment of Blacks in a free Kansas. Conservatives, mostly from western states, led by Jim Lane, opposed slavery in Kansas, but not where it already existed. Their opposition to the expansion of slavery was based on economics, not morality. Without slave labor, more jobs would be available for working-class white men.

What all could agree on, however, was that fraudulent elections had been held, with thousands of Missourians crossing the border and illegally voting, and that an illegitimate legislature had been elected to rule over them. Both factions viewed themselves as having been denied their rights as Americans to hold free and fair elections. The free-staters at Big Springs passed resolutions declaring that the laws of the territorial legislature had "no validity or binding force," that they would resist them "by every peaceable and legal means" within their power and, if necessary, they would "resist them to a bloody issue." The gathering also endorsed a call for a convention to consider drafting a constitution for the admission of Kansas into the Union as a free state.

CHAPTER 29

*O*ctober, 1855— "It's not quite Independence Hall, is it?," Robert said to Monty.

"Indeed, but if we do our job well over the next few weeks," Monty responded, "perhaps it will be as famous someday. This could be the Philadelphia of the West."

Seated on their horses, they were in front of a two-story building in Topeka, about twenty-five miles west of Lawrence. It was late on a pleasant autumn afternoon and the ride over, consuming much of the day, had been uneventful. The structure they were observing was new, almost square in shape, with a smooth limestone facade covering its otherwise rough stone walls. It stood alone on an almost barren street. A couple of small hotels, located on the next block, and a handful of other buildings, were about all there was to the small town of Topeka, which had been founded, as most other towns in Kansas had been, only a year or so earlier. Like Lawrence, Topeka was an enclave for settlers who opposed slavery. Approximately forty delegates, Monty among them, had been chosen by the territory's antislavery voters in a recent election to meet here, starting on October 23, 1855, to draft a constitution for Kansas to be admitted to the Union as a free state. Robert had come along with Monty to report on the constitutional convention for his newspaper.

"We'll be meeting up there," said Monty, pointing to the three large windows on the second floor.

"Here, the fate of Kansas will be decided," stated Robert, slowly, in a deep voice. In his normal tone, he continued, "How's that for the opening line of my first article about the convention?"

Monty shook his head and chuckled. "Dramatic. I like it."

After a loosening of the reins and a few gentle prods with their heels, they guided their horses up the street, to the Chase House, one of Topeka's first hotels, where they would be staying for the duration of the convention. Inside, they were greeted by Charles Robinson.

"Good afternoon, Monty, good to see you."

"And a good afternoon to you, doctor" replied Monty. "I'd like to introduce Robert Geddis, my good friend and a reporter for the *Herald of Freedom*, who will be covering the convention for the newspaper."

After more introductions were made to a few additional delegates who were in the hotel's lobby, Robinson addressed the group and got down to business.

"I have to tell you, gentlemen, that I am not optimistic that the outcome of the convention is going to be entirely pleasing to us. We abolitionists are outnumbered. There are fewer than ten of us among the delegates. The opposition has about fifteen, all former Democrats. Jim Lane is their leader and I hear they're staying over at the Garvey House. We all agree that Kansas should be a free state and that the Missourians are bastards for what they have done, but, beyond that, we don't see eye to eye on much else. Lane and his crowd are no friends of the Black man. Opposed to allowing him to vote, or to having any rights. They even want to forbid free Blacks from living here once Kansas becomes a state."

"What about the rest of the delegates?," asked Monty.

"I suspect that they will line up with Lane's group. Together, they'll have the votes to make him the president of the convention."

Another delegate, Grosvenor Lowry, shook his head in disgust. "Having Jim Lane as the convention's leader will taint our cause," he said. "You've no doubt heard the rumors going around Lawrence about him?"

"That his wife has gone back to Indiana?," asked another delegate "Hardly any shame in that. Life is difficult here, until things get built up more. And the constant threat of violence from the Missourians. I haven't yet brought my wife out here from Massachusetts because of it."

"That's not why she went back home, so I've heard," replied Lowry. "The word is that Lane made advances on a married woman in Lawrence and that his wife left him because of it."

"That's not surprising," added another delegate, who was standing in their circle. "He came here from Indiana a proslavery man. I heard he asked for a divorce from the bogus legislature a couple of months ago and they refused to grant him one. That's when, from what I'm told, he switched over to our side. He's no free-stater from conviction, but out of revenge."

"I warned you about him before, doctor," said Monty, looking directly at Robinson and shaking his head. "Just what we need. A chameleon leading our convention."

CHAPTER 30

ctober, 1855— "Well, Grosvenor, at least you didn't get shot today, or worse," said Monty. "Would hate to have seen you go down in history as the Alexander Hamilton of Kansas."

Everyone laughed.

Monty and several other delegates stood in the lobby of the Chase House after a long and eventful day at the convention.

"We dodged a bullet today. No pun intended," added Dr. Robinson.

The free-state constitutional convention in Topeka got off to a potentially disastrous start, one that Monty knew could have led to the convention's dissolution and be fatal for the cause. A duel threatened to disrupt the convention in its opening days. As expected, Jim Lane was chosen by the delegates to be the body's presiding officer. When Lane heard that a rumor of marital infidelity concerning him had been repeated in Topeka by Grosvenor Lowry, a delegate to the convention, he issued a formal challenge to Lowry for a duel, to take place the following day.

"It would have been the death knell of our cause," Robinson continued. "One delegate to our convention, the president of the body, no less, killing another delegate, or being killed, in a duel. Barbaric. Imagine how it would have played out in the newspapers back East. We would have been the laughingstock of the country."

"I told all of you yesterday that he would back down," Lowry responded. "Like most bullies, he's all bluster. And, of course, there is the fact that my statement about him was true. If I had to die today defending my right to speak the truth, so be it. There are less honorable ways to depart this life."

"I'm glad it all played out as we had planned last night," said Robinson. "I knew when Lane sent over his note late yesterday asking that the duel be delayed for a few hours that he was looking for a way out. Of course, we have Monty here to thank for coming up with our strategy."

"I was confident that he'd never risk getting booted from the convention in order to fight a duel," Monty replied. "It would have damaged his political career. Would have taken him off the stage, and we all know the man *loves* a stage."

"The look on Lane's face," said Lowry, "when Monty rose this morning and offered his resolution that any delegate participating or assisting in any 'hostile meeting' be expelled from the convention, was priceless. Even he recognized the ingenuity of it."

"I knew when he didn't block his chums from voting for it that there would be no duel," another delegate chimed in.

"A face-saving way for all of us to move on to the substance of writing a constitution," said Monty. "He can tell his Democratic friends that he backed down from the duel, not because the charge was true, but because his colleagues begged him to remain part of the convention."

"Unfortunately, gentlemen," Robinson said, "this may be one of our few victories here in Topeka. Keeping one of us from possibly being murdered by one of our colleagues. A rather low bar, I have to say."

"I suppose I'm not including any of this in my article about today's session of the convention?" asked Robert, who had overheard the entire conversation, but had not been permitted to attend the morning session of the convention that day.

"Definitely not," replied Robinson. "The discussion of it was entirely in executive session. Officially off the record."

CHAPTER 31

ovember, 1855— About a dozen men gathered around a long table in the lobby of the Chase House, some perusing specific pages of the twenty-six-page hand-written document spread out before them. Entitled "Constitution of the State of Kansas," it was the product of their labors over the past three weeks. Several sipped from glasses of whiskey that they had brought over from the bar. Despite having finished their task, their mood was not cheerful.

"It is the best that we could get, gentlemen," said Dr. Robinson, holding one of the pages in his hands. "You all know the clause that we need to emphasize." He moved his index finger down the page. "Here it is, Article One, Section Six 'There shall be no slavery in this state, nor involuntary servitude, unless for the punishment of crime.' This is the reason that we all uprooted our lives and came here. No slavery in Kansas. We will accomplish that, if we can get our fellow citizens and Congress to approve it."

"But not much else," said Lowry. "Lane and his crowd voted down our attempt to give Negro men the right to vote."

"We always knew that was going to be an uphill battle, as was my proposal to allow women to vote," Robinson replied.

"But losing by more than a three-to-one margin? I didn't expect that," said Lowry.

"Goddamn Douglas Democrats," said another.

"We talked about this. We decided not to walk out of the convention and split our movement," said the doctor. "What would that have accomplished? We'll fight our battles one at a time. We ensure that there's no slavery here first, then we can move to other things later."

"It's that exclusion clause that sticks in my craw," said Monty. "Not allowing any Blacks to live here once we become a state."

"At least we kept that out of the Constitution," Robinson said. "It just goes to the people as a resolution to vote on, at the same time that they vote on the Constitution. If it passes, it will be up to the first session of the legislature to decide that issue."

"Yes, but it goes to the people as an action of our convention," replied Monty.

"As long as it's not in the Constitution, we can deal with it. We'll just need to have the votes in the legislature, when the time comes, to block it."

Robinson raised his glass. "This is a victory, gentlemen, not a complete victory, but a victory nonetheless. Our free-state movement remains united. Now we need to go back home and sell this document to our people."

* * *

The Topeka Constitution, drafted by a convention of free-staters, was the first constitution for Kansas statehood to be sent to Washington for consideration by Congress. It fell short of what abolitionist delegates to the convention had hoped for. Moreover, the Constitution was sent to the people for a vote along with a separate resolution, passed by the convention, addressing whether the state legislature, once formed, should or should not adopt a law forbidding all Blacks from living in Kansas. Such a prohibition had been enacted in Indiana in 1851 and had been discussed, but not adopted, in a few other western states.

At an election held in December 1855, which was boycotted by proslavery voters, the Topeka Constitution passed by an overwhelming margin. The exclusion provision was also approved, by a smaller, but still significant, amount. Another election was held in January 1856 to elect officers under the Constitution. Charles Robinson was elected governor. Other statewide officers were chosen, including judges and legislators. Within months, free-staters essentially set up a "shadow" government, thumbing their noses at the existing territorial government. Although they took care to make it known that their government would not be "official" until statehood was approved by Congress, they also formed an Executive Committee, with Jim Lane as its chairman, to act as their governing body until that time.

The actions of the free-staters in Kansas did not sit well with Democrats in Washington, who ran the federal government. President Pierce came out firmly against them. In a January 1856 message to Congress, he stated that the territorial legislature elected the previous March, with the votes of crossover Missourians, was "legitimate," despite "irregularities" in the voting. The Topeka Movement of the free-staters was deemed by the president to be "revolutionary" and potentially "treasonable." His Secretary of War, Jefferson Davis, ordered the commanders of the federal forts in Kansas, if requested by the governor of the territory, to suppress all insurrectionary acts and any armed resistance to enforcement of the territory's laws.

CHAPTER 32

ecember, 1855— "Stretch, I'll have another one," Billy said to the bartender at Greeley's in Lecompton, as he took a last gulp of his warm ale. It was early in the evening and the place was mostly empty.

The name of the bar was ironic, it being in Lecompton, a town that had become a proslavery haven in Kansas. It had been named by its original owner after Horace Greeley, the abolitionist editor of the *New York Tribune*. That had been a little over a year ago. The owner, a fellow by the name of Harper, was a free-stater, and proudly so. But when it turned out that most of the newcomers to Lecompton favored the proslavery side, he suddenly sold the place and moved on. Rumor was that threats were made, that if he didn't sell out, the bar would be burned down. Most thought that the new owner, Stretch Parker, was a proslavery man, but no one really knew. He kept mostly quiet and did a lot of slow nodding whenever anyone was talking. Stretch's nickname fit. Standing well over six feet and thin as a reed, he was balding, with his thinning black hair combed back, and with a perpetual stubble on his rugged face. Wendell was his given name, Billy had heard. He was one of those bartenders with an uncanny ability to remember the drinking habits of his customers, even sporadic ones. Stretch told folks he decided to keep the bar's name because the signs out front and on the back wall still looked like new and it wasn't worth the cost and effort of painting over them. Besides, he likely realized, most of his proslavery clientele couldn't or didn't read newspapers, and probably hadn't a clue who Horace Greeley was and what he stood for. If anyone asked, he told them that it was an old family name.

Billy turned to Ned, seated on the stool beside him. "I feel like we should be joining the militia, or doing something." He was referring to all of the activity then going on in and around Lawrence.

"Those Missouri boys can take care of it. They don't need us. What we do for the southern cause through the Lodge is more than enough."

The Lodge, thought Billy. He had never mustered the courage to tell Ned what he really felt about the organization, how he wished that he had never joined it, knowing that it would likely end their friendship. He had told Ned that he was uncomfortable with the nighttime arson raids on the cabins of free-state settlers. Ned replied that he would get used to it. Billy had been on three raids so far, actively participating in the last two. Yes, he kept telling himself, he had vowed to do what the Lodge's leaders told him to, but that didn't mean he had to like it. Still, he thought, he would rather pick up a rifle and fight the free-state men in broad daylight, like a soldier, rather than sneaking around in the dark and burning women and children out of their homes.

* * *

During most of 1855, disputes between the free-state and proslavery populations in the Kansas Territory were largely battles

of words. The free-staters followed their policy of passive resistance to the laws of the new territorial legislature, but stopped
short of active defiance. The town of Lawrence remained, as it
had been since the first group from the New England Emigrant
Aid Company arrived in August 1854, their stronghold. The
proslavery settlers congregated in Lecompton, located a few miles
west of Lawrence, as well as in Leavenworth and Atchison, both
located to the north and east and on the border with Missouri.
In Lawrence, the company built a huge three-story hotel, the
Free State Hotel, intended to be the initial destination for future
emigrants upon their arrival in the territory. To those who favored
slavery, the Free State, with its thick stone walls and parapets on
the roof, appeared to have been built more as a fortress than as
a hotel. The fact that the leaders of the free-state movement met
there to plan and plot their strategy made it a detested place,
and a target, for the opposition. Throughout the year, both the
pro and antislavery factions published their own newspapers,
attacking each other. Their inflammatory stories were reprinted
throughout the East and the South, allowing the rest of the
country to closely follow the tense situation in Kansas.

The Kansas tinderbox was lit in November 1855 by a seemingly
routine occurrence on the frontier—a land dispute between two
neighbors that led to a killing. The events that followed are known
as the Wakarusa War. The death occurred at Hickory Point, about
ten miles south of Lawrence. Charles Dow, a free-stater, was shot
and killed by his neighbor, Frank Coleman, a proslavery man.
Things then swung wildly out of control. In revenge for Dow's
killing, free-staters burned the cabins of a few proslavery families
in the area. A posse led by Samuel Jones, a sheriff under the proslavery territorial government, then arrested a free-state ringleader,
Jacob Branson, who was a friend of the deceased Dow and who
was suspected of organizing the arsons. As Branson was being led

to a jail in Lecompton, a group of free-staters, led by Sam Wood, rescued him from the custody of Jones and his men.

This act of defiance, the forcible seizure of a prisoner from a sheriff and posse operating under the authority of the territorial government, led to a call to arms. The new governor of the Kansas Territory, Wilson Shannon, a Democratic politician from Ohio who had recently been appointed to the post by President Pierce, acceded to the demands for law and order from the proslavery faction and issued a call for assistance to enforce the laws of the territory. A couple of thousand men responded, the majority of whom were from Missouri, and set up camps a few miles southeast of Lawrence, along the Wakarusa River. Months earlier, in March, they had crossed the border into Kansas to vote. Now, they had come to fight.

* * *

"Do you think they will really attack Lawrence?," Billy asked Ned, as Stretch placed the requested tin of fresh ale on the bar.

"They damn well better," Ned responded. "The laws have gotta be respected. They can't steal a prisoner from Sheriff Jones and not expect that there won't be consequences. The free-staters deserve what they're gonna get hit with."

Billy decided it was not a good time to point out to Ned that arson, which they had both engaged in, was also a crime under the territorial laws of Kansas.

"I just hope all of this is over soon," he said to Ned, as both continued to sip their ale. "So we can start planting in the spring. Farming. Getting rid of the Yankees and moving on with our lives."

"When Lawrence is taught a lesson," Ned responded, "we'll be well on our way."

CHAPTER 33

***D**ecember, 1855*— "Good work," shouted Monty, commending the men in his militia unit. "Keep at it. Needs to be at least a foot higher."

He stood in a large pit dug at the intersection of Massachusetts and Henry Streets in Lawrence, a block south of the Free State Hotel. Robert stood by his side. Around them, a circular earthwork, almost one hundred feet in diameter, had risen several feet above the street, and was nearing completion. They had started digging three days earlier. It was one of four redoubts being put up to defend the town from an attack, expected any day now, by proslavery men.

"Lieutenant, have them keep at it for another half hour," Monty instructed Robert, "then give them a break of fifteen minutes before we start our afternoon drill."

"Yessir, captain," Robert responded. "I heard another hundred or so men came into town yesterday to help with our fight."

"Somewhat less than that, but it was a good number. Every extra man will help. General Lane got them organized into new companies this morning. We're still outnumbered, but we'll give them a hell of a fight."

"Any updated information on when the attack will come?"

"Our scouts say by the end of the week. But who knows?"

"What do you think will happen when they find out that the men they are looking for are not here?," asked Robert.

"Nothing. It won't stop them. I'm coming to believe that this whole thing was contrived, part of a plan, that they knew there would be an attempt to rescue Branson, and let it happen, so that they could have a reason to attack Lawrence. We've been a thorn in their side for more than a year now. Folks here had nothing to do with what happened last week. But the bastards don't care. They have the excuse they have been wanting for months to come in here, to kill, and to destroy all we have built."

* * *

While the Missourians camped near the Wakarusa River, the free-staters in Lawrence also prepared for battle. Their leaders, Charles Robinson and James Lane, sent an urgent call across the entire territory for assistance in the town's defense. Robinson led political strategy and Lane was in charge of military preparations. As with the proslavery side, hundreds of free-stater settlers responded and came into Lawrence. Militia units were organized and placed under Lane's direction. Huge circular earthworks were dug on the town's main roads. While the men drilled daily with rifles, the women of Lawrence practiced firing pistols and made cartridges and bandages.

The freed prisoner, Branson, and some of the men who rescued him, had sought refuge in Lawrence. However, at a meeting of the town's citizens, it was decided to ask them to leave. Although the arrest of Branson and his rescue had taken place several miles from Lawrence, all knew that the presence of these men in their midst would be used as a pretext for invading the town. The men complied and left.

While both sides prepared for battle, another violent death occurred. Three free-state militia men, who had been drilling in Lawrence, set out for their homes a few miles away to check on their families. They were intercepted by a patrol of proslavery men and, after some words were exchanged, one of the free-staters, Thomas Barber, was shot and killed. Barber's murder inflamed an already tense situation. His body was taken to Lawrence and displayed at the Free State Hotel.

* * *

"The men are already inside, sir. Corporal Gibson is leading them through," Robert informed Monty. The unit's afternoon drill had ended minutes earlier.

The two of them stood across the street from the Free State Hotel, looking at the line of people that snaked out of the hotel's front door and down Massachusetts Street, almost as far as the eye could see. All had come to view the body of Thomas Barber, the latest martyr for the free-state cause, laid out on a table in a room near the hotel's lobby.

"Good. I want them to see firsthand what we are fighting against. An innocent man gunned down in cold blood. Have our opponents no shame?"

As they were talking, Monty and Robert were startled by a one-horse wagon that had pulled up from behind them, coming to an abrupt stop. They turned and observed the wagon's occupants, five men, the driver and four seated in its bed. All but the driver were clutching either rifles or swords, with more weapons, including pistols and what looked like spears, spread out on the wagon's floor near their feet. The men, covered with dirt from their travels in the open wagon, appeared to have come from some distance to assist in the defense of the town. One of them, who looked to be in his fifties and much older than the others, climbed out of the wagon, still holding his rifle, and walked up to Monty. The man, Monty observed, was of average height and lean, with a square jaw and thin lips. He had mostly black hair, cut short and combed back. His recently shaved face was highlighted by hollow cheeks, wrinkles on his forehead and also around his eyes, which were gray and seemed to be constantly darting about, taking in everything.

"Afternoon," the man said, with authority. "I'm John Brown. Here with my boys. Reporting for duty."

CHAPTER 34

*D*ecember, 1855— "You were with the family that came in by wagon a couple of days ago? I believe you were the driver?," Robert asked.

The questions were directed to a man who was standing alone in front of a dry goods shop on Massachusetts Street. He looked to be about the same age as Robert, early thirties, and he resembled the older man in that group, but with less intense facial features. Both were watching militiamen march by, in formation, with rifles on their shoulders. Robert's unit had finished their daily drill a few minutes earlier and he had remained to observe the others, to see how his men's performance could be improved.

"Yes, you have a keen eye. Maybe they should make you a scout," the man responded. He smiled, extended his right hand, and added, "The older fella is my father. I'm Jason Brown. Pleased to meet you."

"Robert Geddis, Lieutenant Robert Geddis, I guess I should say," Robert replied as they shook hands.

"I saw that the rest of your family, along with some other new arrivals, have already been organized into a new company by General Lane. They've been given the name Liberty Guards. Your father has been named its captain."

"So he has. *Captain* John Brown. Finally living his dream. Here to do battle for the Lord."

Robert detected some sarcasm in the comment.

"You're not joining them?"

"I'm not a fighting man," Jason replied. "I believe in the cause. Despise slavery as much as they do, but I part with them on tactics. My father came to Kansas eager for a fight, to kill men in a holy war to end it. Been preaching to us about this for years. The time has now arrived, he says. My brothers will follow him anywhere and do whatever he says. Told them I would drive the wagon up here, but I'm no killer. I'll do my part, in my own way. I'm going over to one of the tents and help make bandages in a bit."

Robert and Jason continued to talk. Robert explained why he had left Rhode Island and came to Kansas, of his work at the *Herald of Freedom* since his arrival, and of his involvement in the militia. He learned from Jason that he and four of his brothers had come to the territory for the same reasons that he had—for a new start in life and to support Kansas entering the Union as a free state. The Brown brothers, Jason relayed, had arrived from Ohio, at their father's suggestion, in the spring of 1855 and settled near Osawatomie, about thirty-five miles southeast of Lawrence. They brought with them several head of cattle, a few horses, and had purchased a plot of land to begin farming. Their father, Jason said, had been unsuccessful in various business interests and had, over the years, moved the family from state to state. The elder Brown had long been active in the abolitionist cause and, most recently, according to Jason, had been living near and assisting a colony of freed Blacks in upstate New York. When one of Jason's brothers wrote to their father about the election fraud back in the spring, and advised him that the proslavery men had armed themselves and were threatening violence against the free-state settlers, the old man decided to come to Kansas himself. He raised money from his abolitionist friends in New England to purchase a cache of weapons and brought them with him to the territory, joining his sons in Osawatomie just a couple of months ago, in October. When the family heard of the threatened attack on Lawrence, Jason said, his father's always animated eyes had gotten wilder-looking than usual. Armageddon was at hand, he had declared, and the Browns were destined to be in the heat of the battle.

"An interesting man, your father. I'd love to interview him for my newspaper. Our readers will be fascinated by him."

"You would be wasting your breath asking for that now. He's focused on one thing, this upcoming battle."

"As I suppose I should be," replied Robert. "When it's over, if he's willing to talk, get in touch with me."

He handed Jason a card with the name and address of his newspaper.

"Will do." Jason looked down at the card and then paused for a few seconds. "Assuming that both of you survive."

CHAPTER 35

*D*ecember, *1855*— Monty waited until the governor's covered black carriage came to a full stop in front of the Free State Hotel before giving a nod to Robert. He and the others had been standing in the cold December air for almost twenty minutes, waiting for this moment.

"Present arms!," Robert immediately shouted to the men of the Second Militia Company, who were standing, three rows deep, at the order arms position, just to the left of where the carriage now rested. Another militia company, to the carriage's right, was given the same command by one of its lieutenants. The men raised their Sharps rifles from their right side to the front of their body, with the butt of the weapon at knee height, with the left arm bent ninety degrees and left hand grasping the lower portion of the barrel. At the same time, each positioned his right hand lower, with the arm bent at thirty degrees, and grabbed the stock of the weapon. The maneuver was done in unison and with crispness.

Monty looked on, with pride. Not bad, he thought, for a bunch of farmers and merchants with no military experience. The time spent doing drills had been well spent. He had been instructed to have his men in front of the hotel as a show of force for the arrival of Governor Shannon. The word going around Lawrence was that the governor had been in town the day before, in secret meetings, and had also been to the main camp of the proslavery men on the Wakarusa River, in an attempt to negotiate a truce between the two sides. It was a crisis, many thought, of the governor's own making. He had been the one who, after the rescue of Branson from the proslavery posse, had put out a call for men to come and assist in the enforcement of the laws. Some said that the governor now realized that he had overreacted and was shocked that some two thousand men from Missouri had responded to his call, had assembled outside of Lawrence, and were now foaming at the mouth to attack the town.

Accompanied by three men, Governor Shannon was greeted by Charles Robinson and Jim Lane and all then disappeared through the hotel's front doors. Monty gave another nod to Robert, who gave the command of "Order arms!" to the men, who resumed their prior positions.

"What do you think?" Robert asked. "Are they going to resolve it?"

"Well, I don't think the governor would be here for a second time unless they were close to agreeing on something. From my days in Washington City, I learned that as long as there's still talking going on, there's usually progress."

"I've heard," said Robert, "that they are demanding that we surrender our rifles as a part of any agreement."

"Robinson and Lane will never agree to that," responded Monty. "Without our rifles, they would have overrun us months ago, and they'll do it tomorrow if we are stripped of them."

They waited in the December chill in front of the hotel for a couple of hours, but it seemed much longer. Finally, one of the hotel's front doors opened and a man who had arrived with Shannon came out and retrieved a satchel from the carriage.

"It's done. They'll be out soon," Monty heard the man say as he headed back into the hotel.

A few minutes later, the doors opened again and out came Robinson and Lane, followed by Governor Shannon, and then by an entourage of men. All appeared to have a look of satisfaction on their faces, a few shaking hands and patting each other on the back. Monty and Robert looked on as Robinson introduced the governor, who addressed the throng of citizens and soldiers gathered on the street in front of the hotel.

"People of Lawrence," Shannon began, "having been among you and your leaders for the past two days, I find that I have been laboring upon a misunderstanding. You are an estimable and orderly people. I am satisfied by my investigation of the events of the recent past that no one in Lawrence had advance knowledge of, or was involved in, the brazen seizure of a citizen under lawful arrest by the territory's legal authorities, and that none of the perpetrators are here in hiding. I am assured by your leaders that you are a law-abiding people and that you have no intent to resist the legal service of any criminal process, and that you pledge to aid in the execution of the laws when called upon by proper authority."

"My call for men to enforce the laws," the governor continued, "was intended only for men of Kansas and, if Missourians and others have responded, they have come of their own accord. Being satisfied that no laws have been broken by you, there is no reason for an attack upon you. To all who responded to my earlier call to arms, I am directing them to stand down and return to their homes and families."

Robinson and Lane then briefly addressed the crowd, echoing the governor's remarks that the crisis was over. Once they received verification that the enemy was departing, they said, then the militiamen in Lawrence could also then disband. Folks in Lawrence, Robinson confirmed, would be keeping all their weapons.

Monty and Robert noticed expressions of relief on the faces of most in the crowd, but also some of suspicion. After they dismissed their men from formation, they heard comments from a few that the agreement had come too easily and questions of whether secret promises had been made by their leaders.

* * *

After Monty and Robert parted ways, Robert walked up Massachusetts Street and noticed a crowd of about twenty or so, gathered in a half-circle around a speaker. He approached and listened.

"Our leaders are fools. Cowards. This is no victory," Robert heard the man proclaim. "We had them where we wanted them, all in camps on the Wakarusa. We should have attacked and destroyed them! Vengeance is mine, saith the Lord, for the day of the enemy's calamity is at hand, and his doom will come quickly! With one round fired by us, the Missourians would have been defeated by the wrath of God!"

There were a couple of grunts in agreement, but mostly silence among the onlookers.

Robert immediately recognized the man as the father of his newfound friend, Jason. The older man, John Brown, would be leaving Lawrence disappointed and heading back to Osawatomie with his dream of a decisive and victorious battle against slavery unfulfilled. He was, as Robert and everyone else observed, none too happy about it.

CHAPTER 36

*D*ecember, 1855— Stretch placed the amber brews on the bar before Billy and Ned.

"Those Missouri boys are fit to be tied," said Ned. "They're saying the governor tricked them and has disgraced himself and all of us who support the Law-and-Order Party. It was only after that big storm rolled in the other night that they finally gave up and agreed to leave."

"If the truce avoids fighting and killing, what's wrong with that?," responded Billy.

"I gotta agree with them. We got swindled. The folks in Lawrence still have all of their weapons—their Sharps rifles, their cannons, and everything else. They didn't even agree to follow our legislature's laws. Nothing good will come from that."

"You don't think it's over?"

"Hell, no. There's gonna be a battle, Billy, sooner or later. This stand-down won't last long. Those bastards in Lawrence will stir up something, and then we'll be right back where we were last week."

"When do you think that'll happen?," asked Billy.

"In the spring, my best guess. Which means our work for the Lodge over the next few months is gonna be more important than ever."

"You mean we'll be burning more cabins?"

"Damn right. Can't have the free-staters feeling comfortable, thinking that they've won. We need to keep the pressure on them until the Missourians can come back and finish the job."

"That reminds me," Ned continued, "I need you to step up, to take more responsibility. I'll be traveling over the next couple of months, setting up some new Lodge chapters. Before I go, I'll give you a list of targets that we need to get done by the spring. Miles, our chapter president, will line up some members to go out with you. He's here at Greeley's most Saturdays. Keep him posted on what's going on. I'm counting on you."

That's the last thing he wanted to hear, thought Billy, *more* arson. He wanted to refuse, to tell Ned that there's no way he'd do more. He wanted to do less, indeed to have nothing further to do with this campaign of terror against free-staters. But, for some reason, he couldn't do it. He decided, in a roundabout way, to probe what Ned's reaction might be.

"I noticed that that fella, Otis, who was with us that first raid that I went on, hasn't been at any of the recent Lodge meetings. What happened with him?"

"Otis?," replied Ned, "He moved up near Atchison and transferred to the chapter there."

"Transfer, you say? Anybody ever just quit the Lodge?"

"Quit? Who'd ever want to do that? We took an oath. The whole South is depending on us. Why you ask?"

"Just curious."

"There ain't no quitting, Billy." Ned paused, and then let out a small laugh. "At least not whilst you're still breathing."

Billy sat silently at the bar, slowing sipping his ale, disgusted with himself.

CHAPTER 37

*F*ebruary, 1856— Robert had barely slept. He was excited and, at the same time, nervous. He had been unable to think of anything else since he had found out, jotting down questions whenever they came into his head. He was going to interview the elusive abolitionist, John Brown. This could be the story that allowed him to make a name for himself as a journalist, especially if it was picked up by newspapers in the East. His boss at the *Herald of Freedom*, George, had gotten word from one of Brown's sons, who had visited Lawrence recently to purchase supplies, that his father was now willing to talk, to get the word out about his cause. It looked like Robert's suggestion to Jason back in December had paid off.

John Brown was well known in abolitionist circles in the northeast, but little was known about him in Kansas. He had only arrived in October. The interview would require traveling to an as yet unknown location, likely taking two or three days, round trip. George had an edition of the paper to get out and could not spare the time, so he decided to have Robert conduct the interview, much to the young man's delight.

Robert headed southeast from Lawrence early in the afternoon. It was a clear and cold day, with only a slight wind and temperatures hovering only a few degrees above the freezing mark. His instructions were to go to Council City, located on the Santa Fe Trail, and wait at the tavern there around supper-time. Someone would meet him. When he arrived, the place was mostly deserted, as he had expected. No settlers in their right minds, he was confident, would be using the trail to head out west in the dead of winter. He sat at the bar in the tavern, ordered an ale, and waited.

After several minutes, he heard a voice from behind him. "You the newspaperman?"

"Yes," he replied as he turned and observed a man staring at him. The man appeared to be a few years younger than Robert, probably in his mid-twenties. His hair uncombed and his face mostly hidden by a bushy beard, he wore a coarse blue shirt, underneath a buffalo coat, and had red-tipped boots pulled over his pantaloons. Around his waist, two pistols dangled, along with a Bowie knife.

"I'm Frederick Brown, one of his sons."

There was no mistaking, Robert knew, to whom "his" referred to.

"Robert Geddis, pleased to meet you."

They moved to a table and discussed the travel and the con-ditions for the interview. Frederick explained that they would bunk in the dormitory-style room above the tavern that evening and head out early in the morning. It would take a few hours to get to his father, who would meet them at a cabin. Robert had to agree to not reveal where the cabin was located, who owned it, or the names of anyone that he might see there, other than John Brown. After the interview, Frederick would escort Robert back to the tavern. Robert readily agreed to the terms.

The next day, after riding on trails through the woods for about three hours, Robert had no idea where they were. They could have been going in circles, for all he knew. It was a cloudy day and the sun provided no guidance.

During the ride, Frederick told Robert that, in addition to his father, they would be meeting his Aunt Florilla and Uncle Samuel, who owned the cabin. Adair was their last name. Florilla, he said, was his father's half-sister and she and Samuel had moved the previous year to Kansas from Ohio. Both had studied at Oberlin College. Samuel was a Congregationalist minister and had started a church in the area. Robert wondered why Frederick was revealing so much information, things that he had been told, and agreed, could not be included in his article. Perhaps, he decided, it was just boredom on Frederick's part and wanting to make conversation.

Finally, they came to a clearing in the trees and a cabin appeared before them. The warmth that hit Robert's face as soon as Florilla opened the door was a welcome relief. He noticed that the cabin was larger than most, with two large rooms and a loft above. Unlike the rustic appearance of most cabins in Kansas, this one had been made to look like a real home. The walls were whitewashed and a mantel of dark wood, with an ornate clock placed at its center, surrounded a blazing fireplace. The furniture included tables, chairs, and a bookcase that most folks back East would have been proud to have owned. Framed pictures hung on the walls and rugs covered most of the floorspace. After brief introductions, Frederick and his aunt and uncle retreated to the back room and Robert was left alone with John Brown, who was seated in a red upholstered chair to the left of the fireplace. He dragged over a cane-bottomed chair, pulled paper and a pencil out of his coat pocket, and introduced himself.

"Ask what you need to know," Brown said, not rudely, but bordering on it.

Guess there will be no small talk, Robert thought, sizing up the man before him as direct and serious.

The abolitionist sat erect. In answering Robert's questions, he was matter-of-fact, never altering his tone nor attitude. He talked about the history of slavery in the United States, relating actions taken from the time of the founding fathers up through the recent passage of the Kansas-Nebraska Act. This was a knowledgeable man, Robert quickly decided. Brown spoke of his own experience, as a twelve-year-old, of seeing an enslaved boy his own age mercilessly beaten about the head with a shovel, and of his decision in his mid-thirties, after hearing the fate of Elijah Lovejoy, an abolitionist publisher brutally beaten to death by a proslavery mob in Illinois, to dedicate his life to opposing slavery. Doing all that he could to end human bondage, Brown said, was not his choice, but his duty. God had commanded him. Robert asked about Brown's personal life, learning that his first wife died at a young age after the birth of their seventh child, and that he soon remarried, fathering an additional thirteen children with his current wife. Of his twenty offspring, eleven survived to adulthood, seven boys and four girls. Six of his boys were now with him in Kansas. He admitted that he had brought a large supply of weapons with him to Kansas, paid for by his friends. The only time that he refused to answer a question, Robert noted, was when asked for more information about the identity of his financial supporters.

They talked for two hours. Brown must have told Frederick to end the interview then, Robert surmised, as the young man re-entered the room at that precise time and advised that they needed to be on their way back to Council City.

Once back at the tavern, Robert thanked Frederick, who then departed, and he checked into a private room. After dinner, he lit some candles, spread his notes out on a desk, and reflected on the day. There was much about Brown that he admired, but also much that concerned him. Ever since the truce in December, he had believed that things in Kansas could be settled, if not peacefully, at least with minimal bloodshed. Now, he was not so sure. The words for his article came to him quickly, as they sometimes did when he wrote, which was always a relief:

Of all the men who have migrated to Kansas, John Brown may be the one most dedicated to his cause. Fifty-five years old, he has worked in jobs as a tanner, a wool trader, and a farmer, failing at many of them. But most of all, he has for decades been, and remains, an ardent abolitionist. The injustices done to the Black race have consumed him since he was a child. A deeply religious man, he vows that God will have vengeance for this evil.

Kansas to him is but a preliminary to a more important battle—the abolition of slavery in the entire country. Failure in Kansas, he says, will mean failure for the cause. It took the slavers, he notes, a half-century to get full control of the federal government and, now that they have it, "they will never voluntarily relinquish it." If they succeed in Kansas, he firmly believes, "they will have the permanent upper hand."

He presents as an enigma. Calm and stoic in his words, yet enthusiastic about his cause, one senses a volcano lurking beneath a mountain of snow. He is tall and lean, with short dark hair combed back, thin lips, and a prominent chin. But his most noticeable feature is his eyes, deep gray, and moving about more than it seems they should.

Although he is part of the free-state movement in Kansas, he denounces it for its timidity. It is led, he says, by "broken-down politicians from northern states who are willing to sacrifice principles for their own advancement." He castigates the truce that ended the recent hostilities in December. "They were there for the taking," he said, referring to the hundreds of Missourians camped along the Wakarusa River. "We should have acted."

Brown has given much thought to warfare. Forts, earthworks, artillery, and long-range rifles do not impress him. His strategy in battle is offense, not defense. The best fortification, he firmly believes, is "a brave soldier, well-armed, who is willing to fight in close quarters."

He does not conceal his readiness to strike a blow for freedom at the proper moment. But he leaves the questioner much in the dark concerning his plans for the coming months. One thing is certain—he exudes confidence and appears equal to any task he dares to undertake. Kansas, and the nation, will need to keep an eye on him.

As with most articles that he wrote, Robert reviewed it many times, making a few changes with each reading. Finally satisfied, he blew out the candle.

* * *

"I saw your article on John Brown in the *Herald of Freedom*," Monty said to Robert. "Nice work."

The two were meeting to discuss whether any upcoming drills were needed for their militia unit, deciding that they could hold off, as the truce was holding. It had been about two weeks since Robert had met with the abolitionist.

"Thank you. Gotten a lot of favorable comments on it. I'm told that it's been reprinted in newspapers in New York, Boston, and Philadelphia. Hopefully, it will get picked up in a few more cities."

"Interesting fella, your Mr. Brown," commented Monty. "I can't tell whether he's a prophet, or a lunatic."

"That's been bothering me, too. Sometimes, you know, only a thin reed separates one from the other."

CHAPTER 38

*A**pril, 1856*— Monty's sound sleep was interrupted by a loud rapping on his front door. He wasn't sure of the time, but knew it was well past midnight. He also heard a voice, saying something loudly. He grabbed the pistol that he kept in a drawer by his bed and gripped it firmly. That is how most lived in Kansas, always with a weapon nearby. As he approached the door, he recognized the voice as that of Robert. He put the pistol on a nearby table and unlocked and opened the door.

"Glad to see that you are back. Need you to come quickly!" an agitated Robert said. "All hell has broken loose."

"What? Dammit! Come on in," Monty said, as he fumbled around and lit a couple of candles. "Tell me what's happened while I get dressed."

He searched in the near darkness to find the clothes he had taken off before retiring several hours earlier. Monty had just returned that evening to the row home in Lawrence that he was renting, having camped out for the past few days at the site he had selected and purchased for his foundry, a couple of miles up the river. Construction of the new venture had gotten underway and some of the workers from his family's foundry in Ohio were now en route to get the place up and running.

"You've missed a lot. A few days ago, Sheriff Jones was in town and spotted Sam Wood."

"Wood is one of those who rescued Branson back in November, right?"

"Yeah, he was the ringleader of that."

"He was told to stay away from Lawrence, wasn't he?"

"He was, but he came back. Anyway, Jones found out, tried to arrest Wood, and he resisted. Folks in town took up for Wood, shouted some things at Jones and jostled him around, allowing Wood to get away."

"That's just great," said a disappointed Monty, as he put on his boots. "What are people thinking? They're giving the Missourians an excuse on a silver platter to cross over the border again and attack us. Idiots."

"It gets worse. Jones came back today with a platoon of federal troops and, with their help, arrested some of the men who had assaulted him. They put the prisoners under armed guards in a house. About ten o'clock tonight, while in a nearby tent, Jones was shot."

"On purpose?"

"Appears so. There was a crowd around there and they started banging pots and pans and cheering after he fell."

Having finished dressing, Monty grabbed his coat and blew out the candles.

"Let's go."

* * *

An uneasy peace existed in Kansas in the months following the truce in late 1855 that ended the Wakarusa War, punctuated with occasional assaults, arson, poisoning of cattle, and the like, by each side upon the other.

In April 1856, a series of events escalated tension between the two sides, just as the murders of Dow and Barber, and the rescue of Branson, had done a few months earlier. Sheriff Samuel Jones learned that Sam Wood was again in Lawrence. Wood had been the leader of the posse that had taken Branson, by force, from Jones and his posse the previous November. Jones went into Lawrence, found Wood, and attempted to arrest him. The sheriff was harassed and assaulted by a group of people on the street, which allowed Wood to escape. This appeared to be a violation of the terms of the truce negotiated by Governor Shannon, under which the people of Lawrence had agreed to not interfere with lawful criminal process. A second visit a couple of days later met with similar resistance. The third time, Jones brought several United States troops with him. Unwilling to interfere with federal authority, there was no further resistance by people in Lawrence and Jones arrested six men who had impeded his attempt to take Wood into custody a few days earlier. By then, Wood had fled Lawrence again.

That evening, while Sheriff Jones sat in a tent pitched beside a house where his prisoners were being kept, he was shot in the back. Proslavery newspapers reported that he had been murdered, but he survived the attack and soon recovered. The shooting set into motion legal maneuvers by the territorial government to punish the free-staters for their actions. A grand jury was summoned and indicted Charles Robinson, the governor elected by the free-staters under their Topeka Constitution, as well as other state officers elected, for treason. Further, the grand jury found that the Free State Hotel in Lawrence, which served as the headquarters for the free-state movement, and two newspapers in the town, the *Herald of Freedom* and the *Kansas Free*

State, which had been running articles attacking the proslavery government, were public nuisances. Robinson attempted to flee the territory to go back East to embark on a speaking tour to raise money for the cause, but he was arrested in Missouri and taken to Lecompton and held prisoner.

The shooting of Sheriff Jones and the indictments led to calls on both sides for their militias to reassemble. Again, in May, as they had done months earlier during the Wakarusa War, thousands of Missourians gathered outside of Lawrence to attack it, and free-staters throughout the Kansas Territory rushed to the town to defend it.

CHAPTER 39

*M*ay, 1856—Ned stepped out of the front door of his cabin and quickly closed it behind him. Instead of welcoming an unexpected visit from a friend, he looked annoyed. It was not the reception that Billy had expected. The two friends had only seen each other once since Ned had returned in April from traveling around Kansas to set up new Blue Lodge chapters.

It was late afternoon on a cloudless day in mid-May. Billy had planned to make this trip the previous week, but a Lodge obligation (as he had come to think of the raids, and trying to justify them in his own mind) had taken up a couple of days of his time. It had involved a ride down to Gardner. He and two others had burned a cabin belonging to a free-stater there and had stayed out overnight. It had been on the list that Ned had given to Billy a few months ago, locations of places to be burned by the spring. Billy had only done three of the five targets on the list, the minimum number he felt Ned would view as a credible showing. He would come up with excuses for the others. The last cabin had not been occupied, which Billy had confirmed by scouting it out beforehand. As far as he knew from reading the newspapers, no one had died in the raids that he had taken part in. This had been the sixth one, five cabins and a blacksmith shop. He still wanted out, but didn't see a way, especially after his conversation with Ned back in December. He had taken an oath to do what was ordered by the Lodge's leaders and, despite his misgivings, felt honor bound to comply. If he refused to go on the raids, they'd probably burn his cabin next. If he quit the Lodge or told all that he knew about it, well, he didn't want to think what they would do to him.

Despite his qualms about the Blue Lodge, he still enjoyed the company of Ned, the man who had brought him into it. Ned had told Billy that he, too, had not known all that the Lodge did at the time that he had recruited Billy, but an oath was an oath. Soon, Ned kept telling him, the free-staters would leave, and Lodge members like him and Billy would be given a good part of the credit for it. They could then reveal their identities, would be considered heroes, and would step up a few rungs on the ladder of Kansas society. That was Ned's dream. It had once been Billy's, but no longer. He was tired of all the conflict and violence, and ashamed of the role he had played in it. Maybe coming to Kansas had been a mistake. Next year, he was pondering, he'd pull up stakes, move on, and start over again. Maybe in Texas.

"Whatcha doing here, Billy?," Ned asked his unexpected visitor.

"Just passing through on my way to Kansas City. Gonna buy some seed there. Thought I might ask to sleep over."

"It ain't a good time, sorry," Ned responded, tersely.

Billy was taken aback by the response. He thought that Lodge brothers looked out for each other. Was sleeping over for a night too much to ask? He would do it for Ned, without hesitation.

"Sorry to have bothered you," said Billy, as he walked away.

A few seconds later, he heard Ned call his name and turned and looked at him. Ned walked a few steps in front of the cabin.

"Billy, I'm sorry. Already got someone here. It's my uncle. He's passing through and staying over tonight. Ain't seen him for over a year. I woulda introduced you, but he's tired from all the riding and feeling poorly."

"Understood," replied Billy. "Y'all enjoy catching up and your evening."

"You know Jack from the Lodge?" Ned asked. "His cabin is about a mile or so up the road. The one with some cottonwood trees by it. He'll prob'ly take you in for the night."

"I do. Will stop by there. I'll be fine. There's also that tavern just this side of Monticello."

As he walked to his horse, tied at a hitching post, Billy noticed Ned's chestnut gelding, and one other horse, a gray one, in the small corral behind the cabin, confirmation that Ned indeed had a guest. He resumed his ride and headed east.

CHAPTER 40

May, 1856— "I always feared it was going to come to this," Monty said to Robert as he peered through a slit in the wall of the shed where they had taken refuge. He had a look of resignation on his face.

"So did I," responded Robert, "I just didn't think it would happen without our side firing a shot."

It was early afternoon on May 21. Shortly after dawn, everyone in Lawrence who had ventured outside had seen them— hundreds of men standing menacingly at the top of what many settlers were now calling Mount Oread, originally known as Hogback Ridge, which overlooked the town. The latter name had seemed more appropriate, some people thought. Calling it a mountain was a misnomer. More of a high hill, its crest only a couple of hundred feet above, its elevation still gave those occupying it a strategic advantage in any attack on the town. Those with spyglasses watched as more men arrived every hour, and observed that a four-cannon battery was pointed directly at them.

It had started quietly enough, Monty and Robert thought, as they had stood on Massachusetts Street and watched events unfold. Later that morning, a federal marshal on horseback, escorted by a few men, came into town and arrested two fugitives, with no opposition. He even stopped to have a friendly lunch at the Free State Hotel before heading back up the hill. The leaders of the free-state militia gathered in the town had given strict orders to their men to stand down. There would be no armed resistance, no defense to an attack. They were hopelessly outnumbered, and they knew it.

Spies stationed on Mount Oread then rushed down the hill advising of an ominous development. The marshal, upon his return to camp, had transferred the posse of hundreds of men who had gathered, mostly Missouri border ruffians, to the control of Sheriff Samuel Jones. Jones, still recovering from being shot in the back less than a month earlier on his last trip to Lawrence, had a score to settle. He rode into town on a buggy and demanded that the citizens turn over all of their arms, or he would order an attack. It was agreed that one cannon, along with a few weapons that were publicly held, would be turned over, but that any weapons that were privately owned would not. Upset with the response, Jones made further demands. He advised that the Free State Hotel and the town's two newspapers had been declared public nuisances by a grand jury and he was going to destroy them. He gave the hotel's owner two hours to remove the occupants and any furniture that he wanted to salvage. Meanwhile, the hundreds of men that had been on Mount Oread rushed down the hill. At that point, with the decision not to resist having been made, all in town took cover in the nearest safe place they could find. Monty and Robert ducked into the shed of a carpentry shop, up the block and across the street from the hotel, and with a decent view of all that was going on.

"If any man or woman dare stand before you, blow them to hell with a chunk of cold lead," they heard a man standing in front of the mob yell.

"I think that's Atchison," whispered Monty, who had the only clear view of the street. "He used to be a senator from Missouri."

"I've written a couple of articles about him. He really gets 'em stirred up," replied Robert, also whispering.

"They've broken through the door of the *Kansas Free State* and are tossing things out the windows," Monty continued, describing what he was seeing. "Looks like this is gonna get pretty bad."

Both were tense, knowing that the mob could rush into the shed at any moment and kill them. As Monty watched the street, Robert, his heart racing, pointed his Sharps rifle at the door in the front of the shed, his finger resting on the trigger.

As they huddled together in hiding, seeing the attack on Lawrence play out before their eyes, Robert asked a question that Monty had been expecting ever since they first met. He had been surprised that it had not come before now. The threat of impending death, he supposed, made men want answers to lingering questions that had troubled them in life.

"Monty, what's the truth about my brother's death? You were his best friend. I suspect you know."

To Monty, in the half-darkness, with slits of sunlight peering through the thin gaps in the walls of the shed, Robert appeared indistinguishable from his late brother. It was as if Ben himself was pleading with Monty to share all that he knew about his own death. Should he tell the truth? The whole truth? Wouldn't Robert's memory of Ben be enhanced if he knew what really happened? Yes, he and Ben had planned the killing of a man, a man who happened to be the president of the United States, but it was for the greater good, for the fight against slavery.

"What were you and your parents told?," he asked.

"That he was the victim of a burglary in his room in a boarding house in Washington City. Died of a head injury after a struggle and that there were no suspects. Years later, we were told that it had not been a burglary, and that one of his friends had killed him. Something about an argument and that it was an accident. We were told that this friend was now dead himself."

"All of that is true."

"What were they arguing about?," Robert asked.

Monty peered outside. Books and papers were being thrown out of the windows of the *Kansas Free State*, and the same thing was now going on at the *Herald of Freedom*, where Robert worked, located a few buildings up the street. He could see men with axes and sledgehammers rushing into both places, no doubt, he thought, to destroy the printing presses. He watched as a cannon was wheeled to the middle of the street and aimed directly at the Free State Hotel.

Monty decided to tell Robert the truth. He told him that, in 1844, he and Ben had plotted to assassinate President John Tyler, to stop Tyler's annexation of Texas and, with it, the expansion of slavery in the Union. He told Robert that they brought a third conspirator, a friend of theirs, into the scheme and that they almost pulled it off. And then, a few days later, Ben was dead. He relayed that it was not until years later that he learned of an argument between Ben and their friend, arising from the plot's failure, and of the friend having killed Ben during the argument. He explained what the argument had been about and confirmed that, indeed, this friend was now also dead.

Robert's face was expressionless as he took in all of the information.

Outside, the boom of a cannon could be heard, shaking the walls of the shed. Monty looked out and saw that the target was the Free State Hotel. A couple of minutes later, it was fired again. And then again, and again. When the smoke and debris from the blasts cleared, Monty could not help but smile when he saw that the multiple firings of the cannon had little impact on the hotel's thick stone walls.

"My brother, a would-be Brutus in the battle against slavery," Robert finally said, in a matter-of-fact manner. "Seems fitting. He was always so passionate about everything."

"So he was," responded Monty. "And now, here we are, all these years later and a thousand miles away, fighting the same battle."

"But that was different, wasn't it? Kinda taking the law in your own hands? Trying to kill a president to change the course of history?"

Monty was taken aback by the questions, and their tone of disapproval. Maybe, he thought, he shouldn't have told Robert the truth. The last thing he wanted to do was tarnish the young man's memory of his beloved brother.

"Someone else once told me that," Monty replied, recalling what Senator Clay, on his deathbed, had said when he had learned of the plot. "He said it would lead to anarchy."

"Sort of like what is going on out there?"

The booms of the cannon finally stopped. Monty peered out again. The blasts having been ineffective, the hotel had been set on fire. Flames now rose from its first-floor windows and were creeping to the upper floors. As he looked farther up and down the street, he saw that several shops were being broken into and their wares looted.

"It seemed like the right thing to do at the time," Monty said, as he looked back at Robert. "We were young."

"If you could go back in time, would you do it again? Try to kill a president?"

"That president? Tyler? If I knew that it would succeed, and that Ben would not die because of it? Definitely," Monty replied.

Robert stared at him and made no response.

Monty looked out at the mob in the street again, but was deep in thought. He said he would do it again, for sure, and he had always believed that. Ever since the assassination plot in 1844, he had thought of Ben and himself as white knights, fighting for a just cause, and foiled at the last minute by something beyond their control. Was he wrong? If Senator Clay did not think that killing Tyler could be justified, and if Robert agreed, did he need to rethink things? All of a sudden, he was not so cocksure and had doubts about his past that he had not had before.

The noise in the street began to get louder. Monty was still in a semi-daze, deep in thought, his mind not registering what his eyes were seeing. Robert came over, stood next to him, and peered through the cracks.

"They're coming this way!," Robert exclaimed, as he grabbed Monty by the arm. "No time to waste! Come on, I'm getting you out of here. Not gonna let the bastards take you prisoner," he added, as he kicked open the back door of the shed and they both started running as fast as they could.

CHAPTER 41

May, 1856— "Sure do appreciate your hospitality," Monty said to the man seated next to him. It was approaching ten o'clock in the evening. The two were sitting on the porch of the man's isolated cabin. Two lanterns provided some dim light as they chatted.

George Partridge was a free-state settler near Ottawa. Monty and Robert had been hiding out with him for the past three days, ever since they had fled Lawrence after the town's sacking by the proslavery mob. George's wife and two children had gone to bed a couple of hours earlier, and Robert had retired for the night soon afterward, to the nearby barn where he and Monty had been sleeping.

"Glad to do it," George replied, as he wiped his lips, having just taken another taste from the jug of corn whiskey from which the two had been sipping. "Can't have those goddamn ruffians getting their hands on you, militia captain, former congressman, and all. I'll check out the trails around here, and the main road, again in the morning. Hopefully, their patrols will have moved on and you and your friend can be on your way."

As they were talking, both were startled by the sound of hoofbeats, coming at some speed, toward them. George quickly grabbed his rifle, which he always kept by his side, and aimed it toward the noise. Monty felt defenseless, silently cursing himself for having left his pistol in the barn. As the man on horseback got closer, Monty heard him shout, "George, George, don't shoot! It's me, Charles!"

"You damn fool!," George replied, as he lowered his rifle. "I almost killed you, Charles. Why you charging up here like a scalded cat this time of night?"

Charles Kaiser was a longtime friend of George. They were from the same small town in western Pennsylvania and had traveled together to Kansas, with their families, about a year earlier, in the spring of 1855. Both opposed slavery and were looking for a new start in life. Charles had settled on land about fifteen miles southeast of George's, on Pottawatomie Creek. They continued to keep in touch, one visiting the other every month or so.

"There's been some killings down my way. Four or five. All hacked to death. I found out about it this afternoon. On my way to Lawrence to get word of it to the Executive Committee. Been riding for a few hours. Was near here and was hoping I could get some water for my horse and a few minutes of rest."

"Sure, sure, Charles," replied George, as he walked down the steps to the porch and handed his friend one of the lanterns. "Go over there," he continued, as he pointed toward the barn. "There's a full trough of water on the right side."

After his horse's thirst had been satisfied, Charles tied him to a post and came up on the porch. George introduced Monty, advised that Monty's friend was asleep in the barn, and explained why the two of them had been hiding out the past few days.

"Tell me about those killings," Monty asked.

"Men and boys. Taken from their cabins at night and slashed all over with swords. Didn't lay eyes on the bodies myself, but I got it on good authority."

"The dead are free-staters?," asked George.

"No," replied Charles, "word is that they were slavery folk, every one of them."

"So they're now killing each other? Violent bastards," commented Monty.

"No, no, Mr. Monty. Darndest thing. They say free-staters done it. Even know who it was."

"Who says?," asked a skeptical Monty.

"Folks who were there. It happened at three different cabins. A fella who survived at one of them recognized the attacker who looked to be in charge, an older man. Said he lives on a spread with his sons a couple of miles up the creek. Some sort of crazy fella with wild eyes. Old Man Brown, he called him."

"John Brown?," asked Monty.

"Yeah, that's the one. You heard of him?"

"Afraid so. I can vouch for the wild eyes. Something you don't forget. Met him briefly late last year in Lawrence. When was it, December, when we all thought the town was gonna get overrun? He came in with some of his sons and volunteered to help out. General Lane got them set up in some sort of unit. I think they made him an officer. He was none too happy when Governor Shannon negotiated a truce. Tried to get a bunch of men to go out with him and attack the camps of the Missourians down on the Wakarusa after the truce was announced. No one would join him and he finally left."

"My friend," Monty continued, "the one in the barn, is a reporter and came down this way back in the winter, interviewed Brown, and wrote an article for his newspaper. He says the old man is full of fire and brimstone, that he believes there is going to be a holy war here in Kansas over slavery. Blood up to the horses' bridles. That kind of stuff."

"Guess this is his way of starting it," commented George, who had been sipping from the jug of whiskey while Monty and Charles had been talking.

"Would appear so," said Monty. "Revenge for the attack on Lawrence the other day, no doubt."

"An eye for an eye," said Charles.

"You sure this information is true," asked Monty, "and not some crazy rumor that the slavers have started?"

"I swear on the Bible. The fella who told it to me spoke to them that was there. I know him and he don't tell no lies. And a couple of others vouched for it."

Monty closed his eyes for a few seconds and took a deep breath, trying to take in this information and decide how to react to it. "Charles, I need you to do me a favor," he finally said. "When you get to Lawrence and report all of this, get word to General Lane that you came across me. He knows me. I'm a captain in the militia. Make sure he knows that I'm gonna go down to Pottawatomie Creek and investigate and find out if all of this is true. I'll write a report and will either get it to him, or deliver it in person, in the next few days."

"I surely will," said Charles, as he reached for and grabbed the jug from George, took a swig, stood up, and headed toward his horse. "I'll be on my way. You be careful. I don't think they'll look too kindly on free-staters coming down there and investigating killings done by our own men. Folks are all wound up. Wouldn't put it past them to try to kill or capture you."

"Perhaps so. I'll think of something," replied Monty, as he stood up, said good evening to Charles, and walked toward the barn.

Tomorrow, he thought, is going to be a long and interesting day.

CHAPTER 42

ay, 1856— As Monty and Robert rounded a curve on the trail, they saw the cabin before them, surrounded by several people. It was engulfed in mid-afternoon shadows from tall trees that surrounded a clearing in the woods. It looked like any number of cabins they had passed during the day. But this cabin, Monty knew, if what he had been told happened here was true, would soon be the talk of the entire country, North and South. It was crudely built, with a chimney on the left side, made of a combination of stone and brick, and had a small front porch. Probably one room, he guessed, where the family cooked, ate, and the parents slept, with a loft above for the children. Monty was tired, his back was sore from the long ride, and he was looking forward to getting out of his saddle and putting his feet on the ground.

"You got our story straight in your head?," he asked Robert, when they were still a good distance from the cabin.

"For the *third* time, yes." replied Robert, pretending to be annoyed. "We're both reporters, now living in Missouri. You're Marcus Lester, work for the *Kansas City Democrat*, and you're originally from Indiana. I'm William Gaylord, with the *Saint Louis Intelligencer*, originally from Pennsylvania."

"Wait, I thought I was Gaylord?," asked Monty, as he looked at Robert with a puzzled look on his face.

"Stop it! You're just trying to confuse me."

Monty grinned.

"Such a jokester," said Robert, also breaking into a grin. "Keep it up and you'll get both of us killed."

Robert continued, in a more serious tone: "Anyway, we've both been in Kansas for a few weeks reporting on the troubles and are here to get the facts about these killings to write articles for our newspapers. From the proslavery point of view, of course."

"And what's the most important part?," inquired Monty.

Robert grinned again. "That you'll do most of the talking, because my New England accent will give us up as frauds."

"Exactly," said Monty, as they guided their horses the last few yards up to the front of the cabin.

"Good afternoon. Who's in charge?," Monty asked, as he dismounted.

"I guess I am," replied a stout man, wearing spectacles, a leather vest, and a slouch hat. He introduced himself as Gaius Elmore, a deputy for Franklin County. Monty knew what that meant. As an official for the county, the man was part of the proslavery territorial government, the government that Monty and his fellow free-staters did not recognize. Elmore was just the type of man who would arrest Monty, if he knew his true identity.

"Pleased to meet you, Mr. Elmore. I'm Marcus Lester," Monty lied, as he extended his right hand. "I'm a newspaperman. With the *Democrat*, up in Kansas City. This here's William Gaylord, with the *Saint Louis Intelligencer*. We were up near Lawrence and heard about the killings down here. Want to get the word out about them in our papers. We're hoping to get some information about exactly what happened."

"Newspapermen, you say?," replied Elmore. "Good. The whole country needs to hear what those Yankee bastards have done. Evil, pure evil, I tell you."

"We heard abolitionists did this?"

"Damn right they did."

Monty nodded toward Robert, who walked over to his saddlebag, pulled out two writing pads and pencils, and handed one of each to Monty.

"It's spelled E-L-M-O-R-E, is that right?" asked Monty, pencil in hand. "And can you spell the first name for us?"

"It's G-A-I-U-S. Folks usually have a tough time getting that one right."

"Thank you. A name with character. Don't hear it often," said Monty, trying to curry favor with the deputy.

"Family name. On my momma's side."

"Can you tell us what happened?"

"Here's what we know so far," the deputy began. "The killings were at three places, this being the first one. This cabin belongs to the Doyle family. They came here from Tennessee. Six of them—parents, three sons, and a daughter. Most of what we know is from the wife and the surviving son. The family was asleep when there was a knock on the door, sometime after eleven o'clock on Saturday night, and a man asked for directions. The father opened the door and three men came in, one much older than the other two, who were armed with pistols and knives. The old man did most of the talking and appeared to be in charge."

"Any idea if there were others with them?," asked Monty, as he wrote down some notes. He looked over at Robert, who was furiously scribbling in his writing pad. Not hard to tell which one of them was the real reporter, he thought.

"The wife heard them talking to others outside," Elmore continued, "We think at least three more, based on the footprints we have been able to find so far."

"What did they do after they got inside?"

"The old man said they were from something he called the northern army and that Doyle and his three sons were their prisoners and needed to come with them. The wife said she pleaded with him not to take her youngest son, who is in his teens, and he agreed, but took the three others away. The older boys were twenty or so in age. A few minutes later, she said she heard some groaning, the firing of a gun, and then some whooping. Her husband and two sons never came back."

"Who found the bodies?"

"The younger son did, early the next morning, shortly after sunrise. His mother wouldn't let him go out until then. He found his father and oldest brother about two hundred yards away from here, by the road" said Elmore, as he pointed back up the trail that led to the cabin. "The boy then came across his other brother in some brush, a bit closer."

"Tell me about the wounds," Monty asked.

"Mr. Doyle was stabbed in the chest and had a gunshot wound in his forehead. The older boy's head was cut open, a chunk of his jaw was gone and he had been stabbed a few times in the side. The younger boy's head was slashed open, he was stabbed in the chest, and his arms and fingers were cut off."

"Christ Almighty. May God help us," muttered Monty, as he lowered his head in disgust and shook it. He noticed that Robert continued to write everything down. He raised his head, looking directly at Elmore, "And you think you know who did this?"

"Yessir. Mrs. Doyle said that the old man had a crazed look about him. Had a fire in his eyes. That description fits only one man that we know of in these parts. Old Man Brown. John is his given name. He's been around here a few months. Lives with a bunch of his sons on a farm over at Osawatomie, a couple of miles from here. We think it was his boys who were here with him. Some say he's a preacher. At least he quotes scripture a lot. About as much of an abolitionist as one can get, from what I'm told. Tells anyone who will listen that God's wrath is coming and that there's gonna be a war. Word is that he and his sons have got up their own militia."

"How many men in that?" asked Monty.

"Maybe twenty or so, I heard," replied the deputy.

"You had any run-ins with the Browns before?"

"Nope. Just a lot of talk and a few threats from them. At least up to now. We suspect they heard about the doings up in Lawrence last week and that this is their response. Butchering innocent folks."

"This Mr. Doyle, what's his first name?"

"James."

"Did he own any slaves?"

"No sir. But he was on our side. Supported southern institutions, like most of us around here. A member of the Law-and-Order Party, but not active in the politics of it."

"You say there were more killings, other than here?," asked Monty.

"That's right. Two more, further down the creek," said Elmore. "Next one was about an hour later, over at the place of Allen Wilkinson. He was a prominent man around here. Local postmaster and a member of the legislature. Slavery man, of course. What we know is from his wife. Same story as here. They were sleeping and heard a knock on the door. Some men asking for directions. Reluctantly, they let them in. An old man with a wild look about him was in charge. Said her husband was their prisoner and they took him away. His body was found next to the road a ways from his cabin. Hacked by swords, just like the Doyles."

Monty felt sick to his stomach. He looked over at Robert, who was listening attentively and still writing down every word. He continued to question Elmore.

"Tell me about the third place."

"That was at the cabin of James Harris, about a mile from the Wilkinson place. Just across Pottawatomie Creek, near Dutch Henry's Crossing. Harris and his wife had three men, guests, who were sleeping there. About two o'clock in the morning, some men forced open the door. Harris recognized the man in charge as Old Man Brown, whom he had met before. He also identified another of them as one of Brown's sons. They said they were from the northern army. They questioned all of the men and took one who was staying over, William Sherman, away. Harris found his body in the creek the next morning. His head had been split open in two places and some of his brains had been carried off by the water."

"Any idea where Brown and his gang are now?"

"We got posses out everywhere looking for them. Heard they're up near Black Jack."

"Any other violence yet,?" asked Monty.

"Heck, yeah. This has got everybody stirred up. Men roaming around, looking for trouble. A few cabins, belonging to folks on both sides, have been burned. Old Man Brown said he wanted to start a war. Looks like he may have done it."

"And, of course, there was all of that stuff up in Lawrence last week," said Monty. "Those may have been the first shots fired in the battle."

Elmore gave Monty a stern look. "Everybody knows that were justified, Mr. Lester," he said. "And nobody died up there, let alone butchered like animals."

* * *

Late in the evening of May 24, 1856, and extending into the early morning hours of May 25, abolitionist John Brown and four of his sons (Owen, Frederick, Salmon, and Oliver), along with two other men, committed five gruesome murders along Pottawatomie Creek in southeast Kansas, not far from where Brown and his family resided. They had been on their way to Lawrence to help defend the town from the expected attack by proslavery men but, when they learned en route that the attack had already occurred, and that there had been no resistance, Brown was furious and put into motion a plan to strike on his own against the slavers. The victims were taken from their cabins in the middle of the night and were mutilated with broadswords. Some were also shot. All were supporters of slavery, but owned no enslaved people themselves. They were selected by Brown from a list he had of proslavery men in the area. The event is known to history as the "Pottawatomie Massacre."

Brown was associated with the killings almost immediately and was denounced by both the proslavery and free-state sides in Kansas. Although he never publicly admitted his role in the killings, he freely told family and supporters that he had masterminded them, had been present, and had given the orders. God would be his judge, he said. Within a few days, two of his sons (ironically, the two who had *not* participated in the massacre), were captured by proslavery men, turned over to federal authorities, and were imprisoned at Fort Leavenworth for a few months. Brown, his other sons, and their supporters, became guerilla warriors.

The massacre led to an increase in the violence in Kansas. A week later, Brown and his men attacked a proslavery militia company at the Battle of Black Jack. Although outnumbered, Brown's men prevailed and took more than twenty prisoners.

Some historians have called this the first battle of the Civil War, as it was the first time that two organized militia groups, all Americans, fought against each other in armed conflict over slavery. Other skirmishes followed. A couple of months later, at the end of August, a second major engagement was fought at Osawatomie, near where Brown and his family lived. This time, the outcome was different. Brown and his men were routed and one of his sons, Frederick, was killed in the fighting. The proslavery militia then burned the town to the ground.

Over the next couple of years, Brown moved in and out of Kansas, between trips back East to raise money for his cause. Viewed as a murderer and a madman by his opponents, his supporters saw him as a hero. He was never held legally responsible for the killings at Pottawatomie.

* * *

"Thank you, deputy," Monty said to Elmore. "Mind if we go in the cabin and look around?"

"Sure, help yourself. One of my men can give you directions to the two other cabins, if you want to go there."

"We would. Much appreciated. One last question. Any of the victims ever make any threats against the Browns?"

"Nuthin out of the ordinary, that we know of. No more than the kind that has spewed from the lips of the Browns. Hell, Mr. Lester, this is Kansas; if we murdered every man who made a threat 'gainst somebody on the other side, there'd be nobody left to bury the bodies."

"You've been very helpful."

"Look forward to reading your articles," said Elmore. "They'll be in the *Democrat* and the *Intelligencer*, you say?"

"Yes sir."

"The whole country's gotta know about this. This is the true face of those abolitionist bastards."

* * *

After visiting the scenes of the other two killings, and speaking with witnesses there under the same guise as reporters for Missouri newspapers, Monty prepared a report confirming that John Brown, his sons, and a couple of followers, had indeed committed, without provocation, the atrocities at Pottawatomie. He addressed the report to General Jim Lane, who was in charge of military operations for free-staters. He would have addressed it to Charles Robinson, but the doctor had recently been arrested on a charge of treason and was being held a prisoner in Lecompton. Beyond the loss of life, Brown's massacre made Monty angry for the damage it had done to the free-state cause. The nation had just witnessed the sacking of Lawrence by a proslavery mob, in which free-staters were seen, rightly so, Monty thought, as victims and looked upon with sympathy. In one night, John Brown had changed all of that, making the opponents of slavery appear equally lawless and evil. Monty recommended to Lane that the leaders of their movement strongly denounce Brown, hunt him down, and seek to bring him to justice. The man needed to be punished, Monty thought, and free-staters, to regain the high moral ground in the Kansas conflict, ought to be the ones leading the effort.

As Monty was finalizing his report, he received news of another violent act concerning Kansas and slavery, this one in Washington City between members of Congress. In a speech entitled "The Crime Against Kansas," Senator Charles Sumner of Massachusetts, an abolitionist and a member of the new Republican Party, argued for the admission of Kansas into the

Union as a free state. In doing so, he criticized not only his colleague from Illinois, Stephen Douglas, the author of the Kansas-Nebraska Act, but also, in personal terms, Senator Andrew Butler of South Carolina. Butler, as all southern senators, was a strong supporter of slavery. Using imagery, Sumner declared that Butler "has chosen a mistress . . . who . . . though polluted in the eyes of the world, is chaste in his sight. I mean the harlot Slavery." Three days later, as Sumner sat at his desk on the floor of the Senate, he was attacked with a cane by Butler's cousin, Preston Brooks, who was a congressman from South Carolina. Brooks beat Sumner numerous times about the head and shoulders, with blows so hard that he broke his cane, leaving his victim, by the time others finally intervened, an unconscious bloody mess on the floor. Most in the North were outraged by the brutality of the attack, while many in the South praised Brooks for defending southern honor, some sending him replacement canes, including one from the citizens of Charleston inscribed with the words "Hit him again!"

Monty could only shake his head in disgust. What was the country coming to? Over the span of one week, there had been the attack on Lawrence, the massacre at Pottawatomie, and a brutal beating in Congress, where he had previously served. Where was a statesman, he wondered, like his old boss, Henry Clay, when the country needed someone—anyone—to bring it together, to try to make peace? It would not be, he was certain, that nebbish in the White House, Franklin Pierce, controlled by the South, and whom he had come to detest as much as John Tyler, the president he had once tried to assassinate.

When Monty arrived in Lawrence, he learned that General Lane, because of an indictment for treason having been issued against him, was hiding out in a camp near the Nebraska border. After some rest, he rode to the camp and found Lane there, who, due to the indictment, was going by the alias of Joe Cook. Monty delivered his written report on Pottawattamie to Lane and briefly told him what he had found and recommended. He would review it, Lane said. The two had a tepid relationship ever since the Topeka constitutional convention, when he and Monty had been in rival factions, and because Monty had proposed the resolution that had thwarted Lane's duel against another delegate. Since then, Monty had heard that Lane's views had undergone a metamorphosis and that the man who had once said he'd as soon buy a Negro as a mule, and who wanted the convention to exclude all Blacks from Kansas, was now an ardent abolitionist and favored strong action against the slavers. It was all opportunism, Monty was certain, and that Lane had no moral compass. The political winds had shifted and the man didn't want to be left behind. Monty got the impression that Lane wasn't too interested in tracking down John Brown and making him pay for his crimes. Brown's actions had put fear in the hearts of proslavery men and Lane, Monty suspected, was more than willing to overlook the means that Brown had used to do so.

The general quickly shifted the topic of conversation, and gave Monty a new assignment. There had been two more killings, he said, this time of free-staters, somewhere west of Lawrence. The victims had been hacked to death by swords, just like the dead at Pottawatomie. Go investigate those killings, Lane told Monty, and write him a report.

Monty saluted and left Lane's camp. He was frustrated. Was this to be his life from now on, looking into grisly murders and writing reports that his superiors would pay little or no attention to, and possibly never read?

CHAPTER 43

June, 1856— Monty stared at the bloodstains on the coarsely-cut wood floor. He stood on the porch of a cabin about halfway between Lawrence and Lecompton. It had been only a few of days since he had been at Pottawatomie. And now this, the site of more killing.

He had brought Robert with him. After all, this was an official investigation assigned to him by General Lane, and Robert was his top lieutenant. Moreover, Robert's skills as a reporter would likely be beneficial. Robert had just finished writing a detailed article about the Pottawatomie killings. With the printing press of his paper, the *Herald of Freedom*, still out of commission from the attack on Lawrence the previous week, he had sent the piece to Kansas City with instructions that it be telegraphed back East. He hoped that some newspapers there would pick up the article and print it.

"This is where you found them?," Monty asked.

"Yes, sir, one of them. The other one was there, in the dirt, near the bottom of the steps," replied Sergeant Henry Preston, pointing. Preston served in the free-state militia unit that covered the territory to the west of Lawrence.

"Tell me about the wounds."

"Pretty gruesome, sir," replied Preston. "From a sword, likely a two-sided one, from the type and angle of the wounds. The fellow here was slashed across the chest and stabbed through the throat. Also had gashes on the side of his neck and on both arms. The one down there was struck across his back a few times, and on his lower legs. We figure he was trying to run away. Both were in their nightclothes, so musta happened sometime during the night."

"What do you know about them?," inquired Monty.

"They were brothers, James and John Turner. Both were free-staters. From Iowa. Been here since last summer."

"They got family?"

"Yes sir, but still back in Iowa. See those logs over there?"

"Yes."

"Looks like they had started on a second cabin. We suspect they wanted to get that one built and were then going to bring their families out. One cabin for each family."

"Makes sense."

"They political men, active in the Free-State Party?"

"Not that we know of."

"Talk to any of the neighbors yet? They know anything?"

"We did. A couple of them so far. As you can see, it's pretty isolated here. Nobody saw or heard anything. One man, the one who lives that way," said the sergeant, pointing to the north, "told us a couple of things you might be interested in."

"Oh yes, what?"

"He said the brothers had some sort of dispute with the neighbor just south of them a few weeks back. Something about letting their cows drink from a stream on the neighbor's land. He might have pulled a rifle on them and made some threats."

Preston paused, as if unsure whether to continue or not.

"Go ahead. What else?" Monty said. You said *a couple* of things."

"There was one other matter he mentioned, something he heard secondhand. Don't like to speak ill of the dead, but the fella also told us that the younger brother, John, may have been spending some time with a gal in Lecompton."

"And?"

"She's married. So was he."

"Her husband aware of it?"

"We don't know."

Monty looked down and rubbed his forehead a few times.

"Good work, Sergeant Preston. Lieutenant Geddis here will assist you in your investigation. Talk to everyone living within a couple of miles, especially that neighbor to the south. And find out who the one brother's lady friend was, and talk to her and her husband."

"Yessir," replied Preston, as he saluted Monty.

"What do you think, captain?," Robert asked, turning toward Monty. "These killings done by the slavers over what happened at Pottawatomie, or they something else?"

"Either revenge by the slavers, or someone sure wants us to think it was," replied Monty. "Just because we got two sides fighting over slavery here in Kansas doesn't mean the other evils that men do will stop. Folks still gonna steal, still gonna bed other men's wives, and still gonna kill."

As Monty was asking more questions of Sergeant Preston about when the bodies were found, who found them, and where they had been taken, a man on horseback, moving with some speed, rode up to the cabin. He dismounted and Monty recognized him as a corporal in his own unit. The man, who had a look of excitement on his face, stood near the bottom of the steps to the cabin and saluted Monty.

"Good news, sir!," he proudly announced. "We have the killer. Arrested him in his cabin about a couple of hours ago. Heard you would be here and thought you'd want to see him. We got him on his way over here now."

"Excellent work, corporal," replied Monty. "How did you find him so fast?"

"We got a tip, sir, anonymously. Went to his cabin and found a sword under his bed, wrapped in a cloth with blood on it."

"Sure sounds like he's our man," Robert commented to Monty.

"What's his name?," asked Monty.

"I don't have that yet," the corporal responded.

Several minutes later, a wagon pulled up. Monty and Robert watched as two men seated in the back grabbed a third one, who was between them, by his upper arms and manhandled him out of the wagon. The man's feet and hands were bound and a hood was over his head. He was not resisting, perhaps, Monty thought, resigned to his fate. The corporal walked over and pulled off the hood. The man, who appeared to be in his mid-twenties, was trim and fit, had a mane of dark black hair, and a look of fear in his hazel eyes.

Robert stared at the man in disbelief. He recognized him. He could barely get the word past his lips.

"Billy?"

CHAPTER 44

June, 1856— "We've got to help him," Robert implored Monty, "Billy didn't do this."

The two were riding, alone, back to Lawrence from the cabin where the killings had taken place. Monty had ordered that the prisoner be taken, separately, to the militia's jail in Lawrence and kept in isolation in one of the cells there. He and Robert had stayed behind to look inside the cabin and to check out the area around it for anything that might have been overlooked by Sergeant Preston and his men. They found nothing.

"Do you think he recognized you?," Monty asked.

"How could he not have? Isn't like I've changed much and there sure aren't many of us redheads in Kansas. We kinda stick out in a crowd."

"What do you really know about this Billy, other than a couple of conversations that you had with him more than a year ago on a steamship?"

"Enough to know that he saved my life. We talked about a lot of stuff back then. You know how you get a feeling about people? He didn't have to rescue me from those Missouri thugs, but he did. He may be a slavery man, but Billy's no killer. I'm sure of that."

"What about the sword and the bloody rag found in his cabin?"

"Our men were sent there by an anonymous tip. Seems awfully suspicious to me."

"You think your friend is being set up?"

"We already know that the Turners had a neighbor pull a gun on them for trespassing, and one of them was taking liberties with a man's wife. What else don't we know about them yet? Everybody knows there's plenty of slavery men in Kansas itching to kill some free-staters, looking to avenge Pottawatomie. If you had it in for these brothers, why not kill them and try to pin it on some slaver?"

"Could be," replied Monty, "or maybe you've just been reading too many novels."

"Enough of them to know that the obvious answer isn't always the right one. It's just the easiest one. Look at my brother Ben's death. You were there at the time. How many years did the police in Washington City say it was from a burglary? And then it turned out to be from something entirely different."

Monty thought back to his friend Ben's death, recalling the grief he had felt, how he had a different theory than the police about who had killed him and why, and how he had been totally wrong, just as wrong as the police had been. From that experience, he knew well that murders often were not easy to solve. Of one thing he was certain—the free-staters in Kansas were going to want a noose around someone's neck for the vicious murders of the Turners. Billy was in custody for it and proving him innocent was not going to be an easy task.

CHAPTER 45

June, 1856— The crowd in front of the wooden building in Lawrence that served as the militia's jail, about thirty strong, was angry. Two privates with rifles stood by the front entrance. Word had quickly spread around town about the prized prisoner who had been brought there the day before, Billy Rutledge, the proslavery man accused of killing the Turner brothers. As Monty and Robert stood across the street, they heard shouts of "Give him to us!" and "String him up!"

"Let's go this way," Monty said to Robert, as he pointed to an alley next to the adjacent dry goods shop. "Sergeant Preston said to meet him around back and he'll let us in."

"Glad we don't have to walk through them," replied Robert.

"That's for sure," said Monty.

The sergeant was true to his word and, within a couple of minutes, Monty and Robert were dragging two chairs into Billy's cell. The high-ceilinged room was no bigger than a horse stall, with whitewashed walls and a dirt floor. Sunlight filtered in through the two small windows located about ten feet or so from the ground.

Billy, sitting on a cot, staring at the floor, and did not react as Preston opened the door to the cell. He looked scared, Monty thought, and rightfully so, with a mob outside calling for his hanging.

"Mr. Rutledge," Monty began.

"You can call me Billy."

"Very well then . . . Billy, I am Captain Montgomery Tolliver of the Second Unit of the Lawrence Militia. I believe you know my friend here, Lieutenant Robert Geddis."

"I spotted him yesterday. Yes, we've met before," Billy answered, with little emotion. Still seated on the cot, he folded his arms, as if unsure what to make of his visitors.

"Robert tells me you saved his life on a steamboat when you were both traveling out here, that you rescued him from some ruffians."

"Not sure about his life. Definitely from a tarring and feathering."

"You know what you're being charged with?"

"Hacking those two free-staters to death with a sword, yessir." Billy said, as he cocked his head to one side. His voice remained monotone.

"Did you do it, son?," asked Monty.

"Course not," Billy scoffed, as he looked Monty directly in the eyes. His tone was louder and firmer than his prior responses.

"We're here to help you," said Robert.

"Where were you that night," inquired Monty, "when the killings happened?"

"Out," Billy replied, hesitantly, now avoiding Monty's eyes and staring at a corner of the cell.

Monty waited a few seconds for more information, but none was forthcoming.

"Like Robert said, we're trying to help you. Anything you can tell us about that day and night that would be beneficial."

"I left my cabin in the early afternoon," Billy then added. "Needed some time to myself. Slept out under the stars. I do that sometimes. Got home about the same time the next day." The flatness had returned to his voice. His arms remained folded in front of his chest.

"Where did you go?"

"Not exactly sure. Up north, I think. Pretty sure that's the direction I went."

"Anyone see you from the time you left until you got back?"

"Didn't talk to no one, if that's what you mean."

"Is there anyone, Billy, who can say you were not anywhere around the Turners' cabin that day or night, who saw you somewhere else and can verify where you were?"

"No sir, I guess not."

Robert whispered into Monty's ear, asking for some time alone with Billy.

Monty agreed, got up and walked out of the cell. He tried to figure out what he had just seen and heard. He knew first impressions could sometimes be wrong, but Billy had seemed intelligent enough. He didn't seem violent. He hadn't been forthcoming with information, but he wasn't hostile. Once down the hallway, Monty could hear more clearly the noise coming from the crowd outside, shouts demanding Billy's release to them.

* * *

Robert moved his chair closer to Billy's cot, reached out a hand, and briefly placed it firmly on Billy's knee. "Billy, I know you ain't no killer, no butcher," he said. "Captain Tolliver is a good man. We want to get you out of here. I owe a lot to you. Maybe you're right, that those thugs on the steamship wouldn't have killed me. But they woulda slapped hot tar all over my handsome face, scarring it for life." He hoped that the feigned vanity would lead to a breakdown of Billy's evasiveness.

"It ain't that handsome, Robert," replied Billy, with a slight grin. "A little scarring might have added some character."

They both chuckled. Maybe, just maybe, Robert thought, I've gotten through to him.

"Give us some information, tell us what you know," Robert pleaded, "so we can help you."

"I didn't do it, Robert. That's all I know, all that I can tell you." Billy lowered his eyes again and stared at the floor.

"Any idea how a sword like the one used in the killings got under your bed, along with a bloodied cloth?"

"Obviously, somebody set me up, wants me to take the blame for this. I told you, I won't home until the afternoon of the next day. Anybody could of broken in and put that stuff there. Heck, I ain't even sure I locked the door when I left. Never had any reason to."

"You on the bad side of anyone, Billy? Who'd want to do this to you?"

"Nobody that I know of."

Robert was frustrated. After a brief moment of hope, the conversation had returned to where it had started. It was going nowhere. Why didn't Billy trust him, he wondered?

"Come on back," he called down the hallway to Monty, who had been chatting with the sergeant.

Monty reclaimed his seat. "Any progress?"

"Nope," replied Robert, as he stared at Billy, who continued to cast his eyes downward.

The disappointing interview was over.

As Monty and Robert walked out the back door, through the alley and to their horses across the street, both noticed that the crowd in front of the building was still there, and appeared to be a bit larger.

"He's hiding something," said Monty. "If he won't tell us the truth about where he was, it's because he's afraid to."

"Or maybe he knows who the real killer is and is protecting him," Robert speculated.

"One thing's for sure, he doesn't strike me as fool enough to stash a murder weapon and a bloody cloth under his own bed."

"What do we do now?"

"Billy lives near Lecompton. If we're going to find out anything," said Monty, "we're going to have to go there and talk to the folks that have the most information about what's been going on."

"You mean we're going to visit all of the bars?"

"Damn right. Now you're thinking like a reporter."

CHAPTER 46

June, 1856— Monty's eyes darted open in the darkness. He was hot, sweating. It took a few seconds for him to realize that he was in his own bed. Whatever covers he had started with hours ago were now mostly on the floor. Almost instantly, he recalled the dream from which he had suddenly awakened.

The sky hung heavy with dark clouds, but there was no rain. In the distance, he could see prairie grass weaving back and forth in the wind. It had to be somewhere in Kansas, he was sure, but the place was unrecognizable to him. He was being led between two lines of armed soldiers, who were surrounded by an unruly and noisy crowd. He felt pain in his wrists and realized that his hands were tightly bound behind him. One soldier was walking a couple of steps in front of him, while another followed closely behind, jostling him along. As the three made their way to the end of the lines of soldiers, he saw it before him—a gallows with two sets of stairs leading up to it, one on each side. From the top rail hung two nooses, one of which he assumed was meant for him. He was led to the steps, about fifteen or so, on the left side of the gallows. After going up three or four of them, and rising above the crowd, he could hear their shouts—"Murderers!,

Traitors!, Kill them!" As he reached the top of the platform, Monty looked across it and saw another man who had been led up the stairs on the opposite side, with his hands also bound behind him, and with soldiers also at his front and behind. One of the soldiers obscured the man's face. Both Monty and the other man were led up toward the structure's center, until one of the nooses dangled above each of their heads. The shouts of the crowd grew louder. Monty could now clearly see the other man. John Brown looked Monty directly in the eyes and a broad smile came across his rugged face. Then darkness, as a canvas bag was lowered over Monty's head. That was the last thing he remembered before he awakened.

Monty lay in the sweat that dampened his bed. What did it mean? Why should he be subjected to the same fate as John Brown, who had pulled men and boys from their homes in the middle of the night and had them hacked to death. He detested Brown, believed him to be a monster, a traitor to the antislavery cause. He then thought back to more than a decade earlier, and to the failed plot with his late friend, Ben Geddis, to assassinate President John Tyler. They had tried to kill a man, the leader of a nation, over slavery. But that had been different, he told himself. Tyler was guilty, had blood on his hands. He was pushing an aggressive slaveholding agenda on the country by rushing through the Senate a treaty for the annexation of Texas, trying to almost double the enslaved territory in the Union.

When, Monty wondered, does the end not justify the means? He recalled what Henry Clay, on his deathbed, had told him— assassination can never be the answer in a republic and it will lead to anarchy. Robert had seemed to have the same unapproving view when he had been told of the Tyler plot. But change, Monty thought, takes longer without people taking decisive action, like he and Ben had tried to do. Sometimes, it needs a nudge, doesn't it? He thought some more. Then, it hit him. Isn't that what John Brown also thought? Killing, yes, but for the greater good. Was he wrong to have participated in the Tyler plot, or was he, in reality, no different from Brown, both too impatient to wait for the wheel of history to turn, and both willing to murder to speed it along? Monty wondered, in the dream, had Old Man Brown known this about him, and is that why he had looked him in the eye and smiled.

CHAPTER 47

June, 1856— "Hope we have better luck here than we did at the Long Branch and the Prairie Rose," said Robert.

"Patience, my friend," replied Monty. "It's a small town. Somebody in one of these bars has to know something."

Neither had been to Greeley's before. They knew that the clientele was mostly proslavery men, but had also heard that free-staters ventured in from time to time and that all were served and treated fairly. Any concern they had for their safety was relieved by the signs they saw in the front window and above the bar—upon entry, all guns had to be left with Stretch, the bartender. If not, the Sharps rifle that was kept standing upright behind the bar, for all to see, would be used for enforcement. Both complied and handed over their pistols. They seated themselves on a couple of barstools near the back. It was late afternoon and the bar was mostly empty. The place looked a bit less seedy than the others they had been to earlier in the day.

"What'll you have, gentlemen?," asked Stretch.

"A bourbon," Monty replied.

"And an ale for me," added Robert.

After the second round was set before them on the bar, Monty decided it was time to find out if Stretch had any helpful information. He introduced himself and Robert.

"You know a fella named Billy Rutledge?," he asked. "Lives somewhere around here. Young guy. Black hair, kinda long."

"You mean the one they got locked up over in Lawrence for those killings?"

"That's him," replied Monty, relieved that someone finally admitted to at least having heard of Billy, if only because of the charges against him.

"He's been in here a fair amount," said Stretch. "Ain't no regular, but yeah, I know him. Nice fella. Didn't figure him for a killer."

"Know anything about him?"

"He's a Blue Lodger."

Both Monty and Robert were surprised by the statement. They knew plenty about the Blue Lodge, a secret society promoting southern values that had started in Missouri and spread into Kansas. Operating in the shadows, the Lodge was believed to be behind many of the threats made to free-staters traveling through Missouri, and of organizing the massive crossovers of Missouri men to fraudulently vote in Kansas elections. Many free-staters believed that Lodge members did much more than intimidate and cast illegal ballots, that they also stole cattle, started wildfires to destroy crops, put torches to cabins and businesses, and even killed to support the southern cause.

"How do you know that?," asked Monty, barely above a whisper, although there was no one within earshot of them. "They're a secret society."

"Mr. Tolliver, standing back here behind this bar, I got the best seat in the house. I see everything." Stretch continued, "I see them come in here and give their so-called secret hand signals.

One of them puts a finger to the side of the nose. Another responds with a scratch of the forehead. Or something else. And then they start chatting like they'se best friends. It ain't too hard to figure out." The bartender's words were spoken as a man who took pride in observing behavior that most others missed.

"You seen Billy do that?," asked Robert.

"A few times, yeah."

"Sounds like you don't care much for these Blue Lodgers," commented Monty.

"I say if you're gonna do something, do it in the open," said Stretch. "Just the way I was raised, I guess."

"You heard anything about these killings? About who may have done them?"

"No sir, but I'd say most folks who come in here ain't too upset about them, after what happened down at Pottawatomie. Biblical justice, they say. That seems to be the general opinion."

Monty and Robert thanked Stretch for the information, paid their tab, and headed out of Greeley's.

"I could be wrong," said Monty. "But if Billy's a Blue Lodger, then maybe he was involved in the killings, or knows who was."

"Sure could explain why he won't cooperate with us."

"Seems like something those cretins could have done."

"Seems awfully bold for them," replied Robert. "They mostly attack property. The Turners' cabin wasn't burned and their horses and cows weren't touched. Unless the Lodgers are changing their tactics."

"Maybe the killing down at Pottawatomie has caused them to."

"Or," responded Monty, "maybe someone wants us to think it did."

* * *

Billy lay on the uncomfortable cot in his cell and stared at the ceiling. Why didn't he stay in Mississippi, he kept thinking to himself. Had his life there with his brother and his family really been all that bad? He had chased a dream and this is where he ended up. Why, he wondered, had he gone to that meeting in Jackson?

He didn't see a way out of this mess. Whichever route he took, he was certain that he was a dead man. The truth was that he had gone on a raid for the Blue Lodge the night of the Turner killings, near Oskaloosa. They had burned down a sawmill owned by a free-stater. It was one of the places on the list that Ned had given to him. Ned had not gone on that raid, but two other Lodge brothers did. Ned had assured him that this would be the last one, at least for a while. If he told his captors the truth about where he was that evening, they would drop the murder charges, but would hold him for the arson. Likely, they'd then put two and two together and connect him to the other raids he had been on, and force him to tell the names of the Lodge members who had been with him. They'd probably still hang him. If he told the truth and the free-staters didn't kill him, then his Blue Lodge brothers likely would, for violating his oath and ratting out his fellow Lodge members, in order to save his own skin. Or, he could continue to keep quiet and get sentenced to death by the free-staters for the Turner killings. He didn't see an option where his neck did not end up on the wrong side of a noose, or his body riddled with bullets.

He was disgusted with himself. He had no one else to blame for his predicament. He was a good person, he thought, or at least he always had been. But he had helped burn homes and businesses. It was only through a stroke of luck that folks had not been killed. He should have gone with his initial instinct and jumped out of that wagon the night of that first raid when

Ned told him what they were going to do. These were not things that he ever would have done in Mississippi. Moreover, a friend, a Yankee friend (who would have ever believed that?) was trying to help him, and he had shut him out and refused to cooperate. What, he wondered, had Kansas done to him?

CHAPTER 48

July, 1856— Monty sat at a desk in the back room of his rented row house in Lawrence. It was mid-afternoon and he had spent most of the day reviewing maps and finance options for three different parcels of land along the Kansas River, each a few miles west of Lawrence. He would build his foundry on one of these and he needed to make a decision soon. Buy the land, get construction of the foundry underway, get his house built on another piece of land he had already purchased, and then he would send for Theresa and the children. At least that had been the plan, before he left Ohio. How he missed them. It had been more than eight months since he had arrived, a longer time without them than he had expected. But their well-being had to come first. He hadn't anticipated all the violence in Kansas, which had delayed his timetable. It had gotten much worse since the Pottawatomie killings back in the spring. He would not bring his family to Kansas until he felt they would be safe.

He had difficulty concentrating on the land proposals. The riddle of Billy Rutledge kept running through his mind. His intervention with Robert had kept the young man alive so far, but time was running out. A trial was going to be held soon and they had not come up with anything to help in the defense. Some wealthy slavers had offered to pay for a lawyer, but Billy had declined. Monty was convinced that Billy didn't kill the Turners, but the young man was hiding something. What was it? The initial leads that had once looked promising had evaporated into thin air. The neighbor who had pulled a gun on the Turners over cows drinking from his stream said it had only happened one time, that the brothers had apologized, and that they had even invited him over for dinner a few days later and all had joked about it. Others vouched for the character of the neighbor and said he was not a violent man. The so-called affair of John Turner had also turned out to be a useless diversion. The woman in question swore that it was nothing more than a couple of flirtatious conversations, started by her, and that her husband never found out. Both she and her husband had an alibi for the night of the killings that had been verified.

Monty's thoughts were interrupted by a knock on his front door. He opened it and found a boy, no more than ten, staring up at him.

"You Mr. Tolliver?" the boy asked.

"I am."

"Here," said the lad, as he handed Monty an envelope.

He took it, noticed that it was blank, and started to ask the boy who it was from. Before he could get the words out of his mouth, the boy took off running. By the time Monty got down the three steps to the sidewalk, the boy had turned down a nearby alley and had disappeared.

Puzzled, he went back inside, sat at the desk, opened the envelope, and pulled out and read the brief unsigned handwritten note inside.

Billy Rutledge is innocent.

Meet me on north side of Dutch Henry's Crossing. Noon on Tuesday.

Come alone.

Monty buried his face in his hands, a habit that he had when thinking, and which always annoyed Theresa. His first instinct was suspicion. Was this note legitimate, from someone who really wanted to help, or not? It was no secret that he had been asked by General Lane to look into the Turner killings. Plenty of slavers knew this, as well as free-state men. Could this be a plot by the slavers to use his role in the investigation to lure him into a trap, to capture or kill him? As a captain in the militia, he, or his body, would be a good prize. He decided it was a risk that he had to take. He had to go. How could he not, if this could save the life of a young man whom be believed was wrongfully accused of two heinous murders?

CHAPTER 49

July, 1856— Monty had known that Robert would not be happy and would want to travel with him. But the note had said for him to come alone. He finally convinced his friend that not complying as demanded could jeopardize any chance of saving Billy's life.

To get there by noon, he would have to split up the trip of thirty-five or so miles to Dutch Henry's Crossing, which was on Pottawatomie Creek, over two days. He knew the way. It was the same route that he and Robert had taken a few weeks earlier after the attack on Lawrence. He left town in the early afternoon on Monday, making it to Ottawa before sunset. Although he had brought along a blanket and gear, if needed, to camp out overnight, his first choice for accommodations worked out. His knock on the door of the familiar cabin was met by the ever-friendly George Partridge, who gladly let him spend the night again in his barn. After George and his family shared with him their hearty breakfast of fried eggs and smoked ham (the best ham he had eaten, he thought, since arriving in Kansas), he headed out for the remaining part of the trip. George invited him to come back and stay over again in the evening, on his return trip to Lawrence, and he accepted. After about four hours of riding, he arrived at the spot. He took out his pocket watch and was pleased that he was early, as he had intended.

Monty noticed that the width of Pottawatomie Creek narrowed significantly at Dutch Henry's Crossing and the water looked shallow, more like a stream. There was no bridge or ferry in sight. The water could be safely forded on horseback. There was a tavern just beyond the south bank, where the road continued. He was, as instructed, on the north side of the creek and had been waiting about fifteen minutes when he heard some rustling in the woods. He stood still, glancing to his left, trying to pinpoint the location of the noise. Then nothing but silence. Maybe an animal, he speculated. Seconds later, he heard a louder, trudging noise, like footsteps, directly behind him. He turned around, his heart racing. Again, nothing. And then, a dark figure suddenly appeared from behind a large tree. Monty felt his gut tighten, taken aback by the man's menacing appearance. He looked every bit a border ruffian—unkempt, with a beard, muddy clothes, a rifle on his shoulder, and a pistol and knife on his belt. But there was more. He was hiding his identity. Although it was a hot July day, he wore a leather hat, pulled down over half of his forehead, and a red bandana covered his nose, face, and chin. Only his eyes were visible. The lower part of his whiskers extended below the bandana. With most of his facial features hidden, Monty didn't have a clue as to the man's age, or his intentions. Maybe coming here wasn't such a good idea, he thought, remembering that he did have a pistol stashed in his saddle bag.

"Don't mind the rifle. It's empty," the man said. His friendly tone belied his looks. "You Mr. Tolliver?"

"I am," replied Monty, relieved.

"Let's walk into the woods a bit. Never know when somebody's gonna be passing down this road."

Monty followed and led his horse about fifty feet through the trees, until he reached a small clearing, where the man's horse was tied to a tree.

"And who might you be?"

"That ain't important."

"Your note to me? You know something about those murders, those hackings, up around Lawrence?"

"Yessir, I do. Just like the Pottawatomie killings. They was done to start a full-blown war over slavery."

"But the dead at Pottawatomie were slavers, and the others, the two brothers, were free-staters."

"That's the intentions. Kill on both sides. Get them all so riled up that they'll attack and kill each other right and left."

"Who's intentions?," Monty asked.

The man hesitated, moved some dirt around with his right foot, and then stared into the distance. "Old Man Brown started it," he finally said.

"John Brown?," he inquired. "You're saying he *was* involved in the Pottawatomie killings? He's denied it, you know."

"That ain't true. He didn't swing the blades, but he was there and was the one who ordered it be done, in the way that it was done."

"How do you know that?"

"I just know."

"And the killings up near Lawrence?," Monty inquired.

"I'm getting to that. When Brown was on his way to Kansas last fall, he took up with a fella. They traveled together for a while. The fella won't from back East. He was from Ohio, Indiana, or somewhere thereabouts. But in his talk, he could pass for southern. Brown and him spoke a lot and they was of like mind, saw things eye to eye. The fella came from a rich family, had money, and had already bought some land around Lecompton.

Brown came up with a plan and persuaded the man to pose as a southerner when he arrived in Kansas, to live amongst the slavers, become a part of them, and to report back to him."

"You mean the fella was to be Brown's spy?"

"That's right. He worked himself into some sort of prominent position among the slavers. Not sure of the details. He and the old man met every few weeks, and he'd tell of what he learned—names of their leaders, how they was organized, raids they was gonna carry out, what have you. Around the middle of May, the old man went up and met with the fella. Told him that he'd be hearing some big news soon."

"Big news? You mean Pottawatomie?"

"Yessir."

"Middle of May? You're saying what happened at Pottawatomie was planned *before* the attack on Lawrence?"

"That's right. It was gonna happen, sooner or later. Got moved up a bit to make it look like it were a response."

"But what does that have to do with the killing of the Turners?"

"A few days after that happened, the fella showed up at Brown's camp. All proud and all. Told the old man that what was done at Pottawatomie had inspired him, that he had killed those two brothers, the Turners, and made it look like a slavery man done it. Said that Brown had gotten the slavers a chompin' at the bit for war, and what he did would get the free-staters as angry as they were."

"What was Brown's reaction?"

"I weren't there, but from what I was told, he won't fer it or agin it. Said he could see how it might help the cause. Started quoting the scripture about sacrifices, how they are needed from time to time. Told the fella to keep quiet about what he had done, to go back living among the slavers, and to report back to him when he could."

"You're saying this man is really a free-stater, posing as a slaver, that he's working with Brown, and that he killed the Turner brothers and set up Billy Rutledge for it? That Brown didn't order it, but condoned it?"

"Yessir, that's correct. I won't say condoned, but he won't too upset about it."

"Why are you telling me all this? Why go to all this trouble?"

"Cause I know this Rutledge boy had nothing to do with these killings. Mr. Tolliver, I ain't a friend of any slavery man, but I don't want to see one hung for something he didn't do."

Monty took a couple of steps back, unsteady on his feet. He found a nearby rock to sit on, buried his face in his hands, and shook his head slowly from side to side. He needed a minute to take it all in. He was a free-state man. He had uprooted his life to come to Kansas to support this cause. Learning a couple of weeks ago that someone on *his side* had butchered slavery men and boys had been devastating for him. And now, this. Someone on his side had also murdered *two of their own* and had set up an innocent slavery man to hang for it. And it was all done for the purpose of starting an all-out war in Kansas.

"Who is this bastard, this spy?," he demanded.

"I don't know his name," the man said. "Never saw him. Most of what I told you is secondhand, but I know it's true."

"Given your appearance, I assume you're not willing to come to Lawrence and testify as to what you know."

"No sir, can't do that."

"Will you write out a statement for me?"

"Nope. I done told you all I know. You gotta figure out the rest."

Monty watched as the man mounted his horse.

"Don't try following me. Where I'm heading, they shoot strangers on sight. Do your best, Mr. Tolliver, to see that justice is done for that young man."

CHAPTER 50

July, 1856— Monty and Robert slowly nursed their warm pints of ale. They sat at a table in the rear of Greeley's, having just finished their dinners. The place was about half full, it still being early on a Friday evening.

"Stretch ain't a bad cook," commented Robert. "Soup was decent. Pretty good cornbread."

"It's not his cooking skills that I care about. It's whether his information is reliable that concerns me," replied Monty.

"Guess we'll find out soon."

"If we catch John Brown's spy, your friend Billy will soon be a free man."

After Monty's meeting with the masked informant at Dutch Henry's Crossing, he and Robert had gone back to Greeley's and met again with the bartender. Stretch said he liked Billy and, when told that the young man had been set up for the killing of the Turner brothers, he became visibly angry, upset that anyone would do such a thing to Billy. Stretch said that he was more than willing to help and provided more information. Monty and Robert learned from him that Billy was friendly at the bar with a man named Ned Watkins, who had a cabin and some land east of Lecompton. Stretch suspected that Ned was some sort of leader in the Blue Lodge, since he would often come into the bar and initiate hand signals to others, including Billy, who would respond. Some of the men at the bar seemed deferential to him. They'd get to talking and drinking and Ned, the bartender said, usually pulled money out of his pocket and paid the tab for all of them. Stretch also said that Ned had arrived in Kansas sometime last fall, from Illinois. It all matched up with what the informant had said about the man who was secretly working with John Brown. What better way to be a spy, Monty and Robert decided, than to set yourself up as a leader in your enemy's secret society. The bartender also advised that Ned usually came in on Fridays, just after dinnertime.

Certain that Ned was their man, Monty and Robert had come up with a plan. They would go to Greeley's on Friday night. Stretch would identify Ned to them, they would engage him in conversation, and get him to walk out back with them. There, a couple of armed men from Monty's militia unit would be waiting. They would take him into custody and turn him over to General Lane, who would question him and, if satisfied that the informant's story was correct, Lane would hold Ned for the murders and release Billy.

"You got your approach down?," asked Monty.

"Yes," replied Robert, barely above a whisper. "It ain't hard, other than faking a southern accent. I've been practicing and gotten pretty good at it. I'm gonna go up to him and ask for a light for my cigar and chat him up, where he's from, stuff like that. When he says the name of the town that he's from, I'll say my friend in the back is also from there, and to come and meet him. I'll get him to walk this way. You'll be down that hallway near the door. We'll invite him to walk out back and sip some real smooth bourbon that we brought with us and, if he resists, you got your pistol, and we'll force him. Our men out there will grab him and take him away."

Monty nodded and pulled out his pocket watch. A quarter past seven. Another round of ale was ordered and the tin cups were slowly drained. About a half hour later, still no Ned. Stretch walked by, shrugged his shoulders and said he had no explanation, that usually Ned would have arrived at the bar before now. Monty went out back a couple of times to update the two militia men.

Another hour passed. The bar was now full. Finally, Stretch came over with another round of ale and gazed briefly at a man who had just walked in and who stood at the end of the bar.

"That's him," the bartender said.

Monty and Robert gave each other a brief nod. Robert stood up, pulled a cigar out of his pocket, and walked over to the bar.

"Excuse me, mister," Robert said to Ned, holding out his cigar, "you wouldn't have a light, would you?"

CHAPTER 51

ugust, 1856— "Stand down, captain!," General Jim Lane barked. "Another inch and I'll have you arrested." Their faces were only inches apart.

Monty realized that he had gone too far. The veins on Lane's forehead were throbbing, and he was sure that his own were also. He removed his hands from the desk of the man who was the leader of the free-state militia, eased himself backward a couple of steps, and sank back into his chair.

"My apologies, sir." He took a few seconds to compose himself, having just accused Lane of gross incompetence. He then added, "I just don't understand how this could have happened, how he could just be gone."

"You know just as well as I do, captain, that we are a militia, not professional soldiers. Mistakes are made. The men involved are being disciplined."

Monty and Jim Lane were discussing Ned Watkins. Monty and Robert's plan at Greeley's had been carried out flawlessly. Turned out, Ned was a bourbon lover and had willingly gone out back of Greeley's with them, where Monty's men nabbed him and delivered him to a squad of General Lane's men. They, in turn, were to take Ned to Lane's camp, which was near the Nebraska border. There, Lane was to question Ned and weigh the allegations of the informant against the evidence implicating Billy. After doing so, Monty and Robert were confident that Lane would release Billy from custody and arrest Ned. They wanted Lane to issue a statement revealing that Ned was a spy working with John Brown and that Ned had killed the Turner brothers and framed Billy for the deed, to foment an even bloodier war in Kansas over slavery. They also asked Lane to denounce Brown and call for his arrest.

But after Ned had been turned over to Lane's men, the plan had gone awry. As he was being transported to the general's camp, he escaped from custody and had disappeared. Lane advised Monty that, on the way, the horse on which Ned was riding came up lame. Ned, with his hands tied in front of him, was told to dismount. As the soldiers were checking the horse's rear hooves, Ned took off and ran toward a nearby patch of trees. Shots were fired, but missed their target. A search of the area failed to find him. It was assumed, Lane said, that he had made it to the cabin of one of the proslavery settlers in the area, was hidden, and had been moved out of Kansas.

"Will you at least issue a statement clearing Billy of the killings?," Monty inquired of Lane.

"Based on what? Some hearsay tale from a masked man you met in the woods?," replied Lane, dismissively. "It all seems pretty far-fetched to me, spies and all that. I never got to question Watkins. Who knows what he would have said, but I strongly suspect he would have denied everything. It may be unfortunate for your Mr. Rutledge, but this is the reality that we are faced with. There is strong evidence supporting the charges against him. He will remain in custody and will stand trial."

"But . . . ."
"This matter is over. Understood, captain?"
"Yes, sir."
"Dismissed."

CHAPTER 52

ugust, 1856— "Are you going to help, or not?," Robert sternly questioned Monty.

"Maybe General Lane is right," Monty responded, "We don't have any evidence that Watkins killed the Turner brothers, or that he was working with John Brown, other than what the fella at Dutch Henry's Crossing told me."

"Why would he come to you, if it wasn't true?," Robert asked. "What would be his motive for seeking you out, if only to lie to you?"

"I'm not saying he was lying, but most of what he knew was secondhand. Maybe he just misinterpreted things and came up with the wrong conclusions."

"You know it's true. Everything he told you about Brown's spy is the same as what Stretch told us about Watkins—when he came here, where he lived, what he did, that he had money. He knew Billy through the Blue Lodge and, for whatever reason, decided to pin the killings on him."

"I just wish we had questioned Watkins," lamented Monty, "before we turned him over to Lane's men."

"We had no way of knowing he was going to escape before he got to Lane."

"I worry that Billy's rescue of you on the steamship has prevented us from seeing things clearly, weighing them objectively. He *was* evasive with us, and there is evidence against him."

"He's just scared, Monty. Doesn't know if he can trust anyone. We'd probably have done the same if we were in his shoes. Sure wish we could talk to him about what we now know. Get his take on it."

"I'm sure that's my fault. I shouldn't have come down so hard on General Lane about Watkins escaping and demanding Billy's release. His order prohibiting all visitors to Billy is no doubt aimed primarily at me."

"Trust your instincts, Monty. You know Billy's innocent, and he'll never get a fair trial."

Monty took a deep breath, bit his lower lip, and nodded slightly. "You're right. I'm with you," he said to Robert. "This should be interesting. I hope you know something more about planning a jailbreak than I do."

CHAPTER 53

ugust, 1856— Robert crouched behind Monty in the darkness. He rubbed the back of his neck with one hand and tightened his grip on the pistol that he was holding in the other. It was approaching midnight on a Tuesday and the streets of Lawrence were empty. The plan had been put together quickly, over the past couple of days, to make it look like it was the slavers who had rescued Billy. He hoped that nothing had been overlooked. If it had, people could die. Robert knew that they owed a lot to Stretch, who had recruited a few of his customers, slavery men, to sneak into town and create a diversion in front of the jail, while he and Monty broke into it from the back. Stretch had even borrowed some clothes to wear, in the event anyone spotted them. Robert thought that he and Monty looked like true frontier ruffians, with muddy boots, leather vests, slouch hats, and bandanas.

"There it is, right on time," Robert whispered to Monty, pointing to a plume of white smoke, barely visible in the night sky, rising from the street in front of the jail. Then, he heard a series of gunshots, fired into the air, all as planned. "Come on, quickly," he said to Monty, as he stood, pulled his bandana up over his nose, and started to run toward the rear of the jail. "The hay in that wagon won't burn for long."

They were both familiar with the jail and its layout from prior visits. The wooden door was fairly thin and had only a simple lock on it. Robert pulled out a metal lever that he had taken from the printing room at the *Herald of Freedom*, slid it between the door and the frame, and went to work. After a few strong pushes on the lever, the door popped open. They slowly peered in and, although the few burning candles in the room provided only dim light, were satisfied that no one was there. The plan was working. The two overnight guards had taken the bait and had gone out front to see what the fire and gunshots were all about.

"You know where the keys are kept, in that desk," said Monty, pointing. "Bottom drawer, on the right."

"Right," replied Robert, hoping that neither of the guards had thought to grab the keys before rushing out front. "You go down the hallway. Warn me if they come back in. I'll get Billy."

Robert opened the desk drawer and let out a deep sigh, relieved that the keys were there. He grabbed them and walked over to the cells. The area was mostly dark. He knew that there were three cells and that Billy was being kept in the one on the left. The last time he was there, the other two were empty and, from what he could tell, that still appeared to be so. He walked to his left and barely made out a figure, standing, with his fingers wrapped around the bars of the last cell.

"Billy, it's me, Robert," he whispered, as he fumbled with the keys. The second one that he tried in the lock worked and the cell door opened.

"You got clothes, shoes?," Robert quickly asked.

"Put my clothes on when I heard that commotion out front. You do that?"

"Yep."

"They took my boots. Don't know where they put 'em."

Robert glanced down at Billy's bare feet.

"No time to look. Do your best. Follow me. We're not going that far."

As they raced for the back door, Robert heard Monty's voice.

"They're coming back in!" Monty cried.

Robert saw his friend squatting behind a table at the end of the hallway, with his pistol drawn.

"I got Billy!" Robert replied. "Cover us. See you out back."

Once outside, Robert heard three gunshots. His heart sank. He turned and was relieved to see Monty running out the door, only a few seconds behind him. But then, he saw Monty fall, face first, onto the ground. There had not been any additional gunshots. He must have stumbled, Robert guessed. As he started to go back and help, he heard Monty call out, "Go on, I'll catch up."

Two men emerged from the back door of the jail, brandishing rifles. Thinking quickly, Robert reached down, grabbed a good-sized rock, and heaved it as far as he could toward a wooded area to his right, it making noise as it passed through tree branches and landed. The men turned and ran in that direction, away from Monty.

Satisfied that Monty was safe, Robert turned to Billy. "Run!," he said softly, "Down the hill. To the river."

The Kansas River, which formed the northern border of Lawrence, made a southerly turn just before it reached the town. Its banks were about a quarter of a mile from the jail.

"Over there," an almost breathless Robert said to Billy, as they approached the river. "Toward those trees."

A few seconds later, Robert spotted Stretch, exactly where he was supposed to be, holding a lantern, and standing at the stern of a small rowboat.

"That's Stretch, the bartender at Greeley's," he said to Billy. "You know him. Been a big help. He'll get you across the river, to some friends of his, who'll get you to Leavenworth, and then across the border into Missouri. He'll fill you in on everything, how you got set up."

"You're not coming?"

"Afraid this is the end of the road for us, my friend. Wish we had gotten to spend more time together. You stay the hell out of Kansas. Best that we don't try to contact one another. Too risky."

"Agreed. Probably smart."

"Get in! Time's a-wasting," barked Stretch, as he reached out to help Billy into the boat.

Billy grabbed Robert's hand, shook it heartily, and gave him an embrace. "Thank you!," he said, tears welling up in his eyes. "You saved my life."

"You'd do the same for me, I'm sure." Robert winked, it barely visible in the dim light from Stretch's lantern. He paused for a couple of seconds. "Oh . . . that's right. You already did."

Billy smiled.

Once Billy was safely in the rowboat, Robert gave it a strong shove with his foot. He watched as it disappeared into the watery darkness.

As he took a few deep breaths, relieved and thankful that all had gone well, he heard a noise coming up from behind him. Startled, he pulled out his pistol and turned.

"Relax," Monty said, "It's just me. All good?"

"All is good," Robert responded. "Let's get outta here."

CHAPTER 54

A pril, 1857— "You can't turn it down," Monty said to Robert, as forcefully as he could. "It's what you've always wanted."

Robert had just told Monty about his hesitancy to accept an unsolicited job offer that he had received from the *Washington Evening Star*. The editor there had read some of Robert's articles about the Kansas conflict, was impressed, and had sent a letter to Robert with a job offer. It was for a position as a reporter and came with a substantial increase in salary over what he was making at the *Herald of Freedom*. But it would mean moving from Kansas to the nation's capital.

"I don't want to leave the field before the battle is won."

"Nonsense. You earned this. You've done more than your share. A lot of folks back East know about what's been going on here from reading your work—your interview with John Brown, your articles about Pottawatomie, about the Turner murders, and about the fighting. They support us because of the words you have written. You've made it real for them. Not to mention your service in the militia in support of the free-state cause. Your work here is done. You'll be on a bigger stage there and can have more influence than you could ever hope to by staying here."

In truth, from a personal standpoint, Monty would much prefer that Robert stay. With his wife and children still in Ohio, he had grown close to Robert since they had both arrived in Kansas two and a half years earlier. The younger brother of his deceased friend Ben had become his best friend, just as Ben had been. But Monty, a decade older, also felt a need to be a mentor to Robert, who had no family to call upon for advice and guidance. He wanted to persuade Robert to focus on what was best for his own life and career.

"I don't know. We still got fighting going on," replied Robert, still unconvinced. "Congress won't approve our constitution. John Brown is back East plotting God knows what. I don't think we've seen the end of him out here. There's a lot of things I would like to see through to the end."

"We've turned the corner, Robert. More and more free-state settlers are arriving here every month. We outnumber the slavers by a large number now. The time is coming soon when we will no longer be the shadow government of the territory any longer, and we take control."

"You make it sound like it's over."

"Still work to do but, mark my words, Kansas is going to be a free state. You're still young. Go live in Washington City. Experience it. I enjoyed my years there, at least most of them. The *Evening Star* is a respected newspaper. And you're sure to find a suitable wife much easier there than here, where the pickings are, shall we say, rather slim."

"You're going hammer and tongs over this. One might think you want to get rid of me."

"I only want what's best for *you*, my friend."

CHAPTER 55

ugust, 1857— "How much longer Pa?," Josh asked again.

"Five minutes less than when you asked me last time," replied Monty, as he looked to his right and winked at his eleven-year-old stepson. The boy had a right to be impatient. The journey to their new home had been a long one. They had been traveling for almost three weeks, having taken multiple trains from Ohio to St. Louis, a riverboat up the Missouri River to Kansas City, and were now on the last leg of their trip, in a loaded wagon being pulled by two oxen, slowly, through eastern Kansas. It seemed as if the lad had grown a foot since Monty had last seen him. He was tall for his age and lanky, with curly black hair. Theresa said his build and his hair came from his deceased father, but Monty always thought that his facial features—large blue eyes, thin nose, and his pleasant smile—were spitting images of Theresa.

"Here, slide over a bit," Monty added. "You can help me out and take the reins for a while." He watched with joy as Josh's eyes got even wider and the grin that he loved to see appeared.

"No need to pull much on them, Josh, they're moving dreadfully slow as it is," added Theresa, who was sitting on a bench behind Monty and Josh, with Benjie, who was a few months shy of his fourth birthday, close by her side.

Behind them, the large wagon was loaded with satchels and trunks, all filled with clothes, dishes, books, and family keepsakes that they had brought with them on the trip. The family's furniture and other items had been shipped separately from Ohio and, hopefully, would be there when they arrived.

Monty sighed, relieved to have his family together once again. It had been a long time, much longer than he had expected. What he had initially thought would be a separation of only a few months, starting back in late 1854, had, due to the violence and political battles in Kansas, lasted almost three years. Finally, the violence had subsided, at least in the area around Lawrence, and free-staters had more settlers, and the upper hand, over their proslavery opponents. He had gone back to Ohio twice, in the summer of 1855, and again in 1856, for about a month each time, to visit and to make sure that Theresa and the children knew that he had not abandoned them. But it was not until now, in the summer of 1857, that he felt that it was safe to move his family to their new home. In July, he had again returned to Dayton, settled up his affairs there, visited with his parents and siblings, and began the long journey back to Kansas with his wife and boys.

The construction of the foundry, located on the banks of the Kansas River a couple of miles west of Lawrence, had been completed in May. Seven men now worked there, making wagon axles and wheels, boilers, cast iron stoves, tools, and other assorted items. There was no competition from other foundries in the Lawrence area, at least so far, and Monty was confident that the business would grow and that more workers would be hired over the next year. A house for the family, which he had helped construct himself, was located about a half mile from the foundry, closer to town, and had also recently been finished. Made of black walnut, it was one of the larger residences to have been built in Kansas, with four rooms on the ground floor and two bedrooms upstairs. A wide covered porch extended across its front. Satin paper that Monty had ordered from England covered the walls of two of the rooms—in the dining room, a light rose color, with a flower pattern, and, in the parlor, a medium solid green. The other rooms were still rustic, and needed a woman's touch, he thought.

* * *

"It's beautiful," exclaimed Theresa, as she stood in the foyer of her new home, holding Benjie's hand, and having just made a quick tour of the rooms on the first floor, maneuvering between crates and trunks that had, fortunately, already been delivered and which took up much of the space. "Bigger than the house in Dayton and I love the wallpaper in the dining room and parlor."

"I'm glad you like it. Wasn't sure," responded Monty. "I know you like those colors. You can select it for the rest of the rooms."

"Josh, take your brother upstairs to look at your room," Theresa said, placing the hand of her younger child into that of the older.

"The one on the right," Monty added, as the two eager boys ran more than walked up the stairs to the second floor.

"Looks like most of the furniture is here," said Monty. "I have a couple of fellas from the foundry coming over later today to uncrate it and move it around for us."

"Seems like you've thought of everything."

"Well, I've had three years to look forward to and prepare for this day."

"Lots of work to do, but we'll make it into a home in no time."

Monty hugged his wife and gave her a kiss. "We're together again now. That's all that really matters."

CHAPTER 56

*F*ebruary, 1858—Monty was in a good mood, sitting with Theresa in the evening by a blazing fireplace in the parlor of their home. How grateful he was to have his family with him. The boys had gone up to their beds some time ago and were, hopefully, asleep by now. Theresa, per her custom after supper, was reading a novel. It must have a humorous plot, Monty decided, as he noticed her chuckling slightly from time to time.

Monty stared into the fire, felt the warmth of its heat, and reflected on the events of the past few months. While the battle over slavery in Kansas was not over, he was more confident than ever that the end was in sight, with free-staters the victors. A new governor of the territory, Robert Walker, appointed by President James Buchanan, had arrived in the spring and pledged that future elections would be fairly conducted. Free-staters, who had been boycotting elections and rejecting the laws of the "bogus" legislature that had been imposed on them with fraudulent votes, rethought their strategy. As they were now the clear majority of settlers in the territory, and with the new governor having vowed that future elections would be conducted fairly, they decided to participate in voting, to gain control of the new legislature, and overturn the existing proslavery laws. It was working. In an election held in October 1857, although there had been obvious fraud by the slavers in two counties, Governor Walker, holding to his vow that elections would be legitimate, threw out those votes, resulting in free-staters taking control of both houses of the legislature.

Monty thought about the latest news from Washington City, which had been the talk of everyone in Lawrence and at the foundry during the past week. President Buchanan, who favored slavery in Kansas, had lost key political support within his own Democratic Party. It all involved a proposed constitution for Kansas. In the fall, proslavery Kansans had met in Lecompton and drafted a constitution of their own, providing for the admission of Kansas into the Union with slavery. After much political wrangling, this constitution had been voted down, by a large margin, in an election held in January. When the president recently vowed to pursue acceptance of the Lecompton Constitution by Congress, despite its rejection by Kansas voters, Governor Walker, who had been his close friend and political ally, had resigned in protest. Buchanan's decision split the Democratic Party. Even Senator Stephen Douglas, the author of the Kansas-Nebraska Act, had turned on him. Monty knew that there was little chance that Congress would force a slave-state constitution on the unwilling people of Kansas.

"I almost forgot," Theresa said, looking up from her book, interrupting Monty's thoughts. "I went into town today and stopped at the post office. There was a letter for you. From the handwriting on the envelope, looks like it might be from your father."

She walked over to a nearby table, retrieved the letter, and handed it to Monty.

"Thank you, my dear. It is his handwriting."

Monty opened the envelope and read the letter, which was brief. He then felt a few tears run down his cheek and watched as the droplets fell onto the letter, blurring a few of the words.

"What wrong, Monty?," asked a concerned Theresa, "Is everyone in the family all right?"

"Yes, yes, family's good. But there's sad news." He hesitated, wiping his eyes. "It's Delores . . . she's no longer with us."

"Oh, no! What has happened?"

"Father went to the foundry to meet a group coming through on the Underground Railroad and asked the conductor how Raven was doing, as he had not seen her in a while. The man said that she had passed away a couple of months earlier. Said she was at the reins of her horse, leading a wagonload of charges to a safe house, when she had some chest pain. One of the men got out from his hiding place in the wagon and took over. She was able to tell him which house to head to, but by the time they arrived, she was gone."

Monty thought back to that day just outside of Washington City when he had first seen her, at that awful slave auction, and of the joy on her face when he told her, after completing the purchase, that she would be freed. He reflected on her selfless life since then, recalling their unexpected meeting at the foundry in Dayton. That had been almost four years ago. How good it had been to see her again, after all the years, and to learn about all that she had accomplished. She could have gone to Canada and lived a quiet and pleasant life. Instead, she had dedicated herself to a cause, to helping others such as herself flee slavery. Fresh tears began rolling down his cheeks.

Theresa closed her book, walked over to her husband, reached out and squeezed his hands.

"She made a difference in people's lives and she died doing what she loved."

"She surely did. We should all be so fortunate," he replied.

"And never forget, it was your act of kindness that gave her the opportunity."

CHAPTER 57

November, 1859— "These are for you, Mr. Geddis."

"Thank you, Henry," Robert said, as he looked up and took his mail from the clerk's hand. He was seated at his desk in his office at the *Evening Star*. It had been more than two years since he had left Kansas and moved to Washington City. It was not a decision that he regretted. Monty, who he kept in touch with, had been right—being in the nation's capital, at the center of all things political—was exhilarating and good for his career. His writing skills had improved and he was on his way to being recognized as one of the best reporters in the city. Although the subjects of his articles varied, he continued to write about events in Kansas, and of the improving fortunes of the free-staters there. Over the past month, he had been writing about a man familiar to Kansans—John Brown. The abolitionist's failed October raid on the federal arsenal at Harpers Ferry, in Virginia, and his trial and conviction for treason had captured the attention of the entire nation.

He was working on a story about the upcoming 1860 election and had a small mountain of books and papers before him. He could use a break, he thought, and started to open the envelopes and read their contents. The top one was a brief letter (unsigned, as usual) wanting him to investigate some alleged scandal at the Patent Office. He got these fairly often—about the Patent Office, the War Department, the city's prison, or someplace else. He ignored most, believing them to be personal vendettas, someone looking to have a reporter investigate a person who they thought had done them wrong. But he had looked into a few that had attracted his attention, found them to have some merit, and had gotten a couple of good articles published under his byline.

Next was a note from the secretary of Harriet Lane, the niece of President Buchanan and the official hostess for her bachelor uncle, inviting him to a levee at the White House on Saturday next. He smiled and shook his head. Old Buck was still trying to curry favor with reporters. Was there no end to what his staff would do to try to get a favorable story out of Robert? Too little, too late, he thought, convinced that the president was a dead man walking. Just like Pierce, his predecessor, Buchanan was a northern man with southern principles or, as Robert believed, a stooge for the slave power in the South. Doughfaces, they were called. The Democratic Party in 1856 had dumped Pierce after one term and he was sure that the same fate awaited Buchanan at the party's upcoming convention in a few months.

Robert then picked up another envelope addressed to him, with the word "CONFIDENTIAL" written across the bottom. The handwriting was not familiar. He opened it and read the enclosed letter:

Dear Robert:

I hope that you are well. I read your article about John Brown's trial, which was reprinted in a newspaper here in Texas, where I now live. Brown is now headed for the hangman's noose. Without you, I would have met the same fate in Kansas. I am forever grateful.

I know this letter breaks our agreement to not communicate, but I've learned some things since you rescued me. Hard to believe it's been more than three years.

When I crossed the river with Stretch that night, he told me all that you and Mr. Tolliver had found out—that you knew I was in the Blue Lodge, and that my Lodge brother, Ned Watkins, had killed the Turners and set me up for it.

A few months ago, a fella I knew in Kansas from the Lodge passed through my town here. He saw me in a tavern. I tried to avoid him, as I now live under a different name, but he knew it was me. He said he was part of a committee of Lodge brothers that had been looking into Ned's past, going back to the summer of '56, because things about him just didn't square up. They found out his rich daddy was an abolitionist in Illinois and suspected that Ned had been playing them for fools, by pretending to be one of them, and passing information to the enemy.

This fella was one of a group that captured Ned as he was trying to get out of Kansas, around the time you broke me out of jail. They held a Lodge trial for him, and he confessed to all that they suspected. Admitted that he was working as a spy for John Brown ever since he got to Kansas. But he also admitted to more, things they weren't aware of. Ned must have thought they knew about it, and that they'd go easier on him if he was straight with them.

Ned told them that after you and Mr. Tolliver arrested him at Greeley's, he was taken before General

Lane and confessed to him all that he had done—that he had killed the Turner brothers and framed me for it, to impress Brown and to get the free-staters all riled up for war. Ned related that Lane started cursing and said, if word of any of it ever got out, it could destroy their cause—that free-staters couldn't be seen as butchering their own and making it look like the other side did it. The fella said that Ned accepted a deal offered by Lane—if he swore to never breathe a word of what he had done and leave Kansas forever, the general would tell his folks that Ned had escaped, but Lane, instead, would let him go and give him a horse and some money to get to the border.

The fella also cleared up one thing that had always bothered me—why Ned set me up as the killer. Ned told them he picked me because I always hesitated when he ordered me to do raids for the Lodge. He told them he didn't think I was fully committed, and that he hated folks who were not true believers, whichever side they were on.

They convicted Ned and carried out the usual sentence for spies. The fella said that Ned's is one body that will never be found. They kept it all quiet, not wanting other Lodge members to find out that Ned had succeeded in tricking them for so long.

Thought you would want to know.

Your friend always,
Billy

Robert dropped the letter onto his desk, leaned back, and shook his head. Billy's letter confirmed all that he and Monty had believed—Ned had been John Brown's spy, and he had killed the Turners and framed Billy for it, to escalate the fighting in Kansas over slavery. But Billy's letter had revealed more. Ned had not escaped, as General Lane had told them. Instead, Lane had let him go and had orchestrated a cover up. The killing of slavery men by John Brown at Pottawatomie was one thing, but it could have significantly damaged Brown and the entire free-state cause if it were discovered that someone working with Brown, even if acting on his own, had killed free-staters—their own people—to increase the fervor for war. It was a risk, Robert now realized, that Lane had been unwilling to take. Financial support from the East could have dried up. The slavers could have again gained the upper hand.

As a reporter, Robert's mind worked methodically. He now saw most of the pieces of the puzzle fall into place. Except one. It was a question that he had wondered about for three years. *Who* was Monty's informant? It had to be someone inside John Brown's camp. He and Monty had been sure of that. But who? He went over to a table in the corner of his office and grabbed a stack of *Evening Star* papers with articles about Brown's Harpers Ferry raid. He found the article that he needed, with the names of Brown's sons who were there with him. There were three— Watson, Oliver, and Owen. Watson and Oliver had been killed during the raid. The article also listed the names of Brown's sons who took part in the Pottawatomie Massacre in Kansas. Owen and Oliver had also been there, along with Frederick and Salmon. Robert knew that Brown had seven sons. Two names were missing from the lists—John, Jr. and Jason. Robert knew that John, Jr. had led a militia unit in Kansas and, according to the newspaper articles, had shipped weapons to his father for the raid in Virginia. He supported his father fully. That left Jason, the son of Brown that Robert had met briefly in Lawrence.

Jason had said that he was an abolitionist, but that he was not a fighting man, and seemed to mock his father's righteousness. Jason, Robert was now certain, had been the informant.

Satisfied that he now knew all the facts, Robert took a few sheets of paper out of one of the drawers of his desk. He dipped a quill in the brass inkwell. "Dear Monty," he began.

CHAPTER 58

November, 1859— "I have no regrets, Mr. Tolliver, for the actions I took." Jim Lane no longer used the title of captain when addressing the man sitting before him. Monty had resigned his position with the militia the previous year, as hostilities in Kansas had eased. He had just confronted Lane with the information that Robert had received from Billy, without revealing the source. He had expected a denial from Lane but, instead, the man admitted it all, even took pride in it.

"But you let a murderer go and were going to have an innocent man stand trial and hang. You lied and covered up the truth."

"And I'd do it again. Look at what John Brown has accomplished in the years since then. From his prison cell in Charles Town, he is a hero. Folks are singing his praises all over the North and West for what he did at Harpers Ferry. Our side is united as never before. When Virginia hangs him, he will become a martyr. And we will be even stronger and more united. We have a good chance to elect a Republican as president this year. If I had let this thing of Brown's be exposed back in '56, word that a spy he recruited, this Watkins fellow, had murdered some innocent folks on our side, I doubt any of this would be happening. Guilt by association. The man's reputation could have been destroyed."

"Folks may still be interested in knowing about it."

"Not now. No one will now care about John Brown's involvement with Watkins. It's old news. Water over the dam."

"I meant that folks would be interested in knowing about your role in covering it all up."

"You want to expose me as the man who protected John Brown? Go ahead. Shout it from a mountaintop. No one will give a tinker's cuss. It'll just make me more popular than I am already. Because of what I did, slavery's days are numbered. I thought that was something that you wanted."

"I *always* have. A few years ago, at the Topeka convention, you didn't want Negroes to have *any* rights, you wanted to exclude them from a free Kansas. Before then, you *supported* slavery."

"What can I tell you? Times change; people change. Have you never changed your opinions?"

"Only if the change was sincerely arrived at."

"What are you implying?'

"You know damn well what I am implying."

"I confess to being a politician. You were once one, too. You of all people should know that you can't accomplish things if you are no longer on the stage. I'm now the leader of this movement in Kansas, more so than your friend, Dr. Robinson. I intend to be a United States senator when Kansas enters the Union, which will be soon. You don't want to cross me. And don't think that I don't have eyes on your friend, Billy Rutledge. I suspect you know that he's hiding out in Texas. I've been tracking him down for three years, and pretty sure I've found him. He's still a fugitive, you know. Fugitives get shot. It would be a true shame if something were to happen to that young man, after all this time."

241

Monty had had enough. He never cared for Lane, and this conversation only solidified his opinion. Fortunately, with his resignation from the militia the previous year, he no longer needed to answer to the man. He tried to think of a sarcastic or cutting comeback, but was too irritated to think of one. All he could muster was a firm "Good day, sir" as he stood up and stormed out of the room.

Minutes later, as he rode his horse slowly home, to Theresa and the boys, he grudgingly admitted to himself that Lane was probably right. John Brown was about to become a martyr to the antislavery cause and few would care about his association with Ned Watkins and what Ned had done. It was already well known that Brown had blood on his hands from the killings at Pottawatomie and folks denied it, ignored it, or just didn't care. Nor would anyone likely care about Lane's role in hiding the truth about the Turner killings. The man was a chameleon, an opportunist, and a demagogue, but he had played his cards well. In addition to his metamorphosis into an ardent opponent of slavery, he had led several successful militia attacks on the slavers, making him a popular military figure, as well as a political one. And then, perhaps most importantly, there was Lane's not-so-veiled threat against Billy. Monty was not one inclined to tilt at windmills, especially if it put Billy's life at risk. Ever since that day when Lawrence had been attacked, when he and Robert, hiding in a shed, had talked about the assassination of President Tyler that he had attempted with Robert's brother, and Robert's negative reaction to it, Monty had come around to convincing himself that he had been wrong back in 1844, that honorable ends do not justify less than honorable means. Now, once again, he was not so sure. It seemed to have worked out well for Jim Lane.

CHAPTER 59

*D*ecember, 1859— Monty and his family stood in the midst of a large crowd on Delaware Street in Leavenworth watching an approaching carriage that was still a couple of blocks away. It was almost noon on a bitterly cold early December day. Some of the snow from a storm a few days earlier remained on the ground. Theresa, with Benjie standing directly in front of her, cuddled the boy's cheeks with her gloved hands, to help shield them from the temperature, while Monty pulled up his scarf, trying to cover more of his neck and face. Josh, like most excited fourteen-year-old boys, seemed impervious to the cold.

Monty had been looking forward to this day. He hoped it would help him get over the thoughts that had occupied his mind for the past weeks. His meeting with Jim Lane had been almost a month ago. He and Robert had communicated by telegraph a few times since then, using codewords that Robert had suggested in his letter to Monty, the letter that had contained the information received from Billy. They had to be careful. One never knew who in a telegraph office might have access to their words. Monty's last message to his friend in Washington

City had read "To save the lamb, the knave will be spared," to which Robert had responded with "Agreed." They did not know whether Lane would follow through on his threat to kill Billy in Texas, if they revealed Ned Watkins' murder of the Turner brothers, his close ties with John Brown, and Lane's cover up of it all, but decided it was not worth the risk. Not after all this time. Deep down, in any situation, Monty's first instinct was that the truth should come out, but he decided that this was an exception, at least for now, and Robert had agreed. The life of Billy (the "lamb") was worth it. When the time came, Jim Lane ("the knave") could be dealt with.

"It's an open carriage!" shouted a thrilled Josh, staring in the distance. "Looks like some folks are already running alongside it."

"I met him once, you know," Monty said, turning his head toward Theresa.

"Yes, I remember you saying so. In Washington City, when you were in Congress. But you didn't give me any of the details."

"It was on inauguration day, in March of 1849. He was leaving Congress, after one term, and I was being sworn in for my first one. We sat together during the ceremony for Zac Taylor to take over as president. He spun some humorous yarn about his hometown and we both got to laughing so much that I think one of the ushers had a mind to throw us both out."

"They say he tells a good story," replied Theresa.

"He surely does."

"And that his speechmaking is even better," she added.

"I guess we will find out firsthand tonight," replied Monty, adding, "Something that I admire—the ability of a man with his voice and words to hold an audience in his hands and inspire them. In my years working for Senator Clay, I saw, and heard, a master of the craft at work. Sad to say, none of it rubbed off on me."

"You have other talents, my love."

The carriage got closer. Monty could now see that some running beside and behind it were waving American flags and campaign banners. It was black, with red trim, and seated only two people behind the driver. The roof was up, but it provided no protection from the wind and the freezing temperature. Leavenworth's guest of honor had a robe of buffalo fur pulled around him and his rugged face was red. A brass band to Monty's right, twelve members strong, resplendent in blue and gold uniforms, began to play.

"I'm surprised that their lips don't freeze to their mouthpieces," commented Josh.

The black horse pulling the carriage slowed to a crawl and the throng of people erupted in applause and cheers as it passed by. All could now get a good look. There he was, Abraham Lincoln, candidate for the nomination of the new Republican Party for president of the United States. He smiled, nodded his head, and tipped his stovepipe hat to the crowd. The band stepped in front of the carriage, and everyone then followed behind it, for the short distance to the Mansion House, a hotel where a few fortunate callers, including Monty, would be received by the Illinoisan during his stay in Leavenworth. Monty had reserved a room for the night in the same hotel for himself and his family. He watched the lanky Lincoln extricate himself from the carriage and give a final wave to the crowd before disappearing behind the hotel's dark oak doors.

"What time is your meeting with him?," Theresa asked.

"Eleven o'clock in the morning."

"I suspect the boys are hungry for some lunch."

"Definitely. Me, too. We have all afternoon. We'll sate our appetites and then explore the town."

The family walked to a cafe about a block from the hotel. With Lincoln's arrival, it was crowded and they had to wait in line for a table. Fortunately, there was an area for standing just inside the door, and out of the cold temperature.

"Did you hear the news?," a man standing in front of Monty turned and asked.

"Yes, we just watched Mr. Lincoln arrive at the hotel. Quite exciting."

"No, no, not that," replied the man, pointing to a newspaper in his hand. "John Brown was hanged in Virginia yesterday."

"I had not heard. Knew it would be happening soon."

"Sounds like," said the man, "he was defiant to the end. Rode to the gallows in a wagon, proudly sitting up in his own coffin. He told the crowd," the man continued, now holding the folded newspaper in front of his face, and reading, "I am now quite certain that the crimes of this guilty land will never be purged away but with blood."

"He oughta know," said a second man in the line, who had been eavesdropping. "He sure shed enough innocent blood here in Kansas."

"It always amazed me," replied the first man, "how Brown never had to pay for what he did here."

"Sure made me lose respect for the leaders of the abolition cause back East," said a third man, who was standing behind Monty. "They knew he was a cold-blooded killer, but took him back in and asked no questions. They continued to support him and financed his hair-brained scheme at Harpers Ferry."

"And now he'll be viewed as a saint," said the first man.

Monty could only nod his head in agreement.

CHAPTER 60

ecember, 1859— Stockton Hall in Leavenworth was filled to overflowing on a cold Saturday night. Monty and Theresa had good seats in the third row. Monty noticed his wife looking around the room and saw that a smile came to her face.

"Good to see so many women present," Theresa leaned over and said to him. "Women needed to be informed about politics, just as men."

"Indeed they do," Monty responded.

Abraham Lincoln sat on a stage several feet in front of them, in a too-short chair that made his long legs look like those of a grasshopper.

Monty had also surveyed the room. "Looks like a lot of Democrats are curious about him and are here tonight," he said to Theresa.

"How can you tell?"

"Take a deep breath and look at the floor. A lot more of them chew tobacco than we Republicans."

Lincoln was introduced by Mark Delahay, the owner of a newspaper in Leavenworth and an old friend of his from Illinois.

Monty had met Delahay a few months ago at an organizational meeting for the Republican Party in Kansas. Following Delahay's brief remarks, Lincoln stood and began speaking.

"You are, as of now, the people of a territory; but God willing, will soon be the people of a State of the Union. Then, you will have to take a stand on the policy of the national government on domestic slavery. That policy must take one of two directions. It must deal with the institution as being wrong, or as not being wrong."

Monty noted that Lincoln spoke without a podium and without notes. His large hands, with his fingers interlaced, rested in front of his flat stomach.

"From the early actions of the federal government, in relation to the foreign slave trade, the basis of federal representation, in the prohibition of slavery in the territories, in the fugitive slave clause in the constitution, all show plainly that the early policy was based on the idea that slavery is *wrong*, and tolerating it so far, and only so far, as the necessity of its actual presence required."

"Yet, the Kansas-Nebraska Act is based on the opposite idea, the idea that slavery is *not wrong*. You, the people of Kansas, furnish the first example of this new policy. At the end of almost five years of continual struggles, fire, and bloodshed, over this very question, you have framed a Free-State Constitution, under which you will probably be admitted into the Union. You have, at the end of all of this difficulty, attained what we in the old Northwest Territory achieved without any difficulty at all. Compare the actual working of this new policy with that of the old way—the one adopted by Washington and his peers—and ask yourselves if theirs was not the better way."

Monty noticed that Lincoln began to move his hands, making gestures to emphasize his points.

"This new policy," Lincoln continued, "has proved false in all of its promises. They said it would speedily end the nation's slavery agitation. It has done the opposite. They pledged it would give the people of the territories greater control over their own affairs, but it has done the opposite. You have been bedeviled by more outside interference than the people of any other territory have had to tolerate."

"It is curious that those who support popular sovereignty and say they are as much *opposed* to slavery as anyone have never found any proper time and place to oppose it. In their view, slavery cannot be opposed in politics, because that is agitation; it cannot be opposed in the pulpit, because it is not religion; nor in the free states, because it is not there; nor in the slave states, because it is there. Yet these men are never offended by hearing slavery *supported* in any of these places."

"I like his delivery," Theresa whispered into Monty's ear. "Smooth and easy. Logical, and easy to follow."

"Those who think slavery is *right*," Lincoln argued, "should unite on a policy that deals with it as such. They should push for a revival of the slave trade, for carrying the institution into the free states, and demand from Canada the return of all of the former slaves living there. If Canada had as many horses as she has slaves belonging to Americans, I should think it a just cause of war if she did not surrender them on demand."

"On the other hand, those of us who believe slavery is *wrong* should unite on a policy that deals with it as a wrong. We should not be deluded by the deceitful contrivances of those who pretend indifference to the institution, but who, in reality, work to support it."

As he listened, Monty recognized and admired the speaking technique—state the arguments of your opponents, then reduce them to absurdity and show them in a ridiculous light. He remembered that Senator Clay had done this on occasion but, he had to admit, Lincoln was better at it.

"We Republicans are conservative. We are not trying to destroy slavery. The peace of society, and the structure of our government, both require that we should let it alone, and we insist on letting it alone. It is our opponents who wish to change things, by expanding the institution. They say that we Republicans will destroy the Union, that if we elect a president, they won't stand for it. If so, I say to them directly—it is you who will break up the Union. That will be your act, not ours. Do you have cause for such a desperate action? You will find that our policy is *exactly* the policy of the men who made the Union. Nothing more and nothing less."

"When *you* have elected a president, we have submitted, never breaking or attempting to break up the Union. If *we* shall elect a president, it will be our duty to see that you submit. Old John Brown has just been executed, for treason against a state. We cannot object, even though he agreed with us in thinking that slavery is wrong. That cannot excuse violence, bloodshed, and treason. It could avail him nothing that he might think himself right. So, if we constitutionally elect a president, and you seek to destroy the Union, it will be our duty to deal with you as John Brown has been dealt with."

When Lincoln concluded, most in the audience rose, including Monty and Theresa, and there were loud and long cheers, even from some of the Democrats in the room.

"Just over an hour and a half," said Monty, having pulled out his pocket watch.

"I could have listened to him talk for three, or more," replied Theresa.

"Not sure Josh would approve of that. He probably has his hands full with Benjie."

"You're right. We should be getting back to the hotel room."

* * *

After he became president, Abraham Lincoln once mused, if he moved to the West later in life, that it would likely be to Kansas. It was natural that he had a special affection for the place—it was Kansas that had led to his reentry into politics. The popularity of his speeches opposing the Kansas-Nebraska Act, in which he set forth his refined views on slavery, put him on a path that, within six years, would end at the White House.

Lincoln's only visit to Kansas occurred in early December 1859 and lasted a little less than a week. He traveled by train from his home in Springfield, Illinois, to St. Joseph, Missouri, and took a ferry across the Missouri River to Kansas, arriving at Elwood. He visited five towns—Elwood, Troy, Doniplan, Atchison, and Leavenworth—and made well-received speeches at each stop. Most of his time was spent in Leavenworth, where he stayed at the home of an old friend, Mark Delahay, who was a distant cousin by marriage and also a lawyer who had formerly practiced in Springfield. Delahay had become a newspaper editor in Leavenworth and was a leader in the founding of the Republican Party in the territory. It was Delahay who had written to his old friend, Lincoln, who had decided to run for president in 1860, and encouraged him to make a campaign tour through Kansas.

While Lincoln was in Kansas, John Brown was hanged in Virginia for treason over his failed raid at Harpers Ferry, which had occurred less than two months earlier. Brown was well known to Lincoln's Kansas audiences, from three years earlier, when he had participated in and ordered the massacre of five proslavery men at Pottawatomie Creek, actions for which he was never arrested and which were often overlooked, or outright denied, by his supporters. His hanging gave Lincoln the opportunity, during his speeches in Kansas, to laud the abolitionist for his devotion to the cause of ending slavery, but to denounce him for the killing and other crimes that he had committed.

CHAPTER 61

ecember, 1859— Monty entered the open doorway of a second-floor suite in the Mansion House. He had arrived early, a habit instilled in him by his always punctual parents. A burly man, who introduced himself as Ward Lamon, advised that things were running a few minutes behind schedule. He pointed to a chair where Monty could wait and then went and stood, almost at attention, beside a door that led to the next room, where Abraham Lincoln was meeting with Kansans who wanted to assist in his campaign for president. Monty's letter to Lincoln, written a few weeks earlier and offering his support, had landed him a spot on the schedule.

Although not yet a state, meaning no electoral votes would be cast by Kansas in the upcoming 1860 presidential election, the Republican Party had decided that the territory would have voting delegates at its nominating convention the coming summer. In a close contest, a handful of delegates could decide the outcome. This is what had brought Lincoln to Kansas.

Monty took a seat and unfolded a copy of the *Leavenworth Daily Times* that he had purchased in the lobby. He began reading the front-page article about Lincoln's speech the previous evening:

Oratory is an art. Yet, there is often no marrow to the speaker's words, no food for reflection or thought. Usually, it is all passion and vehemence, of shallow feeling or animal impulse, and nothing more. Mr. Lincoln, to the contrary, takes a broad common-sense view of principles and measures, and presents and argues them with strength. He is clear and solid, and is true to principle.

Monty glanced up at Lamon, still standing like a sentry by the doorway, and avoiding any eye contact. He then refocused on the newspaper article:

Lincoln stands by the Constitution of the Union, and will do so as long as he lives. Either the slaveholder has, he argues, under the Constitution, the right to bring his human chattels into the Territories of the Union, or he has not. If he has, we must submit. If he has not, we must restrain him. Lincoln repudiates popular sovereignty with a force of logic which cannot be successfully resisted—with a power of reasoning which no mind can overthrow.

Mr. Lincoln's visit will do good for the people of Kansas. No man can speak as he speaks without sowing seed which bear rich fruit.

Monty refolded the paper and placed it on his lap. A couple of minutes later, the door that Lamon was guarding opened. A startled Lamon walked through it, emerging seconds later and escorting an elderly man, who Monty did not recognize, to the hallway.

"Mr. Tolliver, thank you for your patience. Mr. Lincoln will see you now," said Lamon, as he motioned for Monty to enter the adjacent room of the suite.

"Thank you," replied Monty, handing the newspaper to Lamon as he walked past him. "Good article on the front page that you may find of interest."

Lincoln, who was sitting on an overstuffed red and gold striped armchair, rose and extended his hand. Monty observed that he was dressed in the standard attire of politicians of the day, including himself when he had been in Congress, consisting of a black wool frock coat and trousers, black silk vest, white shirt, and black cravat. He was taller than Monty had remembered, towering a few inches above Monty's own six-foot frame.

"Good morning, Mr. Tolliver. We meet again."

"And a good morning to you, sir. I wasn't sure if you would recall me."

"I surely do. Enjoyed our chat at the inauguration. Any man who worked for Henry Clay sticks out in my mind. Refresh my memory, how long did you work for the senator?"

"About four years, in the late '30s and early '40s. I also got to spend some time with him over his last few months, in 1852, when I was in Congress."

"A great man. My political idol."

"I read that you said as much in one of your debates with Senator Douglas last year."

"So I did, and proud to have done so. I'm glad you asked to meet with me. I understand that you've been active in the founding of our Republican Party here in Kansas."

"I have. We're still getting organized. A lot of former Whigs, but bringing in some others as well."

"Glad to hear it. Tell me, Mr. Tolliver, your assessment of the current status of the race for our nomination here in Kansas?"

"Please call me Monty. I don't see Governor Chase or Mr. Bates as factors here. I keep in touch with political friends back home and they tell me that Chase is struggling for support outside of Ohio. His will be more of a favorite son candidacy, if you ask me. Mr. Bates, I think, is even weaker here. His being from Missouri, with all that we have endured from those folks over the past few years, well, most Kansans would never consider him. I think it is a two-man race between you and Senator Seward, although I have to say I suspect that he has the majority, as of now. We have been through so much here that most favor a strong approach to dealing with the slavers, which he supports."

"He has a weakness, I believe. I think our friend Mr. Seward has misanalysed the situation, spouting off about there being a 'higher law' and that an 'irrepressible conflict' is coming. I am reminded of the story of the farmer's young boy who came running from the barn into the house, all excited. Out of breath, he says: 'Pa, Pa, the hired hand and Sis are up in the hayloft. The hired hand has dropped his pants and Sis has pulled her skirt all the way up! Pa, I think they are a fixin' to pee on the hay!' The farmer put his hands on the agitated boy's shoulder and replied, 'Son, you got the facts right, but you're drawing the wrong conclusion.'"

"Seward has got his facts right" Lincoln continued, "about the South and slavery, but his solution as to how to fix it goes down the wrong road. His language speaks of what sounds like a holy war and an attack upon our southern brethren. Just like Old John Brown, he's a Moses having been to the mountaintop. That kind of talk scares folks. This election will be won or lost in the border states. A New Yorker can't win any of those with talk like that. I can win there."

"I agree, makes a lot of sense."

"I'm a God-fearing man, Monty, but there's no 'higher law' that we are bound by in this situation. In my view, we must deal with the Constitution, as it is. I am convinced that the Constitution tolerates slavery only where it already exists and stands squarely against its expansion, here in Kansas or anywhere else."

"You laid it out very impressively in your speech last night. I wish the whole country could have heard it," Monty replied.

Overnight, he had given Lincoln's words a lot of thought. Lincoln's propose way forward—following the Constitution and the laws—wouldn't satisfy the extremists on either side of the slavery issue, but Monty was convinced that it was the correct path to follow.

"Thank you. Can I count on your support," Lincoln inquired, "and your help here?"

"Yes, sir. I'm with you, one hundred percent. Looking forward to it."

"Glad to hear it!" Lincoln stood up, shook Monty's hand, and steered him toward the door. "My next appointment is with another gentleman who will also be working on my campaign here in Kansas. If he's already here, I'd like you to meet him."

Lincoln opened the door.

Monty took a few steps and his heart sank. There, seated in the same chair where he had waited minutes earlier was a man he knew, and detested.

"Jim," said Lincoln, "thank you for coming in again. I'd like you to meet Monty Tolliver, if you don't know him already. Monty, this is Jim Lane. The two of you will be working closely together on my campaign over the next year. Two former congressmen, one who used to be a Whig and one a reformed Democrat, both now Republicans and pulling oars in the same direction. With both of you on board, how can I lose?"

Lane and Monty stared icily at each other.

"We've met," muttered Monty.

AUTHOR'S NOTES

Many of the events discussed in this book concerning the "Bleeding Kansas" era from 1854 to 1859 occurred and are historically accurate, including the settling of the Kansas Territory by those opposed to slavery and those favoring it, the role of the New England Emigrant Aid Company, Missourians crossing the border and determining the outcome of Kansas elections, the existence of secret societies, and the violence, including the Wakarusa War, the attack on Lawrence, and John Brown's Pottawatomie Massacre. (The murder of the Turner brothers and the investigation of it by the fictional characters in the book are creations of the author).

Estimates vary as to the number of people killed as a result of the conflict over slavery in Kansas during these years, with some going into the hundreds. Kansas eventually entered the Union as a free state in January 1861. The battles over slavery that were fought there in the 1850s would soon be repeated on a larger stage, between the entire North and South, with the outbreak of the Civil War in April 1861.

More information follows about the historical figures, places, and events in the book.

Eli Thayer:

Born in 1819, Thayer was a Massachusetts educator and reformer who established the New England Emigrant Aid Company with the purpose of populating Kansas with settlers opposed to slavery. Under the popular sovereignty doctrine of the Kansas-Nebraska Act, the side with the most voters living in the territory would determine whether slavery would exist there or not. More than two thousand New Englanders, all opposed to slavery, were transplanted to Kansas by Thayer's company. Historians differ over whether this effort was determinative of the outcome, as a larger number of settlers to Kansas, who also opposed slavery, came from states that are now known as the Midwest. Despite this, there is no doubt that Thayer's work resulted in the founding of several towns in Kansas, that his company became a focal point for the antislavery cause, and that it kept the issue of expansion of slavery on the front burner of American politics. Several of the company's agents became political leaders in Kansas, both before and after statehood.

Southerners, especially those in neighboring Missouri, believed that Thayer and his company had great power and influence in Kansas. They detested him and openly issued calls for his execution.

Thayer was elected to Congress from Massachusetts in 1856, serving for two terms as a Republican. In 1857, he was behind the founding of a new town in western Virginia, called Ceredo, with the goal of introducing northern manufacturing methods there and colonizing it with northern settlers opposed to slavery. The new venture was not successful, attracting fewer than five hundred people, and was abandoned with the start of the Civil War. In later years, Thayer focused on his business interests and promoting certain inventions.

Massachusetts Senator Charles Sumner, an abolitionist who was nearly caned to death in Congress for a speech opposing slavery in Kansas, left no doubt about his opinion of Thayer's importance in American history. "Kansas should have been named [after] Thayer!," Sumner proclaimed, "I would rather have accomplished all that he has done than to be the hero of the Battle of New Orleans."

Thayer died in 1899 at the age of seventy-nine.

Free State Hotel:

Built and initially owned by the New England Emigrant Aid Company, this three-story hotel in Lawrence, Kansas, had thick stone walls and resembled a fortress. It became the *de facto* headquarters of the free-state movement in the Kansas Territory, which also made it a target of those Kansas settlers and nearby Missourians who wanted Kansas to enter the Union as an enslaved state. After being declared a public nuisance by a proslavery grand jury, the hotel was attacked by a mob during the sacking of Lawrence on May 21, 1856. When cannon fire failed to penetrate its walls, it was set afire and destroyed.

The hotel was rebuilt, only to suffer the same fate a few years later during the Civil War. On August 21, 1863, a group of Confederate guerilla raiders, led by William Quantrill, attacked and burned Lawrence, including the Free State Hotel, and killed approximately one hundred and fifty people.

After the war, the hotel was rebuilt again and opened as the Eldridge Hotel, named after its then owner, Shalor Eldridge, who had leased the original hotel from the New England Emigrant Aid Company. Due to deterioration, the hotel was torn down and rebuilt in 1925. After a period of conversion into apartments, investors refurbished and restored the site as a hotel, opening it in 1985. Today, the Eldridge Hotel stands on the original site of the Free State Hotel, at Massachusetts and Seventh Streets, and is one of Lawrence's finest and most historic hotels.

Charles Robinson:

A Massachusetts doctor, Robinson arrived in Kansas in August 1854 with one of the first groups of free-state settlers sent by the New England Emigrant Aid Company. He was an agent for the company and quickly became a leader of those in the territory opposed to slavery. Elected the "shadow" governor of Kansas under the Topeka Constitution (which never went into effect), the proslavery territorial government indicted him for treason and he was held prisoner for several months. At a trial in 1857, he was acquitted of all changes.

Robinson's chief rival for leadership of free-staters in Kansas was James Lane. Although they cooperated to some extent during the height of the "Bleeding Kansas" era, they later became political enemies. The two men were a contrast in style, with Robinson steady and cautious and Lane erratic and impulsive.

When Kansas entered the Union as the thirty-fourth state in early 1861, Robinson was elected its first governor. Lane's supporters in the Kansas legislature sought to remove him from office over a scandal concerning the sale of state bonds. They succeeded in impeaching him in the Kansas House of Representatives, but he was acquitted in the Senate.

In his later years, Robinson served in the Kansas legislature and was involved in various educational causes. He died in 1894.

James Lane:

Born in Indiana, Lane was initially a staunch proslavery Democrat and was elected lieutenant governor of that state and, later, a member of Congress. In 1854, he voted in Congress for the Kansas-Nebraska Act and moved to the Kansas Territory the following year. Over the course of a couple of years after his arrival in Kansas, Lane shifted from being a slavery supporter to an ardent abolitionist. Historians differ over his motives. Some believe that he had a sincere change of convictions, while others opine that he acted out of revenge for personal slights, or was a political chameleon, as he saw that the free-state movement was gaining support in Kansas and wanted to be on the winning side. One historian has described Lane as "an unscrupulous opportunist . . . violent, paranoid, and highly unbalanced."

Having had military experience in the Mexican War, Lane was made the leader of the militia of free-staters in Kansas. In the fall of 1856, he led several successful attacks against proslavery forces. He was also a highly effective speaker and traveled around the country to drum up support for the free-state cause in Kansas. He and Charles Robinson became bitter political rivals within the free-state movement.

When Kansas became a state in 1861, Lane became one of its senators in Washington. While serving in the Senate, he also organized several volunteer military units in Kansas, known as the Kansas Brigade, and led them into battle. He crossed the border into Missouri and, in one notorious engagement, attacked, looted, and burned Osceola, a town of three-thousand people, which had little military significance. The raid was criticized by his superiors in the Union Army.

After Lincoln's assassination, Lane supported President Andrew Johnson's weak reconstruction polices toward the former

Confederacy. In doing so, he fell out of favor with the Radical Republicans who controlled Congress. He began to be questioned about alleged financial improprieties. In 1866, while riding in a carriage with a relative in Kansas, Lane jumped out, put a pistol in his mouth, and pulled the trigger. Lane's suicide, combined with erratic behavior over his life, have led many to believe that he suffered from mental instability.

Kansas Constitutions:

During the "Bleeding Kansas" era, four separate state constitutions were drafted for Kansas, three by the free-staters and one by those who favored slavery. Approval of a constitution by both houses of Congress was required for statehood.

The first, the Topeka Constitution, drafted by free-staters in late 1855, prohibited slavery, but also permitted the legislature to exclude all free Blacks from Kansas once it became a state. It was approved by voters, along with the exclusion provision, in an election that was boycotted by proslavery men. This constitution narrowly passed the House of Representatives, but stalled in the Senate, where the South had more power.

Two years later, in October 1857, proslavery men in the territory met in Lecompton and drafted their own constitution, which had a torturous political history. It had two potential slavery clauses, one providing for slavery and the other excluding it. However, only the slavery clauses, not the full constitution itself, were submitted to the voters. In an election held in December 1857, which free-staters boycotted, and in which many fraudulent votes were cast, the constitution with the slavery clause was approved. All of this caused a split in the national Democratic Party. President James Buchanan, a Democrat, embraced the Lecompton Constitution, with its provision for slavery in Kansas, and urged Congress to approve it. However, Democratic Senator Stephen Douglas of Illinois, the man who had drafted the Kansas-Nebraska Act, broke with Buchanan and opposed the constitution on the grounds that the full document had not been submitted to voters for approval, and over the reports of fraud in the election. In January 1858, a second vote was held, this time with free-staters participating, and the entire Lecompton Constitution was voted down by an overwhelming margin.

With their Topeka Constitution stalled in Congress, free-staters met in Leavenworth in March 1858 and drafted another constitution. This one was more progressive than their original product. Not only did it prohibit slavery in Kansas, it also permitted free Blacks to remain in the state and, moreover, provided that the issue of suffrage for Black males would be submitted to the people for a vote. Although approved by voters in Kansas, the Leavenworth Constitution, with its potential for Black voting rights, was considered too radical in Washington and was never brought up for a vote in Congress.

In 1859, with the territorial government then firmly in the hands of free-staters, one final attempt to draft a state constitution was made. A fourth constitutional convention was held in the small town of Wyandotte, near Kansas City, in July. This constitution prohibited slavery, allowed free Blacks to remain, but did not provide a path for Black suffrage. It was approved by the voters of Kansas in October and sent to Congress. In early 1860, it passed the House by a large margin but, as with the Topeka Constitution three years earlier, it stalled in the southern-dominated Senate. With 1860 being an election year, one in which slavery was the dominant national issue, it became clear that no vote would be held in the Senate until the outcome of the election was known. Shortly after the election of Abraham Lincoln, several states in the lower South seceded from the Union. With their secession, the votes to block the Wyandotte Constitution in the Senate were gone. In January 1861, both houses of Congress approved it by large margins and a lame-duck Democratic president, James Buchanan, who had been pushing the proslavery Lecompton Constitution for most of his term, reluctantly signed the Wyandotte Constitution into law. To this day, with amendments, it remains the constitution of the State of Kansas.

John Brown:

Born in Connecticut in 1800, John Brown had long been active in the abolitionist cause by the time he arrived in Kansas in 1855. Over his life, he tried his hand at various trades, with little success. He moved his large family around to several states, including Ohio, Pennsylvania, Massachusetts, and New York. With the passage of the Kansas-Nebraska Act, he encouraged several of his adult sons to move to Kansas to help make it a free state. When violence broke out in Kansas, he followed his sons there, bringing numerous weapons that had been paid for by his supporters in the northeast. Brown believed that God had called him to take decisive and violent action to end slavery in the United States. His Pottawatomie Massacre was denounced both in Kansas and nationally. Although his name was associated with the killings from the time that they occurred, he never publicly acknowledged his role in them and continued to raise money for his cause.

Brown next became the focus of the nation's attention in October 1859, three years after the events at Potawatomie, when he and a band of followers, including several of his sons, attacked a federal arsenal at Harpers Ferry, Virginia (now West Virginia) in an attempt to obtain weapons. It was the first step in Brown's plan to persuade enslaved people in Virginia to revolt, to arm them, and to organize them as guerilla warriors operating from camps in the Appalachian Mountains. The raid ended in failure, with two of Brown's sons, and several others, killed. A wounded Brown was arrested, tried, and convicted of treason by the State of Virginia. From his jail cell, he wrote numerous letters to family and supporters, many of which were printed in newspapers. His trial was a national sensation. Throughout it, Brown remained calm and dignified, justified his actions, was resigned to his fate, and even complimented his jailors and the court for their fair treatment of him. When Brown was hanged on December 2, 1859, he became a martyr to the abolitionist cause. Within a couple of years, Union troops in the Civil War would be marching to and singing the lyrics of a popular song entitled "John Brown's Body," which proclaimed "John Brown's body lies a-mouldering in the grave. His soul is marching on."

Jason Brown:

Born in 1823, Jason Brown was the second oldest son of John Brown and his first wife. Along with several of his brothers, and his wife and three-year-old son, Jason moved from Ohio to Kansas in 1855. Tragically, during the journey, his son died of cholera. Jason is the only one of John Brown's sons who did not approve of his father's violent means to oppose slavery. He did not participate in the Pottawatomie Massacre in Kansas, nor the later raid at Harpers Ferry in Virginia. Jason was an abolitionist, but also a pacifist. He has been described as "gentle and mild mannered, and very sensitive." When he confronted his father on the day after the events at Pottawatomie, the elder Brown admitted to having been there and ordering the killings, although he denied taking part in them himself. An angry Jason denounced the massacre as a "wicked act," to which his father replied, "God is my judge."

Despite not taking part in the Pottawatomie killings, Jason and his brother, John, Jr. (who also had not been present, but who supported his father's actions), were captured by proslavery forces in Kansas, were beaten, and held were held as prisoners for a few months before being released. (The book takes liberties with Jason's location and activities in the weeks shortly after the massacre, as he was imprisoned at the time of the fictional meeting with Monty Tolliver). He left Kansas shortly after his release and moved back to Ohio.

After the Civil War, Jason moved to California and lived there for several years with one of his brothers in the mountains above Monterey. He was active in temperance organizations. Late in life, he moved back to Ohio, where he died in 1912 at the age of eighty-eight.

ACKNOWLEDGEMENTS

I would like to express my appreciation to those readers of my last book, *And Tyler No More*, who encouraged me to continue on the path of historical fiction and who wanted to know more about the life of Monty Tolliver. I am grateful to Larry Giambelluca for reading a draft of the book and for his insight. My thanks to Aaron Redfern at Historical Editorial for developmental editing of the initial draft of the book, and to Dee Marley at White Rabbit Arts for designing the book's cover. As always, I thank my cherished wife, Beth, for her invaluable help and support.

ABOUT THE AUTHOR

Stan Haynes, an attorney, spent his legal career as a litigator with a Baltimore law firm. A graduate of the College of William & Mary and of the University of Virginia School of Law, he has had a lifelong interest in American political history. In addition to *And Union No More*, he has written another historical fiction book, *And Tyler No More*, set in the 1840s. He is also the author of two books on the history of presidential nominating conventions, *The First American Political Conventions* and *President-Making in the Gilded Age*. He resides in Maryland. Visit his website at www.stanhaynes.com

www.ingramcontent.com/pod-product-compliance
Lightning Source LLC
Chambersburg PA
CBHW030810210726
48290CB00002B/515